All the Dogs are Dancing

J.M. Goguen

A NineStar Press Publication

Published by NineStar Press
P.O. Box 91792,
Albuquerque, New Mexico, 87199 USA.
www.ninestarpress.com

All the Dogs are Dancing

Printed in the USA
First Edition
October, 2018

Print ISBN: 978-1-949340-97-6

Also available in eBook, ISBN: 978-1-949340-94-5

Warning: This book contains sexual content, which may only be suitable for mature readers, and depictions of violence and abuse of an adult child by a parent.

Burner's world revolved around three things: protecting the wolf pack of Maine, keeping an eye on his best friend Aaron, and helping prepare enough summer food to take on the long road to Quebec for the winter months. But in the ruins of an old shopping mall on a hot summer night, his world crashes.

Now Burner has to face monsters he thought were just stories told to scare pups, and he must traverse a world he's only seen in old magazines. Meanwhile, his best friend Aaron is dealing with monsters of his own and Burner will do whatever it takes to keep them both safe, even if it means finally admitting how he really feels.

Chapter One

EAST COAST OF MAINE, SUMMER, TWENTY YEARS
AFTER THE DARKNESS

Crickets chirped in the background of the campfire's light. The aroma of hot, dry grass, charred fish, and wild dill filled the air. Five boys ranging in ages from four to eight sat huddled together, watching intently as scarred fingers expertly checked the skewered fish. It was a simple lesson; an easy cooking strategy when out in the wild. Eating raw fish could result in sickness, or worse, death. Teaching the boys early on how to cook would save them trouble later should they get separated or wander off.

It was one of the first things Fern taught me, and he was teaching the boys of the pack. Without burning his fingers, Fern squeezed the sides of the fish, and the boys shifted, glancing at each other. They were hungry, their stomachs grumbling loud enough that even I could hear them from my spot several feet away, but Fern needed them to focus before they ate, as sleep would come too easily with a full belly, and they needed to learn the dangers in the world.

"Do you know who the Deadwalkers are?" Fern's voice rumbled up from deep in his chest. With his scarred face, straggly white hair, opalescent yellow eyes, and broken-fanged grin, Fern looked frightening, at least to the young pups. They just hadn't seen him fight yet.

"They aren't real," Riley said. His gaze was fixed on the fish, and without looking, he shoved another boy who had crept closer to the fire away. Riley was a young pup, new to our pack this summer, and the first time away from his mother too.

A smile spread across Fern's face, the sight of his fangs causing the boys to inch away. "Oh, but they are. You see, they live in the old cities, in buildings taller than the water tower in the Old Town, and they devour everything in their path..."

"Mom always told me they weren't real," Aaron whispered to me.

Aaron and I were several feet away from the boys to the side of the campfire. Close enough to see clearly, but far enough that the boys ignored us. We weren't as nearly as interesting as Fern or the food, but we were to set an example to the boys on how to behave. At least, that's what Fern had told me when I made the fire while Aaron cleared the area for us to sit.

I glanced at Aaron. He was curled in on himself, his knees drawn close to his chest and his arms wrapped tightly around his legs. His black hair was peppered with white streaks as the result of a sickness he'd had before he turned Wolf. "Mom told me they were stories to scare the new pups, to keep them from wandering off at night," he murmured.

"You didn't wander." My fishing net was on my lap. I was trying to fix the large hole a lobster had made that morning with some cord I'd found in one of the nearby huts. It seemed like something was always breaking and needing repairing. Thankfully the moon was almost full, and the additional light helped me to see what I was doing.

"Burner, you always wandered," Aaron said, and for the first time in two months since his mother passed, he chuckled. "Fern always had to go hunt you down, and then Den Mother would be pissed off at him for losing you."

I tried not to smile because it was true. I'd wander off to the Old Town and when Fern would catch up to me, we would walk around the buildings and houses. He would tell me stories from his childhood, about the old world.

I always thought it sounded like a horrible, boring, dead world.

"Fern told me once that most of his scars came from Den Mother," I joked. I twisted the cord and net together with practiced ease, tying them in a knot.

Aaron laughed, really laughed, the sound carrying into the sky and echoing amongst the silent trees. I was glad to see a part of my friend was still alive inside. It made me smile too.

"Do you two think Deadwalkers are a joke?" Fern demanded.

The young pups were watching us, their trance on the fish, and Fern, broken.

Aaron and I shared a look.

"No, Alpha, they are as real as you and me," I said. There was no laughter in my voice. No humor, just the firm, unquestioning tone Fern expected me to have when we spoke of pack matters.

Satisfied, Fern nodded. He picked up one of the skewers, examining the fish closely. The pups returned their attention to Fern, or rather, how he was testing the fish. He started speaking again, and Aaron waited a few moments before he leaned closer to me, his breath tickling my ear. "Do you think they *are* real?"

"I don't know. I've never seen one, not even in the Old Town." I ducked my head, pretending to pick at the net.

Aaron stared at the fire, falling into silence. I peeked sideways at him when he suddenly sniffed, hot tears spilling down his cheeks. "I miss Mom," he choked and buried his face in his crossed arms.

I looked hopelessly at Fern. When he saw Aaron, he motioned for us to go. Net in hand, I stood up and squeezed Aaron's shoulder.

"C'mon, I'll walk you home," I soothed.

"I don't want to go home." Aaron stood. His right hand was cupping his eyes, his lips downturned.

Wordlessly, I let go of his shoulder and took him by the hand. Together, we left the campfire and slipped into the dark of the night.

Chapter Two

THE KITCHEN WAS alive with Den daughters hustling back and forth, shouting at each other in their own unique languages, and cooking enough food to feed a hundred normal men in a room barely large enough to hold twenty. I'd arisen before them at dawn to catch the morning light, and to snag a part of the long kitchen table to try to fix my net. But as my frustration grew, and the morning turned to afternoon, I was forced to admit that it was completely, and utterly, useless. The hole was bigger, and the knots I'd made snapped under pressure, or refused to tighten.

I sighed, sitting back in the wooden chair and stretching my arms above my head, trying to pop my back and ease the cramped muscles. I yawned, then sagged forward, my arms dropping to my sides as I finally noticed the cup of cold elk tea, and the two young daughters, roughly four and five, sitting across from me, staring at me.

I stared back at them and glanced at the others. Nobody was paying any attention to us, so I stuck my tongue out and blew a raspberry at them. The two daughters looked at each other before they stuck out their tongues at me. Suddenly they froze, and like frogs who'd caught a fly pulled their tongues back into their mouths and sat up in their chairs.

The heady smell of cooked lobster caught my senses before a chipped white platter was placed next to my cup. I grabbed the armful of heavy netting, pulled it off the table, and kicked it beneath.

"Do you want my crochet hooks?" a soft and lyrical voice teased. My cheeks heated.

I blamed the growing heat from the two ovens.

"Nah, Jess, I think I'm good." I pulled the platter closer to me.

Jess, or Jessica as the others called her, was wearing a white cotton dress that ended just above her knees. Her long red hair was tied back into a messy bun, with wisps of red escaping. Her skin was milky pale and caused the heavily inked black "M" under her right eye to seem bigger then it was.

"I'll ask Fern if I can head into the Old Town to find another net." I picked up the lobster, testing the strength of the shell before I turned it around to face me. It had been a big one, at least four pounds. Even in death the little bastard somehow looked victorious. Gripping the claws, I broke the shell at the joints and scooped out the meat. The two daughters gasped. I stretched across the table to hand it to them. They squealed, sharing the meat between them.

Jess hummed in response. "You should take Aaron with you; let him visit his mom." Her soft copper eyes watched my every move.

"You think Rock will allow it?" I took the other claw and cracked it in half. I offered it up to her.

"I think Fern should have killed Rock years ago." Jessica plucked the entire claw from my hands. "Just take Aaron with you. If Rock comes looking, my girls will cover for you."

I grabbed the tail of the lobster and pulled the shell off. I shoved it in my mouth and chewed slowly. "Your girls?" I mumbled.

Jessica smiled. "Trust me, Burner." She picked up the platter with the lobster remains on it while I licked my fingers clean. She tsked, shaking her head. "See that, Emily? Misha? What do we do with dirty fingers?"

"Wash them at the sink," the two girls chimed.

I rolled my eyes.

Daughters.

As the room grew hotter, and the two daughters were tasked with removing the ends from a pile of green beans, I took my cup and quietly left through the back door. One of the daughters would find a use for the netting. Maybe a sewing project, or to help pea shoots climb in the garden. I didn't know, but stepping out of the kitchen was a relief. Even though it was late summer, it was much cooler outside than inside. I took a moment to savor the sunshine, leaning my back against the white peeling paint of the house.

"Chatting up Jessica?" A sly and tired voice broke my moment of quiet.

"Not the way you want to." I held up my mug at the two sun-bleached figures approaching me.

Albe and Danbe were identical twins with dirty blond hair and canines a bit too long for their mouths. They wore ripped jean shorts, moth-eaten tank tops, and were an inch or two taller than me. Both of them carried three medium-sized codfish in their hands, no doubt caught without poles. I waved my free hand at Danbe's catch. He flashed back a toothy grin. I'd never heard him speak, and he couldn't hear us speak, but he was our finest fisherman.

"Looks like a good catch."

"Really good," Albe agreed. "Fern told us to start salting the fish tomorrow, says we're going to head inland earlier this year."

"Is everybody at the beach?" I made an ocean wave-like motion with my hand before closing it then opening it to point at the path toward the beach.

Albe frowned. "Not entirely sure." He turned to Danbe, shrugging.

Danbe thought for a moment before he readjusted his haul of fish and mock combed his hair before digging at the air.

"Eric's digging for clams." Albe glanced at me, confused. "Why?"

"Got to speak to Fern, you seen him?"

"Fern? I saw him by the pier, he's trying to teach the new pups how to fish." Albe nudged Danbe's side and walked past me. He disappeared through the open kitchen door. Danbe gave me another smile and followed.

I finished my cup and leaned down to leave it safe in a tuft of grass away from any chance of it being kicked and broken. I pushed off the house and followed the worn path that Albe and Danbe had taken, walking past the herb gardens loaded with bees buzzing madly toward the pier.

Chapter Three

THE WOODEN PIER was a remnant of Fern's old world. He'd patched it over the years, cannibalizing the outer walls of nearby houses to use as new decking. Flecks of multi-colored paint would stick to wet feet, and the wrong step could result in splinters. The pillars that supported the deck were made of concrete that was home to generations of mussels. Fern told me once that people would scrape off the mussels to keep the concrete clean. I thought that was stupid. Why give up a good meal? Fern just laughed in response.

I spied Fern and the pups from last night at the end of the pier. They watched him with rapt attention as he demonstrated how to properly hold a fishing rod, how to tie off the weight and bait. Mindful of splinters, I approached them.

"Fern, do you have a moment?"

The pups turned at my voice and Fern handed the rod to a tall, skinny pup with dark skin and black hair. "Here, Danny, show the others how to flick the rod, just like I showed you." Immediately, the boys clamored around Danny, focusing on his hands. Danny stood taller, puffing out his chest as he demonstrated the movement to the others.

Fern loomed over the boys and me. Technically he was one of the tallest wolves I'd ever met. "What's up?"

"Remember the lobster I caught yesterday?" I crossed my arms.

"The one that destroyed your net?" Fern frowned. "You were working on it last night at the fire."

"Yeah, I spent all morning trying to fix it, but short of cutting apart another net and sewing it together, it's not going to work." I sighed.

"What's your plan?" Fern turned to watch the pups and make sure they didn't hurt one another. Danny was leading the boys, giving each of them a chance to cast.

"I was wondering if I could head into the Old Town and try and find another one."

"On your own?" Fern's focus was still on the pups.

I hesitated, turning my gaze to watch the pups too. "I was thinking...I'd take Aaron with me. I got a laugh out of him last night. I thought it'd be good to take him away for a day, or two," I added the last part. It was late in the day and getting to Old Town would take a while.

Fern was silent, watching the pups with a critical eye. "Do you have Rock's permission to take Aaron with you?"

"Yes."

Fern turned to me. His eyes glinted in the sunlight. A knowing smile drifted across his face. He knew I was lying.

"Just make sure to be back by tomorrow's sunset. I don't need Mother scarring anymore of my handsome features. Make sure to take the Old Cemetery Road, understand?"

"Yes, Fern."

"Good luck with finding a new net." Fern walked back toward the pups. He patted Danny on the back before kneeling. "Now, can any of you tell me how to use the pop-top of old beer and soda cans as fishing hooks?"

Quietly, I left Fern and the pups. I just had to hunt down Aaron.

Aaron and Rock lived in a separate house from the central pack, just a few minutes' walk through the woods along an overgrown mossy trail. They didn't live near the waterfront like we did, and Rock kept their doors locked at all times. We barely closed the doors in the main house because it got too hot in the summer, and the cool breeze off the ocean at night was a relief, allowing everyone to get a decent night's rest.

I sidestepped a pile of broken liquor bottles, mindful of the sharp tinted glass. That was another difference between houses; alcohol was banned in the main house, but Rock drank freely and often. I pushed aside some hanging rotting branches decorated with goat's beard and made a mental note to clear the path in the next few days. Rock could suffer, but Aaron would appreciate the help. Surrounded by old tall trees, the little blue house with peeled blue paint was shaded from the sun. Yelling from inside made me slow my pace.

"You little shit, come back here!" Rock roared.

The front door slammed open, and Aaron raced out into the yard. I hugged a nearby tree, watching as Aaron spun around on his heel, taking a few cautious steps back, and Rock stumbled out the door after him. Rock was old and tall, like Fern, but that was where the similarities ended. Rock had short-cropped, gray and black hair, and was as vicious as a wounded mountain lion. Jess compared his scent to that of a dead, week-old skunk.

"You leave me alone!" Aaron screamed. He was trembling, his hands curled into fists.

"Don't you take that tone with me, boy." Rock snarled. He tried to take another step forward before he fell to the ground. He shook his head, waving at imaginary flies. "You're just like your mother," he spat, "useless and a waste of air."

Aaron stopped trembling. Instead, he growled low in his throat, his curled fingers turning to claws, his muscles shifting underneath the slightly tanned skin of his back.

Aaron wouldn't stand a chance against Rock, even if the man was drunk.

I searched around my feet until I found a small copper-colored pebble. I picked it up, testing the weight. Not too big to leave a bruise, but small enough to fly forward. I chucked it at Aaron's back. Startled, Aaron glanced over his shoulder and I stepped out from behind the tree. His shoulders sagged when he saw it was me, and his face started to crumble. He hated it when I saw him and Rock fighting.

The tension escalated a hundredfold.

"What are you doing here?" Rock sneered. He struggled to stand on unsteady legs, finally succeeding, somewhat. He was balancing his hands on his knees, his face purple while he tried to catch his breath.

"The Den daughters need Aaron and me to help them. They said they wanted to make clams for supper." I kept a careful eye on Rock. I could fight him, land a few punches and bites, but then I'd have to face the Elders for my actions. I could be banished as a threat to the pack. Or worse, wear the traitor's name of Lee.

Rock stared at me stupidly before he burst into laughter. It echoed in the clearing. Aaron bowed his head, trembling once more. "Doing woman's work? What'd I tell you, Aaron? Fern's gone and made bitches out of this entire pack!"

If Rock expected me to rise to the bait, he was wrong. Jessica was right: Fern should have killed Rock years ago. He was nothing more than a petty wolf with horrible control issues who was a bigger threat to the pack than any Hunter. Aaron lifted his head again and met my eyes. I nodded toward the path, and a split-second later, he took off running with me hot on his heels. Rock screamed bloody murder behind us. He would try to follow us, but we were too fast.

When we couldn't hear him anymore and were deep in the woods, Aaron stopped. He dropped to his hands and knees, his head hanging down. Between gasps of breath, painful sobs bubbled up from his chest. I knelt next to him, rubbing his back, and catching my own breath.

"Let's visit your mom."

Chapter Four

THERE WERE THREE roads to Old Town. The main road, which we didn't bother with because it left us to open for attack from animals like bears, white striped tigers, and wild boars. The second road led through a maze of old houses where animals preferred to make dens in the remains of the overgrown gardens and collapsed buildings. The third, and the most scenic, was Old Cemetery Road.

Once upon a time, the land had been a farm, but grass as tall as Fern filled the empty land, providing places to hide, and hunt, if someone knew what they were looking for. The skeletal remains of a glass greenhouse towered near the far corner and provided the barest of shelter when it rained. The tall grass meant you had to take your time; you had to walk carefully and mind your step.

Aaron didn't speak. He wiped his eyes, sniffing back tears while I led us through the thicket, the cicadas providing a summer heartbeat. I'd glance over my shoulder every now and then to make sure he was behind me. He was staring at my bare feet, avoiding my gaze. His wrists were bruised purple, and his cheek was turning a similar shade. He would heal eventually, physically at least. The bruises would fade within a day and he would look like he did last night at the fire. No outward signs of pain, but inside was another matter.

I wished I could kill Rock.

I stopped, and he bumped into my back. His startled eyes met mine. I nodded my head to my left. He stepped next to me and together we pushed aside the grass, walking side by side.

"I didn't realize that clams lived inland." Aaron's voice was soft.

"You haven't heard of the rare inland clam? I heard it's really popular with the Wolves of Newfoundland." I sidestepped a piece of old steel jutting up from the ground.

"Careful, you're starting to sound like a Den daughter."

"It's a beehive in there," I groaned. "I was in the kitchen this morning, trying to fix my net, and they were just buzzing around and ensuring everything was in its place."

"Was Den Mother there?"

"No." I frowned. "I think she was upstairs with the Elders, making sure they were okay."

"Did you get it fixed? The net, I mean?" Aaron rubbed his wrists, the color shifting from purple to black.

"I wish, but Fern gave me permission to go to Old Town to look for a new one." I stopped and jumped up, trying to see over the tall grass and failing miserably. Why couldn't I be taller, damn it?

"Good try, Burner." The corners of Aaron's lips turned upward.

"Then you look," I shot back.

Aaron frowned, his lips twisting before he yelped in surprise when I grabbed him around his waist and lifted him. He grabbed my shoulders, his blunt nails trying to dig in to steady himself. "Burner!"

"Do you see anything?" I was trying to stand in place, but Aaron started to wiggle in my grip, so I tightened my arms around him, holding him firm. "Aaron?"

"Put me down, right now," Aaron barked.

"Do you see the hill?"

"Put me down!"

I let him go. Aaron landed on his feet, turning away from me.

"So? What did you see?" I crossed my arms.

He spun around and shoved me. Hard. I stumbled back into the grass, catching myself before I fell on my ass. "Aaron, what the hell?"

"You bastard!" Aaron spat, his face crimson. He stormed away in a totally different direction, quickly disappearing from view. It took me a few minutes before I realized he was going to *leave* me in the grass.

"Aaron, wait up." I chased after him, blindly pushing my way through the grass, suddenly worried that he might go do something stupid like the day after his mother died. "Aaron!"

I found him fifty feet from where he'd shoved me, frozen solid mid-step.

I grabbed his arm. "Look, I'm sorry—"

"Shh." He shook his head, his focus ahead of him. Instead of speaking, he pointed a few steps ahead of him. Frowning, I tilted my head, looking to where he was pointing, and felt like someone had thrown me into a lake in the middle of winter.

Twelve sleeping piglets nestled together on a bedding of grass. All alone.

Where was the mother?

Unblinking, I ran my hand down his arm. I grasped his fingers with mine and lowered his arm. With my other hand, I hooked my fingers into the belt loop on the back of his shredded denim shorts and tugged backward.

We'd managed two steps back when one of the piglets opened its eyes and noticed us. I took another step back. Aaron started to tremble and fear drowned out my senses.

The piglet lifted his head, his tiny brown snout sniffing the air, and squealed. The other piglets all lifted their heads in response and squealed in distress. Beyond them, just out of sight of the tall grass, a heavy *snort* filled the air.

I didn't need to yell or shout. I squeezed Aaron's hand hard enough to bruise and bolted as the mother boar charged through the grass and chased after us. I blindly pushed aside the grass, Aaron right behind me, and the boar behind us shrieking and howling in displeasure, her heavy tusks aimed at our legs.

We could have killed it. We could have shifted on a dime and turned around, and attacked, but she had piglets. Little ones who wouldn't survive without her, and Aaron hadn't been able to join us for a hunt, let alone kill anything, in months. So, I ground my jaw and hoped that the sow would just chase us to the edge of its territory and give up.

Unfortunately, I didn't count on there being other boars in the area.

We tore through another nesting ground, almost tripping over a different group of piglets who squealed in distress and panic. *That* sow saw the one chasing us and went after it, giving us enough space to disappear into the tall grass.

"Burner, that way," Aaron panted behind me, pointing twelve degrees to our right.

I followed his directions and within moments we burst through the tall grass and found ourselves in front of a giant steel gate with a cemetery looming uphill.

I let go of Aaron's hand and collapsed onto the ground, gasping for breath. Aaron collapsed next to me, rolling onto his back as he tried desperately to catch his own breath. We were both drenched in sweat and the grass seeds stuck to our skin and hair.

"That was, was..." Aaron stumbled.

"Insane? Stupid?" I offered. I sucked in a few deep breaths, willing to calm my racing heart. Aaron nodded wordlessly and mimicked my actions until our breathing had calmed. I fell to my side, gazing up the hill. The sun had already crested the ceiling of the sky and was starting to make its descent.

"Yeah, that," Aaron laughed.

I hummed in agreement, giving myself a few more minutes before I pushed myself to my feet and brushed off my knees. I held my hand out to Aaron. He grabbed it and hauled himself up. He looked to the cemetery on the top of the hill, a lone elm tree perched at the very top.

"Let's go."

Chapter Five

WHEN AARON'S MOTHER Charlotte died, Fern and I dug her grave while Rock drank himself into a stupor and Aaron suffered a complete meltdown. Den Mother and Jess washed and prepared her body for burial. The Elders—well, the one Elder still able to shift to human and communicate—told us that only the Den Mother and her Chosen could safely handle the body.

Eric, Albe, and Danbe were tasked with guarding the house while Fern and I worked. The other daughters...well, they mourned as only Den daughters can. They shifted into wolves and howled themselves sick, not eating or drinking until Charlotte was wrapped in her shroud and buried complete with flowers, pictures, her hairbrush, and a locket of Aaron's hair (Den Mother had me hold him down so he would stay still long enough to get the hair).

Afterward, when we'd all said our goodbyes and thanked her for the life she had given to the pack. Rock was supposed to stand guard over her grave for five days and five nights. Instead, he disappeared that night and didn't return to the pack for two weeks. Fern stood guard in his place. Not sleeping or eating, only moving to chase off any predators that came too close to investigate. A living statue guarding her grave with sharp teeth and deadly fighting abilities.

The night of her burial, I found Aaron at the edge of the dock, his feet dangling over the edge, holding a silver knife wrapped in a crochet blanket Charlotte had made, and quietly talking to the moon overhead. I almost drowned us both when I raced down the path, across the pier, and tackled him into the water.

Sometimes, I have nightmares about what would have happened if I hadn't noticed the figure at the edge of the dock from the window of the second floor of the house.

The graveyard hadn't changed, but Aaron's reaction had.

His steps slowed, his eyebrows drew up, as we approached the top of the hill, passing the graves marked with stone plaques and wooden crosses decorated with weeds and summer flowers. The names of people buried here long forgotten and all that remained were the faint scent of chemicals and old bones. The view of Old Town sprawled wild with broken concrete and burned houses was a sharp contrast to the grasslands we had passed. Aaron hesitated when he got to the top, to the grave protected by the shadow of the elm trees' wide branches.

Aaron sniffed the air and exhaled a shaky breath. "I can't..."

I squeezed his shoulder, letting go as he knelt next to the mound marked with a simple wooden cross.

"I can't smell her anymore." Aaron's voice cracked. He bowed his head and dug his fingers into the fresh green grass.

"I can."

Aaron peered up at me. I tried to smile and failed. My words stuck uncomfortably tight in my throat. "You, you smell like her. So, she's not really gone, she's still here, with you. Because you...carry her scent, but not exactly like hers, but..." I rambled.

Aaron looked back down, running his hands through the soft green. "Go get your net, Burner. I'll be here when you come back."

Uncertain, I rubbed my neck. "Aaron, I—"

"I won't do anything stupid. Just, go."

I nodded and quietly made my way through the graves down the hillside to Old Town. I shot Aaron one last glance and saw him lying next to Charlotte's grave, his face buried in the crook of his arm.

The last time I'd been in the mall was three, four, summers ago when a pup who'd traveled with us from Quebec decided to ignore Fern's rules and wandered off during the night. Jess had awoken me sometime before dawn, frantic that one of the pups was missing and that Den Mother would punish her for losing him. Jess couldn't go to Fern because he would awaken the entire pack and make everyone search for the pup.

So, after slipping out of the bedroom I shared with Albe, Danbe, and Eric, I padded down the stairs and snuck out of the kitchen door. Jess distracted Fern, who slept downstairs, by telling him she thought she'd heard a noise in the attic. It'd worked, and I slunk off into the woods in my wolf form, tracking the pup's scent.

A part of me was a bit impressed with how far he'd made it, all the way to Old Town, and into the basement of the mall, but another part was horrified that'd he traveled so far on such little legs when he'd been warned about predators. It all leveled out when I found him trapped in a room, stuck in his wolf form, and his voice cracked from howling for so long. He'd whined when I found him, but he was safely back with the pack by supper.

Fern punished me for losing a pup, but Jess fed me extra meal servings for two weeks afterward, so it wasn't all bad.

I'd almost forgotten about the old rusted cars strategically locked in place against the glass door entrances on the first floor. The hot concrete of the parking lot burned my feet. I hopped several times, making my way around the building and toward the back of the mall and its rusty steel gates.

I stopped in my tracks when I turned the corner and into the shade the building provided. The closed gates were thrown wide open. Animals couldn't open them, and when I left with the pup, I'd made sure the gates were shut tight. Uncertain, I sniffed the air and picked up the scent of dust and mold. Curious and cautious, I crept into the mall.

Chapter Six

SOUNDS OF A hundred ants marching across the tiled floor echoed in the empty mall. The back entrance led into a long dark hallway, which opened into a section of the mall where the skylights streamed light. There were tracks, not barefoot, but boot prints. They disappeared into the supermarket, and I abandoned them.

It wasn't unusual for people to come to the mall and search for food. They couldn't hunt like wolves, and they were often too sick, or weak, to go after animals. Sometimes in the autumn, when we wrapped up the salted fish and smoked meat to take to Quebec, Den Mother would send Fern to leave some food in the mall before we left.

"Mercy in the dark days," she would say as she prepared the crate.

On the very rare occasion, Fern found women and children in the mall. He'd bring them back to the pack and they would travel with us to Quebec. It only happened a handful of times, and the last time was nearly seven years ago. If Fern ever saw men, he never brought them back.

Never.

I slipped back into the shadows and edged along the windows of the shops. I needed to get to the second floor. The sunlight flooding in through the roof and glass doors was turning a bright orange hue. I found the stairs with the dust-covered, spider-web-decorated handrails and went up to the second floor, my bare feet hot against the cool tiles.

The second floor was a lot like the first floor of the mall—full of useless crap. Shoes that fell apart after a first rainfall, pants and shirts and dresses that had rotted into rags long ago. Dull jewelry and hats covered in cobwebs and ruined with age.

Except for the one store that wasn't completely useless. Well, technically two.

The other was a bookstore with mostly bare shelves. The paper made for good kindling and the picture books were entertaining to the pups. I loved the magazines with the images of Fern's world. The pictures of clothing, food, and oceans around the world. I'd had a stack of them I'd hoarded over the years. Unfortunately, they met their demise during a particularly cold spring when we'd needed something to light the hearth fire so the pups and the Elders would keep warm.

Aaron liked to read the books about space, the stars, and the colonies that circled the world. If he'd had a bad day with Rock, he'd join me out by the water and read aloud while I cast my net at dusk. I made a mental note to dig around in the bookstore after I got my net in case there was a book he hadn't read yet.

A big black-and-white patterned ball outside the shop's open door was still there. I patted the top of it; my handprint perfectly shaped in the dust. I entered the store. I wasn't interested in what Fern told me was sports gear, or the clothes, or the useless shoes. I was interested in what was deep in the back of the store.

Stepping over the scattered shoes and hats on the floor, I continued until I reached the far back of the store where the light was dim at best. Shifting through the supplies and hidden behind a few boxes, I found what I wanted: a long cardboard box with the image of a net stretched by a large metal frame, as people kicked a smaller version of the black and white ball outside the shop into the net.

I opened the side of the cardboard box and pulled out the net. It was woven metallic cloth, and it was strong. I doubted it would rot anytime soon, or get a lobster stuck. Grinning, I tucked it under my arm, but just as I was about to leave, a new sound echoed above the sound of ants endlessly marching.

Sniffing.

I frowned and watched the entrance to the store. Maybe Aaron had followed me, or it was someone else from the pack, or the foreigner who'd wandered into the grocery store. To my surprise, a little red-colored puppy waddled into the shop with its nose to the ground. It was following my scent and was only distracted twice by the shoes scattered on the floor before it returned to my scent.

Patiently, I waited until it approached my feet. I reached down and picked it up by the scruff of its neck. Startled, the puppy squealed and started to wiggle like a worm on a fisherman's hook. Its little mouth snapped at me, small sharp teeth gnashing at air. When we were eye to eye, the puppy stopped, and its red ears drooped flat against its head.

"Can you change back?" I urged.

The puppy's blank look spoke volumes.

"Do you feel that burning buzz in your head?"

The puppy shook its head.

"Look for the burn."

It was getting darker inside the mall, and I guessed roughly half an hour till sunset. The puppy yipped in my hand. I put him back on the floor when he began to change. Bones and skin shifted until a red-headed boy lay in front of me. He was gasping for breath.

"You okay, Riley?" I knelt next to him.

"My back hurts," Riley whined. He struggled to sit up and failed. He fell back onto the floor and curled into a ball with his arms wrapped around his head. "My head hurts, real bad!"

The scar where he'd been bitten on his side, right above his hip, was an angry shade of red.

I patted his head. "I know. It gets better." I waited for him to calm before I spoke again. "What are you doing here, Riley?"

Riley sniffed. "Following you and Aaron, but I saw Aaron in the graveyard, and he was crying, so I followed your scent cuz I didn't want to bother him."

"You shouldn't have followed us," I warned. "It's dangerous outside the pack house."

"I know," Riley sulked.

"You are too young to be on your own, and there are things out there that could hurt you." I had a momentary sense of déjà vu. Was this how Fern felt when I wandered off?

"Like the black pig?" Riley glanced at the store shelves.

"You mean the sows outside?" I was alarmed. Had he stumbled upon both litters too? Riley looked up at me. His blue eyes flickered madly with dark yellow streaks.

"No, the two-legged pig downstairs."

I stared at Riley.

"The two-legged pig?" I said slowly. That couldn't be right.

"The two-legged *black* pig," Riley corrected. Standing up, he glanced over his shoulder. "I have a tail," he chirped. He began turning in a circle, as he tried to catch his red, bushy tail.

I grabbed his arm and dragged him out of the store. In the process, I tore a man-sized, faded, blue striped shirt off a nearby hanger and dressed him. People didn't look like black pigs. People wore clothes that stunk of sweat, and rot, and were infested with mites and fleas.

Pigs did not walk on two legs.

Riley tried to talk, but I shushed him with a vicious hiss, as we descended the stairs. My brain buzzed and my pulse raced. This was a dangerous situation, I had to get Riley out of here before the pig found us, I needed to get back to Aaron, and—

"Burner, look! The black pig!" Riley yelled. He ripped his arm from my grasp and pointed toward the supermarket store entrance.

Indeed, there was a two-legged black pig. It was as tall as me but slimmer in shape. Its skin was shiny, and it had no scent. Its eyes were black and huge, and its snout had a round canister attached to the side of it.

It stared at us.

"Can we eat it?" Riley chirped.

Slowly, I pushed Riley behind me. I passed him the net. "Go find Aaron," I whispered.

The pig tilted its head.

"But, Burner," Riley whined.

"Go find Aaron. Now!" I snapped. I stepped forward, my eyes on the pig while Riley ran for the exit. When I couldn't hear him anymore, I took another step forward.

"Can you change your skin?" The buzz in my brain turned to molten heat. My skin prickled, my muscles twitched. "Are you people? Are you sick?"

The pig tilted its head again, as if it was looking behind me, then, like an avalanche, I heard *them* pouring out from the surrounding stores: boots, whispers, the click of metal.

A long thin *shrink* as an arrow flew past my head and straight at the pig.

The pig caught it mid-air before it could impale its face.

More arrows flew from behind me and two sank into the meat of my right shoulder. I stumbled forward, my eyes wide, the pain blinding my vision. The pig fled toward the supermarket's entrance, and five people surrounded me, armed with crossbows, rifles, and axes. They wore ankle-length jackets, green sweaters, and brown pants with dozens of pockets. Their mouths were covered with black clothes, and they all had the same armband on their upper arms with the image of a wolf's skull pierced with a spear. *Hunters.* They were Hunters. How could I have not noticed them?

Trying to rip the arrows out of my shoulder, I let the burn in my brain take me.

My muscles tried to shift, my bones tried to break apart, and my brain burned as hot as the center of the sun because it wasn't working, everything was *wrong*. I wasn't shifting into my wolf skin. Gasping for breath like I was being held under water, I collapsed to my knees, the arrows burning in their places. My vision started to blur.

"This must be one of the wild dogs we were told about," a male Hunter said. His armband was silver edged. "Is this him?"

I growled low in my throat, fighting the rising panic.

"According to our assets description," a female Hunter began. She shouldered her rifle and pulled out a folded piece of paper. She walked around me, and I tried to grab her jacket, but she stayed out of reach. "This is him. The one they call 'Burner.' He has the scars on his back."

Another male Hunter whistled. "So, we've got a future wild Alpha?"

"Who else could handle two arrows and still be conscious?" A different female Hunter chimed in.

I squeezed my eyes shut, my stomach turning and hot bile trying to flood my throat. The arrows, were they poisoned?

"Let's just kill him and be done with it. We need our energy, and bullets, if we're going to take on the Den Mother with team two." The silver-edged Hunter snapped his fingers and the Hunter with the crossbow raised it, aiming for my head.

"Now, hold on, hold on." The Hunter who'd whistled placed his hand on the crossbow and pushed it down so it aimed at the ground. "I've got a better idea."

I collapsed onto my side. The walls and floors were starting to bleed together. The Hunters' voices were turning into booming, thundering tones.

"I say we take this dog—" The Hunter kicked my legs and I whimpered. "—and sell him at the Butcher's Harbor down in Boston. I'm betting Lucky would want him for the arena."

There was a silence as the Hunters looked at each other, then the one with the silver-edged armband spoke. "Shoot him again with those arrows of yours, Ada. Henry, collar him and tie him up. We'll pick him up afterward."

The Hunter, Henry, reached into his pocket and pulled out a silver collar edged with small red buttons. He wrapped it around my neck, the metal lightly pinching the flesh as it clicked shut, and a weird buzzing sound, almost like a trapped bee, filled my ears. I tried to claw at him while the one he'd called Ada raised the crossbow and fired the arrow directly at my chest.

A guttural cry escaped my lips and I started shaking uncontrollably.

"All right," Silver Armband began again, "let's move out and—ughck!"

Instantly, the others turned to Silver on guard, their weapons raised. He dropped his rifle and lifted his hands to paw at his throat as blood spurted from his mouth. He fell to the floor dead. Standing behind him was the black pig who'd fled, holding a large bloody knife.

"This is our prey, back off!" the Hunters cried.

"I'm not interested in him," the pig replied, its voice muffled.

My eyes slid shut. I felt my body relaxing against my will, my mind a muddled mess as the Hunters screamed "Fire!" and thunder filled the air.

Chapter Seven

I WAS FLOATING on the cotton of a dandelion. Not a worry in the world, not a problem, or issue. My joints were liquid. I felt like a marionette that had been left to lie on the ground. There was no pain, just warmth, and relaxation.

Had I always been in pain?

"Can you hear me?"

Fighting the weight keeping my eyes closed, I opened them and witnessed the sparkling brilliance of the stars overhead.

"Are you awake? Can you hear my voice?

I rolled my head toward the voice and realized there was a pillow of some sort beneath my head. I was lying next to a fire. I stared at the flickering orange and red flames. The black pig, who sat cross-legged on the other side of the fire, was watching me. I smiled, my lips twisting and grimacing at the movement.

"Are you going to eat me?" I slurred.

The pig startled.

"I think I'm too tough, and you don't have any big pig tusks to rip me apart."

"You think I'm a pig?" Its voice was muffled.

I smiled wider, but my smile disappeared when the pig reached up and started to pull off its face. Horror and curiosity nestled in my stomach while it peeled the mask away. Behind the mask was a girl my age, with brown eyes, short-cut black hair, and tanned skin like mine. Stretching across her cheekbones and the bridge of her nose was a mad scramble of tattooed stars. It looked similar to a never-ending star symbol from one ear across her nose to her other ear.

"Still think I'm a pig?" the girl mused.

I stared.

"I think you're still feeling the poison those bastards injected you with. Don't worry, it should pass through your system by daybreak. My name is September 24th Amon."

"That's a long name," I mumbled.

September laughed. My eyes were playing tricks on me because her laughter made the world wobble, even the flames. "It is, but what is yours?"

"Burner of the Maine Pack." The smoke of the fire made me want to rub my eyes, but my arms were too heavy. Couldn't someone pull the strings so I could move?

"Maine? The Maine pack still exists? I thought I was still in the Appalachians... What can you tell me about the New Hampshire pack?" September's brows came together in a frown.

"New Hampshire? That's a long trip," I mumbled, again. "The pups always want to investigate the houses on the back roads. Fern likes to play poker with the Alpha there."

"Do you have a lot of pups in Maine?" I didn't realize it, but she held a book in her hands. I think she was writing. The pencil scraping on paper echoed in my ears.

"Five." I was falling into her eyes.

"And Den daughters?"

"Four." There was a speck of red in her black eyes too.

"And Elders? Young men? Who is your Alpha?" September wrote in her book.

"Four elders, five males my age, Fern is our Alpha." I frowned.

Something was wrong. The hairs on my arms and legs were rising, my brain was starting to burn, but it was a strange burn I'd never felt before. September broke my gaze, and I gasped. I had stopped breathing. I coughed, and she looked in her lap. I flinched as she ripped a piece of paper from her book and set the leather-bound tome aside. She crept around the fire and kneeled next to me and took my hand. She wasn't wearing a glove. Her hand was cool to the touch.

"Give this to your leader, your Fern." She placed the paper in my hand and squeezed it shut. "Do not let anyone else see this, do you understand?"

I nodded then groaned as my head throbbed at the movement and my neck ached. "Why are you doing this? Why are you helping me?" The burn was starting to recede. In its place, exhaustion was creeping in.

September stroked my hair. "Because we're not all monsters, and I always pay my debts."

"Debts?" I mumbled.

Suddenly, the flames flickered and a flash of light far off to the distance caught both September's and my attention. September frowned. "Burner, what's over there?"

I craned my neck, my eyes falling half shut. Beyond Cemetery Hill was the distant glow of white, then yellow, then nothing except the howling wind that tugged at something deep within me.

"Home," I croaked. September drew in a sharp breath. "Home is there."

September stood up. She grabbed her mask off the ground and walked toward the edge of the roof when she paused and turned back to me. "Remember: we're not all monsters. Say it, Burner, say it!"

Cotton was filling my mouth, making it hard to speak.

"We're not all monsters," I slurred.

September nodded. She pulled on her mask and jumped off the edge, disappearing into the night.

Chapter Eight

THE SUN WAS too bright, and I was in a great deal of agony. I covered my face, groaning at the tightness in my shoulder. My stomach roiled and saliva flooded my mouth. I rolled to my hands and knees, the world spinning around me. I vomited bile, blood, and green slime that tasted like burning tires. My throat was tight and I coughed, spitting out the last of the green when I touched my throat and felt the cool metallic collar.

Suddenly, the world stopped spinning.

I ran my hand along the collar, around the rim, trying to find the hook to disconnect it, or a clasp, or something. A frantic panic settled in as I stood, my legs not quite right, stumbling around the rooftop while I tried to *pull* it off. I dug my fingers into the side, hissing, and pulled harder, the metal groaning under the pressure.

An angry bee buzzed in my inner ear before the world went white and I was back on the ground, withering and shrieking in agony.

I let go of the collar, gasping for breath, panicking, and blinking rapidly as the pain stopped. What the hell was wrapped around my neck? I swallowed, bracing myself. I tried to pull the collar again when I received another ripple of pain.

"Shit, shit, shit, shit."

I had to get out of the mall. I needed to find those Hunters and get them to tell me how to take off the damn collar, I needed to get home, I—*what's that?*

Crumpled on the ground, next to last night's campfire, was a piece of paper and a leather-bound notebook. Everything came crashing back to me and I sucked in a deep breath, letting it out.

September 24th Amon.

She was real.

I bent down and picked up the book, along with the crumpled paper, and studied the smooth, cursive writing.

Where did she go?

Before I realized it, before I consciously grasped what I was doing, I was racing down the rooftop stairs of the mall and back inside. September went toward the light, toward home. I'd get there faster if I shifted and I did just that. Well, tried to anyway.

I skidded halfway across the mall floor, howling in agony as the collar buzzed to life. The cool metal quickly heated enough to mark my neck and I stopped shifting, panting as the metal rapidly cooled in response.

Those goddamn Hunters!

Snarling, I staggered to my feet and made my way back to where I'd last seen the Hunters in the mall. One of them had to have a key, had to have *something* that could remove this damnation from my neck. As I climbed down the stairs, I discovered to my horror that the Hunters who had cornered me yesterday were already dead, their bodies burned. Not a touch of clothing remained.

September must have done this, but why would she leave the collar around my neck? Unless she was working with the Hunters to attack the pack, but why would she kill them? I rubbed my forehead, my head pounding and my ears ringing.

I had to get back to the pack. I had to get home.

On unsteady feet, I made my way to the back entrance and started on the long journey home.

Chapter Nine

THE HOUSE WAS gone.

The rooms that I'd lived in, the rooms the daughters, the Elders, the pups slept in, the kitchen and living room, all gone. All that remained were the crackling skeletons of burned old pipes, small fires struggling in vain to devour the charred remains of kitchen tables and furniture. The stench of flesh and gunpowder led me directly to the pack house.

It was all gone.

If only I'd been stronger. If only I'd moved faster and killed those Hunters, or fought that damn poison, or—or something! I could have done something! I could have saved my pack, and now they were gone. I went searching for a fucking stupid fishing net. I *abandoned* my pack.

How the hell could I go back to Quebec? How could I face the Den Mothers there? Or Andre the Alpha? How could I tell them, "I'm the only survivor, because I wasn't *there*."

This was my fault.

I rocked back and forth, burying my face in my ash-covered hands, my tears stinging the blisters I'd gotten trying to dig through the remains to find someone, *anyone*, alive.

A wet, cold something touched my elbow and I gasped, jerking my head to see what it was. Smaller than average, a coal-colored wolf with a patch of white behind its ear stared at me.

"A-Aaron?"

The wolf nosed my arm again and without another word, I got to my feet. Aaron's copper green eyes flickered and with a soft "woo," he nudged my hand with his nose.

"I can't shift, Aaron." My lips soured. I pointed at my collar. "I'm stuck like this. Did...did anybody else survive? What happened? Was it the Hunters?"

Aaron hesitated before he gave another "woo." He led me away from the remains of the house and onto the path toward the house where he and Rock lived. It didn't take long before I heard the pups crying and tasted the heavy copper on the air. I swallowed, faltering in my steps the closer we got until we arrived, and I saw the horror of the hunt first hand.

Den Mother, the core of our pack, was in her wolf form outside the house. She was twice as big as Fern when he shifted, but she was far deadlier. Her white fur was stained red and her breathing was ragged. There were dozens of arrows sticking out of her body, no doubt also poisoned.

Jess was at her side in her human form with dried blood splattered across her face and body. Her arms and legs were covered in purple bruises, and her hair was loose. Three other daughters—Shelly, Nell, and Yu—surrounded Den Mother too.

"Hold her down," Jess wiped her forehead. "Mother, please, don't move." She reached for one of the arrows. Grasping it in one hand, she placed her other hand next to the entry spot and started to pull.

Den Mother reared her head back and snapped at Jess's hands while Yu and Nell tried desperately to hold her down.

"Mother, *please!*" Jess pleaded. "We have to remove them or else you won't heal!"

Den Mother lifted her head again and howled. Aaron cowered behind me, his ears flat against his skull and whimpered. I clamped my hands against my own ears, grimacing at the sound while Shelly, Yu, and Nell cried out in agony and let her go. Jess held on, blood trickling from her ears.

"Stop!"

I raced to Jess's side and, with all my weight, grabbed Den Mother by the scruff of her neck to hold her down. She snarled when she saw me, her jaws dripping with saliva.

"Pull them out," I ordered. Startled, Jess nodded. Yu and Shelly glanced at me before they too started to try to pull the arrows free. Den Mother's howls changed to blood-boiling shrieks and my teeth started to lengthen, and my hands turned to claws, against my will.

She was summoning the pack to fight for her, forcing those nearby to shift in her defense. Shelly and Nell were trembling, their backs arching, their jaws breaking. I couldn't shift, and that damn buzzing and burning sensation was back and—

Shit.

I screamed my voice raw as what felt like lightning sailed through my body and my neck burned as hot as the center of the sun.

Then it stopped.

When I managed to breathe again, and my lungs didn't taste like charcoal, I lifted my head. Aaron's hands were covered in blood, but he was human. He must have shifted while I was being shocked. With a twist of his wrist, he removed the last arrow from Den Mother and cast it aside next to the others. Yu and Shelly were passed out on the grass while Jess was vomiting off to the side, and Den Mother? She was passed out as well, her limbs twitching, her eyes squeezed shut.

Of course, he'd be the only one who wasn't affected. He wasn't tied to the pack as the others and I were.

"Why does she have to be like this? Why is she *always* so stubborn? If she'd stayed still, I could have gotten them out *hours* ago," Jess complained. She wiped her mouth with the back of her arm. "Thank you."

Aaron didn't answer. He was staring, transfixed, at the blood on his hands.

"This is my fault," he whispered while Jess turned to Nell and Shelly and tried to shake them awake.

I shoved myself up and shook my head, trying to rid myself of that high-pitched humming in my ears. "Where is everybody else? Where's Fern?"

Aaron's head snapped up. Jess stilled. She swallowed, hard.

"There were Hunters, Burner. Dozens of them. They shot Fern and Albe and Danbe and Eric with those arrows. The Hunters dragged them away in nets. They would have taken the pups too, but Den Mother attacked. Where *were* you? Why weren't you here?"

Because I was sick and spilling my guts to a woman in black leather with a weird facial tattoo and an even weirder name, who killed a group of Hunters atop the roof of the mall. That would only lead to more questions, and at that moment, I didn't think it mattered.

"Burner was attacked by the Hunters, but he got shot with an arrow like the others. He managed to kill them, but he was too weak to come with Riley and me," Aaron answered. "He told me to take Riley back, in case another group was coming for the pack."

Jess looked at Aaron and me. "Is this true, Burner?"

Aaron wiped his hand on his thighs and grabbed a nearby blanket. He wrapped it around his waist to hide his nudity. "Excuse me, I need to wash my hands."

"Yeah, yeah, it's true," I lied, frowning at Aaron's back. Why did he say that? I focused on Jess once more. "Where are the pups?"

"Inside the house. While Fern and the others attacked the Hunters, Den Mother had us take the pups and Elders out of the house to bring them here. I know I was supposed to stay with them, but I couldn't leave her." Jess stroked Den Mother's white fur. "When the Hunters captured Fern and the others, well... She drew as many Hunters as she could into the house, turned on the gas to the stove, and kicked the lit kerosene lamp we keep by the front door into it. The light was so bright, Burner. It was like daytime."

So, that was the light I saw.

Jess shrugged, then rubbed her forehead, her mouth starting to tremble. "I, um, she was going to burn with them, they'd shot her with the arrows by that point, and I-I dragged her out of the fire and back here." She sniffled then laughed. "She bit me, but, I-I, I don't—" Her voice wavered. I grabbed her, hugging her tight. She wrapped her arms around my neck and started to cry.

"Burner? Is that you?"

I looked past Jess's shoulder and saw little Riley, tear-stained, and holding Danny's hand in the doorway of the house. Danny was faintly trembling. It didn't take a wolf's nose to smell the terror coming off him.

"I'm here," I rasped. "Are you two okay?"

They didn't respond. They stared beyond us, into the woods. I followed their gaze and saw a single Hunter in shredded clothing, his back to us, his arm bloodied and bitten, his head bowed. His back heaved with huge breaths as his body shifted and black fur shot through his exposed skin.

Oh, God.

A Hound. The Hunter was turning into a damned Hound! I didn't think they were real. I thought they were just a fairy tale Fern told us so we wouldn't bite people. They couldn't think. They couldn't shift back and forth. They were stuck, causing havoc, and killing everything and anything until they were killed, but Fern always told me they listened to some words. Words he'd told me once years and years ago. What the hell were they?

It must have followed Aaron and me to the house.

Slowly, I pushed Jess away. She lifted her head, her brows drawn up in confusion, but when she saw the Hunter, her face paled. She looked between Den Mother and the pups.

"Burner, the Elders want to speak to you... What's going on?" Aaron reappeared at the door and stopped in his tracks.

The Hound, gurgling and groaning, slowly turned to face us at Aaron's voice. His body twitched, and half his face was shifted into a wolf's head. He opened his jaw, a guttural growl emerging past his cracked lips as he stepped toward us.

Silently, Aaron pulled Riley and Danny inside before he stepped out and closed the door behind him. Jess covered Den Mother's body with hers, her eyes darting to Shelly, Yu, and Nell still passed out in the grass. Slowly, I grabbed one of the poisoned arrows and stood, my eyes fixed on the Hound. Drooling white foam, the Hound took another step toward us. Aaron shifted into his wolf form, lowering his head, and flattening his ears.

"*Назад,*" a voice drifted from the upstairs window of the house.

The Hound stopped, its head tilting to the side at the words, its expression turning blank.

"*Назад, назад!*" the voice above said. The Hound whined and shook its head, starting to walk in a circle. "Now, do it now!"

Without another word, I leaped for the Hound while Aaron skirted in front of it, distracting it. I raced behind it and raised the arrow above my head and plunged it into the Hound's exposed spine. The Hound shrieked, its head shaking back and forth, spinning around like a whirlwind until it froze. It took one step forward and fell to the ground, dead.

"*Хорошо, хорошо,* come here, here," the voice drifted down to us. I turned to Jess.

She was staring up at the window, her eyes wide. "I've never heard her speak," she whispered.

Aaron sniffed the Hound and sneezed. He shook his head and backed away.

Without another word, I entered the house, patting Danny and Riley on their heads as I passed them. They both peered out of the door, watching Jess and Aaron. I climbed the stairs, wrinkling my nose at the scent of mold and stale air, careful of the numerous liquor bottles that lined each step.

I got to the top, pausing at the three doors. One was a bathroom, another was certainly Aaron's room. I hesitated, uncertain if I should enter or not. His sheets were rumpled, and there were stacks of books everywhere, but there were claw marks on the wall too. I was about to close his door when I noticed the padlock on the outside.

Why did his door lock from the outside?

Swallowing, I turned and entered what had to be Rock's room. The mattress was shredded, the blankets and pillows ripped too. The wardrobe was broken, and the floor was scattered with broken porcelain. But looking out of the window was a petite, white-haired, ancient woman wearing a beige-colored robe. She was murmuring in another language, stroking the head of a yellow and gray wolf who snored loudly in response. There were two others curled tightly around each other, slowly breathing as they slept on a piece of carpet.

Elders.

The old woman turned her head, her eyes solid white, and she smiled. Only her canines were left in her otherwise empty mouth. "горелка? Is that you?" She looked at the wall.

"I, I don't understand, Elder." I took another step into the room.

Her head swiveled toward me. She hemmed and hummed, patting her lap. "What is word… папоротник always knew the good words…"

"I'm Burner?" I offered. She paused before nodding.

"да, that is right. Bern-er. I am Мария,"

I frowned, trying to figure out the words before I blinked. "Maria?" I offered, again.

Maria nodded. "Yes, good. You understand?"

"I think so." Carefully, I approached her. "What is it, Maria? Elder?"

Maria looked out the window, her face turning upward as a cool breeze swept in. "When I was a girl, а гунтер, a Hunter came to our village. My father, the Alpha, and his chosen killed him. But like а чума, a plague, more Hunters soon followed." The wolf on her lap stirred and she gently shushed him, before tilting her head again. "We leave home, leave the village, and come here, to America." Her leathery fingers danced in the streams of sunlight. "But still they find us, and then, the world turns to ash and darkness and the monsters roam free."

"Elder…what are you talking about?" I crossed my arms.

Maria smiled her toothless smile. "More will come. We must move the den. We must join our brothers and sisters and await the hard cold."

My eyes widened. "The pack! You want us to move the pack?"

"Yes."

"But the Hunters took Fern, Albe, Danbe, and Eric. We can't leave them behind. We need to bring them back," I argued.

Maria's smile dropped and she frowned, shaking her head then nodding. "Yes, yes. We must talk. Shoo, shoo." She waved her hand at me. "Go, we must talk."

Without another word spoken, I left the room and headed downstairs. Back outside, a sickening sensation was starting to curl in my gut that everything was going to change.

Chapter Ten

"THERE ISN'T ANY food," Yu whispered.

"What about the storehouse? Or the cellar? There should be something there." Nell's voice was soft.

"The gas pipe came up from the cellar, everything is probably destroyed." Shelly sighed.

Shelly, Yu, Nell were standing in the corner of the living room/kitchen. Den Mother was stretched out on the couch in her human form and covered with a blanket. Her face was clean of blood, but her white hair still had spatters of red mingled within. Her face was turned to the side and the blanket slowly rose up and down with each breath.

Riley and the other young pups were curled up on the floor, a threadbare comforter thrown over them. Danny had tried to stand guard, his back perched against Den Mother's couch, but he'd fallen asleep. Jess had gone up to the Elders' room shortly after I came down.

I was sitting at the table, my fingers curled around a glass of cold water while Aaron delicately traced the collar around my neck. His fingers were cool to the touch. He was close to my neck, his face a mixture of raw curiosity and horror.

"Does it hurt?"

"When I try to shift," I said, "and I tried to pull it off but it felt like this bee was trapped in my ear. It gave me a headache, that's for sure."

Aaron's brows furrowed. "Maybe it's a protective measure against people interfering with it to ensure the wearer's obedience."

I raised my eyebrows. "English?"

Aaron's lips twitched. "No touch the shock collar."

"Right." I sighed.

"Burner? Can you come here?" Shelly called me from the group. I glanced at Aaron and he shrugged his shoulders. I got up from my spot at the table and joined them. Yu and Nell exchanged nervous glances while Shelly waved for Aaron to join us. Aaron frowned but stood beside me, crossing his arms over his chest.

"What is it?"

"There isn't any food, and I don't know how we're supposed to make it the week to join the Quebec pack," Nell said. She kept her voice low.

"What about the storehouse?" Aaron offered. Shelly shook her blonde head.

"No, it's gone."

I pursed my lips, even as Jess came downstairs, her face pale, her eyes darting from Den Mother to the pups to our little group. She wrung her hands in front of her before she went to Den Mother's side and gently shook her shoulder, hurriedly whispering for her to wake up.

Den Mother's golden eyes fluttered open. She blinked tiredly at Jess, taking in the room, the stench of blood and gunpowder, and lastly us before she let out a deep breath. Jess leaned closer, frantically whispering so low even I couldn't hear her. Judging by Aaron's quizzical expression, neither could he. We waited, even as Den Mother sat up, staring at the pups, her face turning grim. She nodded a few times while Jess's hands shook.

"I understand," Den Mother finally said aloud. She rubbed Jess's back and Jess's shoulders sank as she knelt next to the pups on the floor. Den Mother stood, the blanket wrapped tight around her tall body. She was slightly bent forward, the ceiling too low for her to stand straight up. I swallowed as her golden eyes fixed first on me, then Aaron. She extended a long arm, her clawed hand beckoning us to follow her out of the home.

Once we were outside, she was able to stand at full height and she breathed in deep. Den Mother was taller than Fern by at least a foot, her face more angular, her limbs longer. The way she moved was hard to describe, but it was smooth and unlike Fern and myself. Fern told me once that all Den Mothers were like her, and from my experience with the Quebec and New Hampshire packs, he was right.

She turned, her attention focusing on Aaron and myself. I fought the nervous twitch in my cheek as she stared at me first, then Aaron, who swallowed loudly in response.

"Where is your father?"

Aaron's mouth parted, his eyes widening as Den Mother moved swiftly closer to him. Their faces were inches from one another as she loomed over him.

"Where. Is. Your. Father?" Den Mother hissed.

"I-I don't know where he is," Aaron stumbled.

Her eyes narrowed. She did the same to me, her lips slightly peeled back exposing rows of sharpened teeth. "Where is Fern?"

"The Hunters have him," I replied, staring into her golden eyes. "I told the Elders. They want to move the pack, but we can't abandon Fern and the others."

Den Mother stepped back, her eyes flickering up to the windows where a glimpse of silver hair could be seen. She tilted her head, nodding to herself before she looked at Aaron and me.

"There is more to your story, isn't there, Burner?" My name was a rumbled purr on her lips. I swallowed.

"Yes," I admitted, even as Aaron shot me a surprised look.

"Speak."

I drew in a deep breath and told Den Mother everything. I told her about the mall, about the Hunters and the collar and the city they mentioned, about the strange girl with the strange name. I pulled out the note from my pocket; I had honestly forgotten about it with everything going on and held it open to her. Her golden eyes flashed in alarm. She gripped my shoulders with her clawed fingers, digging into the flesh.

"Repeat her name," she rasped.

"Sep...September 24th Amon," I managed, flinching as her grip tightened and blood spilled down my arms.

"Deadwalker," Den Mother hissed like a snake, her eyes turning to slits.

I shot Aaron a panicked look as Den Mother drew me closer to her, sniffing and petting my hair. Aaron nervously took a step back while Den Mother scented me and rubbed her cheek against my head before she shoved me aside, ripped the note from my hand, and walked back into the house.

Aaron didn't say anything, not a single peep. I was too stunned to speak.

Deadwalkers were real? They... Weren't they just a story?

Den Mother emerged once again with Jess, Nell, Shelly, and Yu at her side, helping Maria to stand. Aaron and I both dropped to our knees, our heads bowed as Den Mother lovingly took Maria's hands in hers and led her to us. Maria blindly gazed off into the distance, her fingers touching my face, rubbing across my forehead, through my hair, along my cheeks and lips. When she let go and did the same to Aaron, I realized she was feeling us to see what we looked like.

Maria smiled and let go of Aaron's face. She reached blindly for Den Mother who once more took her hands, letting out a soothing rumble from her chest. Instantly I felt at ease, but Aaron's shoulders were hunched forward. Her power wouldn't work on him.

"Burner." Maria sighed, her voice soft and filled with sorrow.

"Yes, Elder?"

"You must find папоротник, ah, Fern, you must find him and the others and bring them home. They must come home." Maria's voice grew firm. "You must save them."

My mouth opened. I lifted my head. "W-what?"

"How is he supposed to do that?" Aaron sputtered.

Maria squeezed Den Mother's hand, speaking in that strange language of hers. Den Mother rumbled deep in her chest again. Jessica cleared her throat and translated for them.

"They say you must go to the graveyard, and...oh, Den Mother, no. That's too cruel." Jess sighed. Den Mother peered down at her, and Jess relented. "You must... There is a tin box buried atop of Charlotte." Aaron froze. I bit my bottom lip. "There are binoculars and Fern's map from when he journeyed here during the two years of darkness, and—how do you know they went there?" Jess interrupted Den Mother and Maria.

"Because the note the Deadwalker gave Burner, and his own words, told me." Den Mother's voice was low, husky, and dangerous. Her gaze was on me once more. "The note says he's wearing a Hunter's collar, a device to trap wolves and make them unable to fight. Burner told me the Hunters wanted to take him to Boston. That is where the others are being taken to be sold to the dog pits." Den Mother's voice lowered into a threatening growl. I shivered, goosebumps rising along my arms.

"It could be a trap," Jess urged.

"No." Maria shook her head, her silver hair shimmering in the sunlight. "It is greed. Burner, you must save them. You must bring them back to Quebec, use Fern's map to guide you there and back."

"Yes, Den Mother. Yes, Maria." I bowed my head again, my heart in my throat.

"We must leave at once." Maria looked up toward Den Mother. "Take the pups, take the Elders and daughters, we must head North before dusk sets upon us."

"Of course, Elder," Den Mother soothed.

Wordlessly, Shelly, Nell, Yu, and Jess turned to return to the house when Aaron spoke, his voice quiet.

"Wait."

I glanced at him. His jaw was clenched, his hands curled into fists. "You're... you're going to send Burner away with a map, and binoculars, on his own to save the pack?" His voice rose with each word. "Do you realize how stupid that is? What if he dies? What if he's caught by People Eaters? Or, another Deadwalker? Or Hunters? God, Burner, do you even know *how* to read a map?" he snapped at me.

I ground my jaw, glaring at him. "I'd figure it out."

Aaron shook his head, his lips turned upside down. "He can't go by himself, it's too dangerous—"

"Which is why you are going with him," Den Mother purred.

Aaron blinked, his mouth opening then closing. "What?" He squawked, the frustration and anger gone from his voice.

"You would never betray him," she said in that same tone. Aaron jerked his gaze down to stare at the grass he'd ripped up. "Who else to help guide him than one who only has Burner's best *interest* at heart, as Charlotte would say. Am I right?"

Aaron's ears turned pink, his face unreadable, but he shakily nodded his head.

I scowled at him. What was he getting all red about? Of course, he had my best interests at heart, we'd been friends since we were pups.

"When do we leave?" I broke the sudden silence as Maria's face turned to pity.

"At once, my dear pups, at once."

Chapter Eleven

AARON AND I needed supplies, but everything that had been stored in the pack house was ash, floating inland on the ocean's breeze. The daughters stripped every herb plant they could find, dug up every garlic bulb, potato, radish, and vegetable not trampled or ruined. They took it with them as they packed what little they had before setting foot on the road.

We stood at a crossroad. Den Mother, Jess, the daughters, Elders, and the pups stood on one side, and Aaron and I on the other. There was a sick curling sensation in my gut that told me I would never see them again, but I stomped it down.

We would save Fern, Eric, Albe, Danbe and yes, even Rock. We would get home and the pack would be together once more. I turned away from them, my bare feet burning on the summer-soaked pavement, even as Jessica and Riley and Danny started to cry. Aaron waved goodbye to them before joining me.

Neither of us spoke for a long time, not until we stood at the base of the cemetery once more.

"I don't...I can't." Aaron's voice cracked, his body starting to tremble. I gripped his arm.

"I want you to go to the mall and get everything we need," I said.

He stared at my hand, a far deeper shade of amber than his own pale skin. His gaze crawled up my arm to my face, his eyes searching mine. There was relief in his blue and gold-flecked eyes. Relief and sorrow.

"But..."

"Backpacks, pants, shirts, whatever you think we need."

Aaron looked away and nodded. "Shoes, a water bottle, too, I think. We can't walk barefoot the entire time and water might be sparse."

"See?" My lips curled slightly. "I wouldn't have thought of that. I would've settled for a dirty brown puddle."

Aaron gagged. "Burner, that's just disgusting."

I laughed and let go of his arm. I shoved him. "Go on, to the mall."

I waited until he disappeared around the hill of the cemetery before I started up, trying not to think of what I was about to do, what Aaron and I were setting out to do. If I was brutally honest with myself, I was glad Aaron was coming with me, That I had someone on my side, someone willing to face whatever may come. Namely rescuing Fern and the others from Hunters. God only knows what else was out there but the word came unwillingly to my mind:

Deadwalker.

Once, when I was twelve, Fern and I had gone for a walk through the Old Town, exploring the houses, avoiding the lions that made their dens in the shadows of humanity. We went into a building with a giant cross atop the roof and stained-glass windows. The door had been locked from the outside with a two-by-four shoved into the handles. Fern had pulled it out and cracked it open, peering around cautiously, before throwing the doors open wide.

I'd thrown up in the overgrown bushes next to the doors at the stench.

The stench... I could never place my finger on it. All I knew was that the odor somehow crawled its way through my nose and nestled into the back of my throat. It was within the building Fern called a church at the very end near an altar that I saw it. Or at least what Fern had claimed was a Deadwalker nailed to a crucifix. Its naked body was skinny and leathery, almost looking like jerky.

"They're real, Burner. They've always been real." Fern's voice had carried in the building. "They stay in the cities. Promise me you'll keep away from the towns and cities. Those are no places for wolves. You must fight Burner, no matter what."

A day later after being in the church, I came down with a horrible flu and afterward I thought I'd hallucinated the entire experience. I hadn't. That crucified Deadwalker was real. There were others, and one had, for whatever reason, saved me last night.

I took the final steps to the top, gazing out at the mall. Aaron's shadow cast long across the parking lot as he walked, heading for the back loading bay doors. I watched him until he was out of sight before I turned my focus to Charlotte's grave.

I knelt, my hands spreading across the dirt.

"I am so sorry for what I'm about to do," I whispered.

There was no response.

I clawed out handfuls of dirt, sinking deeper and deeper into the soil, sweating under the sunlight as it poured through the branches of the elm tree. The tree provided some shade, but not nearly enough, and the wind that ruffled my hair helped a little. I was sinking deeper into Charlotte's grave, my back and forehead were drenched in sweat, making my eyes sting as some dripped in my eyes. Whoever buried the tin box buried it deep. As I disappeared into the hole, I started to panic.

Had I missed it? Was it already in the dirt I had dug out? No, that wasn't possible. I was so caught up in my thoughts that when my fingers snagged fabric, I froze.

Charlotte's shroud.

I wiped my forehead with the back of my arm and panted as I sat back on my heels. Her shroud was underneath me, but... Maybe she was holding it in her arms? I took a heavy breath, grateful Aaron wasn't here watching me as I deftly pulled open the folds of cloth, grimacing at the sight I was about to see.

Except I didn't see anything because the shroud was empty.

Charlotte's body, and the tin box, were gone.

"No." I swallowed, my heart starting to race. "No, no, no, no!" I ripped the shroud out of the grave and dug deeper, dirt forcing its way under my nails as I desperately clawed my way down.

"Burner! Are you still up there?" Aaron called from a distance and I froze. Hurriedly, I shoved the shroud back inside the grave and crawled out. The sun was setting, but I could see Aaron waving his arms from on top of the mall.

"Y-yeah! I'm still here! Did you find everything?" I yelled back.

"I did! I'm coming back!" Aaron called.

I stared at the empty grave, at the empty shroud.

Fuck, shit, goddamn it, *fuck*!

Aaron could *not* learn Charlotte was missing. *Fuck, okay, Burner, concentrate!*

Hurriedly, I shoved the dirt back into the grave, my breathing ragged, but by the time I was done, Aaron was hiking up to me, his arms loaded with stuffed backpacks and boots. I stumbled away from Charlotte's grave, my limbs trembling as Aaron stopped short. He looked at me, then his mother's grave and back to me.

"What happened?"

I swallowed.

"Burner?"

Your mother's gone. "The tin box is gone," I blurted.

Aaron's eyes widened. He dropped the backpacks, moving to step toward the grave. "What? Are you sure?"

I stepped in front of him, blocking him. "I'm sure. I checked. It's not there."

His brows furrowed. "Did...did you go deep enough?"

"Yes," I panted.

"Did you see—?"

"The tin box is gone." My voice was firm with no room for doubt. "It isn't there anymore, Aaron."

Aaron took a step back, eyeing my dirt-covered body before he cleared his throat. "I found some clean clothes for you."

"Oh, good," I sighed, brushing the dirt off one of my arms. "Give it here."

"You're way too filthy."

I wrinkled my nose before I rolled my eyes. "Fine. Let's head for Oyster Lake. I'll get all nice and shiny and clean. Then we can figure out what to do next. Happy?"

"Happy."

I grabbed one of the backpacks and shooed Aaron in front of me, casting one last glance at Charlotte's empty grave before I followed him down the hill.

By the time we got to Oyster Lake, I was exhausted, miserable, and dragging my feet, but as soon as I spied the cool fresh water, I dropped the backpack and shoved Aaron aside. I raced down the rotting wood dock and dived head first into the lake. Aaron stumbled before he regained his footing and dropped his backpack next to mine, but instead of following me into the cool and refreshing water, he headed for the small fishing shack. I surfaced just in time to watch as he entered the store. I dove back under, getting my bearings as I swam back toward the dock.

Oyster Lake was given this name because of the oysters, mussels, whatever, that grew there once upon a time. Now mussels happily lived in clusters along the pier's stands. I took my time, ripping several off and tossing them back on top of the decking until I had enough to feed a small army. There were a few lotus plants preparing to bloom, so I swam further down to their roots. I pulled a few from the soil and dragged them back up to the top.

When I crawled out, I saw the tentative glow of a campfire with a metal cooking pan on top of the grill and Aaron sitting cross-legged next to it, a map spread out before him, twirling a marker between his fingers.

I carried my prize of mussels and lotus roots toward him. Without saying a word, I dumped the shellfish into the pan and presented him with one of the plants.

Startled, Aaron stared at it, then me.

"What is that?"

"Something really tasty." I flashed a grin. "Do you have a knife?"

Aaron patted himself, but I sucked my teeth. "Never mind, there's gotta be one in there." I dropped the roots and headed inside the shack, squinting as my eyes adjusted to the darkness. I looked around until I spotted a nice bowie knife on display. I did some more digging and found a few sealed cans of butter sauce along with some old, but dry, tins of herbs. I brought my bounty back to the campfire where Aaron was trying to shake the water off his map, an annoyed expression on his face.

"What's that?" I wiped some water from my eyes, flinging it to the side. I grabbed the lotus root and cut it off before I peeled the skin and started slicing it thinly, dropping the slices alongside the mussels.

"This is a map," Aaron said, as if that explained everything.

I peeled open the tin and licked the sauce. After twenty years it still tasted buttery. I shrugged and dumped it into the pan, enjoying the hissing sound that filled the air.

"Is it like Fern's?" I popped open the herbs and sprinkled some on top before I stirred everything together with the bowie knife.

"I don't know," Aaron replied honestly, "what I do know is that it's for a list of campsites along the Appalachian trail, and that trail will lead us to straight to Boston."

"What about the main highway?"

"Too dangerous." Aaron shook his head. "There could be Hunters, People Eaters, who knows what's waiting there. There are a few shortcuts to get from where we are to there, but it'll take some time, that's for sure."

I huffed, shifting the mussels, my stomach growling at the delicious smell of the cooking food. "The Hunters probably took the highway with those, those..." I rolled my hand in midair. "Things people in the old world drove."

Aaron raised an eyebrow. "You mean a car?"

"Yeah, that." I sniffed.

"Hmmm... it would have taken some time to get to the main highway from the pack house, and every car I've ever seen is dead." Aaron's eyes drifted across the map. "It could take them four to five days at the most to get past all the debris set up to shield the pack..."

"You mean they could still be out here?" I looked around, listening carefully for any sounds, any movements, anything, but only the buzz of cicadas danced in my ears.

"Possibly." Aaron's voice was soft and honest. "Either way, they have a jumpstart on us, and Boston is the only location info we have."

"And you think the trail, the apple raisin—"

"Appalachian."

"Right, the Appalachian trail will lead us straight to Boston?"

"Yes."

I studied the mussels and the frying lotus root before I nodded. "Then let's do that, but right now, I think we're ready to eat."

Chapter Twelve

WHEN AARON SAID that the Appalachian Trail would be easier for us to navigate, I think he meant it'd be easier to navigate in our wolf forms. Which I couldn't shift into because my stupid shock collar wouldn't let me. A point driven home when Aaron encouraged me to at least try. I ended up biting my bottom lip bloody and clawing at my throat, racked with violent tremors while Aaron begged me to stop.

He wouldn't meet my eyes for a good while after that and I rubbed the skin around my neck, tugging every now and then on the collar, mindful of where I stepped. I was wearing the jeans and thin jacket over a T-shirt he'd gotten for me. I'd rolled the jeans up to my calves, refusing to wear the boots until things either got to be too muddy or the ground too hard on my feet. The backpacks he'd picked up converted from standard, normal backpacks for humans to wear to ones for dogs to be strapped into and carry the weight on the sides.

It was pretty ingenious, actually. He'd slipped into his wolf form and I had strapped him in before he led the way, stopping occasionally to make sure I was following him. If I'd been able to shift, we could have made double, no, triple, the time needed to get to Boston. But I couldn't shift. I was stuck, and I hated it.

Eventually, we reached an even pace and marched along the trail for days, taking breaks when we could, trapping small game to eat here and there, but the urge to continue, to find the others, was driving us onward past rotted signs and green plaques stuck on rocks. Past campgrounds we skirted around and streams we filled our water bottles with. We were too far from the pack house to even think about turning back and following the others to Quebec.

We were entirely on our own.

We would need to take a break longer than five minutes, find someplace safe for the both of us to sleep at the same time. Eventually, when the sky turned dark and filled with stars that faded away with the morning sun, my eyes were drooping. Even Aaron's pace slowed, his head bowed, his nose barely above the ground. We were pushing our limit.

I grabbed the handle on the back of Aaron's backpack and stopped him. He looked up at me, puzzled. I pointed toward a sign with a picture of a cabin and barbeque pit. Aaron hesitated, his gold eyes examining the sign. I pulled the map from my pocket and unfolded it on the dry ground. Aaron looked it over before he nodded reluctantly. I refolded the map, tucked it into the pocket of my jacket, and we started down the path.

The sun was overhead by the time we got to the collapsing cabins. Most of them were without roofs or siding. Aaron whined unhappily. I patted his side.

"Just stay here, okay? I'll be right back."

Aaron didn't bother with a *woo*, just collapsed onto the ground. He shut his eyes while I searched the triangle-shaped log cabins, looking for at least one that we could sleep inside for a few hours. There were about twenty and most of them were destroyed. Others were trashed and covered with paint on the inside. About to give up, I entered one in the middle, a sign I couldn't read on the front. The door was slightly stuck, but I shouldered it open and peeked inside.

The glass windows had kept the weather out, preserving the sun-bleached carpet. I think at one time it was an office with a metal desk and chair. A curtain covered a wall and I brushed it aside, pausing at the sight of hundreds of pictures of men, women, and children that greeted me. There were notes with words and numbers on them. I traced the red scribble below a picture of two little boys that looked like Danny but wearing brand new, old-world-styled clothes.

Who were they?

I was so caught up, staring at the ghosts of people, fascinated by the perfect brilliant smiles and the backgrounds of buildings, bedrooms, homes and gardens, the different types of people, some pale like Aaron, some darker skinned. A few were covered in freckles like Jess, and others a deep hue like my own. Not to mention the various types of hair color and styles. The pictures almost looked like they were taken from my magazines. I greedily absorbed every detail of the people smiling back at me.

There should be enough space in one of my backpacks to take the pictures with me. Aaron, when he'd gotten enough sleep, could tell me what the words said.

"Oh, well," I breathed and stepped back. I pulled off my backpack and propped it against the desk. I tugged off my jacket and laid it on the table, grateful to let my skin breathe in the warm room. This room was as good as any, and at least the floor was mostly clean and dry. I turned around, meaning to leave the office and drag Aaron inside, when I saw him through the window surrounded by six ragged people wielding axes and hammers.

Aaron was still in his wolf form, his ears flattened against his head, his tail curled between his legs. His entire body was trembling. He looked at each and every person as they eyed him hungrily.

Why the hell hadn't he barked!

"It's okay, boy, shh, it's okay. You're a good boy, aren't you?" a man, missing most of his teeth with a long beard and rotted gumboots, soothed. He had one hand out. The other held a large rusted knife behind his back.

"Carl, look at that backpack, there has to be someone nearby," another man, skinny and wearing a patched business suit, said. He looked around the camp and I dropped to my knees below the window, quietly panting.

"I don't care, Hugh. I want that fucking dog," the man who'd been called Carl said. The responding murmuring of the others in the group made me shudder.

I crept on my hands and knees toward the door and peeked around the edge. Aaron was trying to hide, to make himself look smaller. A man tried to grab the backpack handle and Aaron skirted away, almost too close to another man. The circle was getting smaller and smaller. Aaron was whining, terrified.

Why the hell wasn't he fighting back?

I acted without thinking. I pushed myself to my feet and stepped out of the office. The group was ignoring me, so I cleared my throat, loudly, "He's mine."

Aaron literally sagged with relief while the group turned to me.

Carl, I guess the leader, nodded at Aaron. "He's yours?"

"That's right." My voice was firm and without question.

"Hey, we'd trade you for him," Hugh offered, eyeing Aaron. "We got some bullets if you have a gun."

"No trade," I said. My eyes narrowed. I curled my hands into fists.

"You all alone, son?" Carl lifted his chin, bloodshot eyes scanning the log cabins.

"No. I'm with my friend." I gestured to Aaron.

Carl, Hugh, and the others glanced at each other before bursting out laughing. I waited for them to stop before I stepped toward them. "I don't want any trouble. My friend and I are going to go now."

"Sorry, can't do that." Carl stroked his beard. "See, we haven't eaten in days, and it's been years since I saw a dog this fat, and we are *really* hungry. So, run along, or else we'll butcher and cook you too."

I smiled, peeling my lips back, my canines slightly longer than normal. The collar was starting to buzz. "If you don't leave, I'm going to rip out your fucking hearts and eat them, do you understand?" I growled low in my throat.

The blood drained from Hugh's face while the others hesitantly stepped back. "Carl, *Carl,* he's one of *them!*"

"No, he isn't! It's sunlight. They can't walk in the sun. Just some stupid shit kid. Come on," Carl snapped. "There's six of us and one of him. I don't care if we eat him or the dog. Let's do this!"

Before he could act, I ran straight at Carl, his eyes widening in surprise as I punched him hard in the gut. He dropped to his knees. I spun on my heel, kicking another one on the side of the leg and hearing the bone snap in half. He dropped, screaming and clutching his leg, blood spurting from the exposed wound.

"Aaron, run!" I shouted, rapidly backing up as two others wearing ill-fitting clothes came toward me with axes raised. But Aaron didn't move. He remained frozen in his spot, his golden eyes wide in panic even as Carol grabbed his rusty knife and crawled toward him.

"*Run!*" I roared. I was grabbed from behind by filthy hands, my arms trapped at my side. I slammed my head back and connected with someone's nose, but whoever had me didn't let go. They cursed, and I used the momentum to raise my legs and kick a man wielding a hammer in the chest. He gasped, dropping it, as he hugged himself, trying to draw in air.

I slammed my head back again, blood sinking in my hair. The man let go, allowing me to raise my arms and elbow his ribcage. He shrieked, and I took off, running toward Aaron's frozen frame as he stared at Carol who raised the knife above his head. I was about to deck him again when a gunshot echoed in the air and I panicked. Evidently, it was enough to stir Aaron from his stunned state because he bolted toward the path that we'd taken with me hot on his tail.

We ran, dipping into side trails, along deer trails, desperate to put enough space between them and *us*. The only reason we stopped was because Aaron's paw caught an upturned tree root and he tumbled down a hill. I chased after him, panting and straining for air as I reached his still form. I knelt next to him, pulling open his eyes, patting his nose.

"Aaron," I gulped, almost sick from the amount of adrenaline pumping through my body, "Aaron, wake up."

His eyes moved, and he squirmed in my arms. I let him go and he rolled to his feet, shifting into his human form.

"Get it off, get it off!" He hissed, pawing at the straps that were too tight for him. With bloodied and rough fingers, I opened the locks and straps. Aaron collapsed back onto the ground, the wet leaves sticking to his naked flesh as he scrubbed his face with his hands, his entire frame trembling. "What...what the hell... Those people, who *were* those people?"

I fell backward onto the ground, sucking in deep lungfuls of air and willing my heart to calm. The sky rumbled softly overhead and it began to rain. Aaron continued muttering to himself. When I thought I could talk, I did.

"Why didn't you howl?"

Aaron froze, his startled eyes meeting mine. "*What?*"

I sat up, my arms at my side supporting me. "Why didn't you *howl?*"

"I-I don't... I mean..."

I shook my head. "No, better yet, why the hell didn't you fight back?" My voice was rising. Aaron looked away, shame burning his face. "They could have fucking killed us. Actually, they were going to kill *you* and *eat* you! You know how to fight, so *why didn't you fucking fight back!*" I roared.

When he didn't respond, I threw my arms into the air. "Goddamn it, they aren't piglets. They aren't small furry fucking animals, they are people and—"

"I'm sorry!" Aaron spat out. His eyes were squeezed tight, his lips curved down. He dug at the leaves. "I-I just froze. There were so many, Burner, and they had axes, and I didn't even notice them I was so tired. I'm *sorry!*"

"Some fucking wolf you are," I snarled, grabbing the backpack and getting to my feet. I started climbing back up the hill.

"Where are you going?" Aaron asked.

"We have to go back; I left my jacket and backpack in the office. The map is still there," I finished. I got to where Aaron had tripped and paused. It was pissing down rain, and within moments, our tracks would be gone. Yeah, a wolf's sense of smell was good, but it wasn't strong enough to survive a heavy rainstorm.

We didn't have a map and who knew what little trail we were on. I growled, kicking a pile of dead leaves.

"God*damn it!*"

Aaron soon joined me, his teeth chattering quietly. I didn't bother to turn and look at him. I threw the backpack at his feet and brushed past him, going further down the trail. "Put on some fucking clothes. We have to go."

I didn't bother waiting for a reply, or even for him to dress. I blinked past the rain, growling low in my throat as Aaron eventually caught up.

What the hell were we supposed to do now?

The thought raced through my mind as we walked.

It never stopped raining. I didn't speak to Aaron for hours. The only reason I was still walking was because of the anger and frustration coursing through my body. If Aaron had wanted to stop, he didn't say anything. He desperately did his best to keep up, hampered by the godawful mud that tried to suck us into the ground.

We crossed a bridge. The wind had started to pick up and it made the wood and steel beams creak under us as we crossed. Behind me, Aaron was whispering to himself, telling himself it would be okay. That everything would be fine. I snorted, scanning the other side and noting a shack on top of a platform towering over the forest not too far away. It was getting dark again, and as much as I wanted to keep walking, we were heading for a massive storm.

I made my way up to it, climbing the steel steps with Aaron right behind me. When we got to the top, I pushed the door open and eyed the room. It had a wooden desk pushed against one side, a man-sized closet lying on the ground, a small stove near a corner, a plain steel bed with a moth-eaten mattress on top of it. There were a few cooking pots and pans hanging over a sink. Wordlessly, I entered, momentarily grateful for the reprieve from the growing storm outside.

Aaron stood outside the door, uncertainty on his face. I glared at him.

"Get inside and shut the damn door."

Aaron bowed his head, entering and shutting the door behind him, blocking out the wind and rain. He padded to the opposite end of the room, as far away from me as he could be. I didn't bother looking at him as I pulled off my T-shirt and kicked off my boots.

I fell onto the bed and, within seconds, was dead to the world.

Dimly, I awoke at some point when the storm was at its worst. Aaron's back was pressed against mine, his hands covering his ears. He was quietly whimpering as the building groaned on its stands. I waited for him to fall silent, but when he didn't, I huffed and rolled over in the narrow space, curling tight around him. I pillowed my head on my arm and reached over him, covering his eyes with my hand, and feeling the telltale wetness of tears as he stilled next to me.

"I'm hungry and exhausted. I'm not mad at you, I'm mad at those People Eaters for fucking everything up. Do you understand?" I whispered.

Aaron mutely nodded.

I sighed and hid my face in the crook of his neck. "Then please just go to sleep."

I waited until his breathing slowed and he relaxed before I wrapped my arm around his waist, curled my fingers under his side, and let myself fall asleep.

Chapter Thirteen

"B-B-BURNER." AARON'S TEETH were chattering. I groaned, hiding my face in his hair. The wall against my bare back was icy to the touch. Thankfully, the scars on my lower back meant I could only feel part of it. Still, I pulled Aaron closer, digging my fingers into his shirt, my breathing easing once more.

"Burner," Aaron tried again. His hands gripped my wrists and arms. I sighed, reluctantly peeking one eye open. He had slightly turned his head, peering back at me with worried eyes.

"What?" My voice was thick with sleep.

"It snowed."

I blinked. Slowly. His eyes searched mine. I scowled at him.

"Bullshit."

Aaron waved at the room. I let go of him, sitting up, and instantly regretted my mistake. Without his warmth, my body was covered in goosebumps from the cold. I looked out of the windows.

Nothing but miles and miles of white snow for as far as the eye could see. I climbed over Aaron and out of the bed, my toes stinging at the bitter cold floor as I passed every window, small white clouds of white escaping my mouth as I breathed. Outside, the limbs of trees were heavy with snow, and when I scanned for the bridge we had crossed last night, it was gone. Broken. We couldn't go back.

The bed creaked under Aaron's weight and his socked feet were silent on the linoleum floor as he joined me at the window.

"What are we going to do now?" Mist drifted from his mouth.

I rubbed my arms, the cold starting to dig in my flesh. "I don't know. We can't stay here."

Aaron didn't say anything. Instead, he turned around and picked up my shirt from the floor. He grimaced as he held it up. It was frozen solid. "I don't think you can wear this."

"No." I scanned the room again, noting the closet. "Here, help me lift it. Maybe there's something inside I can wear."

Wordlessly, we stood on each side of the closet and lifted it back to its standing position. It was locked with a small eye and hook on the outside. I flipped it and pulled open the doors only for a pile of bones to spill out and a skull to roll across the floor. Aaron yelped, jumping onto the bed as the skull rolled past his feet.

"*W-what the hell?*" Aaron sputtered.

Mouth parted, I stared at the bones, not quite formulating what exactly I was looking at. Leg bones, remains of the spine, ribs, feet, and hands still inside the closet, alongside the rotted remains of a tartan hunting jacket and crumbling pants. A suitcase was wedged into a space next to it. I went to close the doors when I noticed the claw marks on the inside. I ran the pads of my fingers across them, frowning.

"Who would put a skeleton in there? Better yet, *why* is there a skeleton in there?" Aaron's annoyed and panicked voice carried in the small room.

"I think...whoever our skeleton was, hid inside of the closet, and somehow the latch closed, and they tried to open the door, but it made the closet fall forward, and they were trapped within and eventually died," I offered.

"That's...really sad," Aaron murmured.

I pulled out the leather suitcase and thumbed the lock. There had to be a set of clothes inside. Hopefully, they weren't rotten. "If we're lucky, there's a key in his pocket," I said. I checked the pockets, turning them inside out, and ignoring the remains of dead moths that coated my fingers with a fine silver powder. I reached into the back pockets. When I felt something sharp, I pulled it out. It was small, and weirdly shaped key, with a chain attached to it. I dropped the suitcase to the floor and held the key to Aaron. He shrugged, reluctant to step down.

"The skull isn't going to eat you," I said. "I think he's long dead."

"Oh, ha-ha. It's not like Fern made you dig up half-rotted bodies to clean them up," Aaron growled.

I paused. "Rock...made you dig up bodies?"

Aaron looked away. The old bedsprings squealed under his feet as he shifted on the bed. "Yeah, and no, I don't know why he made me do it. I'm just glad he left Mom alone."

I didn't respond because I was starting to suspect Rock *had* dug up Charlotte. But, why? Why would he do that? I hadn't seen any bodies at the house. What the hell was Rock up to? I shook my head and tried to use the key on the lock, only to realize it wasn't anywhere near the proper size or shape. I sighed and tossed the key with the chain to Aaron.

"Catch."

Aaron fumbled, forcing him to hop onto the floor. He raced over to the table and sat on it, his eyes narrowed. "You did that on purpose."

"I have no idea what you're talking about." I picked up the suitcase and held it to my chest, my fingers gripping the front on each side, the metal lock groaning under stress.

"You're smirking!"

"I am not." I grinned back at him.

Arron rolled his eyes, the corner of his lips twitching. I focused again on the suitcase, scowling as it refused to open, until the locks snapped apart and the floor was covered with stacks of green paper.

"Huh."

Curiosity must have gotten the better of Aaron because he was next to me in an instant. He picked up one green bundle and flipped through it. "This is money. I think it's about...five thousand dollars' worth?" He glanced toward the bed. "Why would someone hide in a closet with a suitcase full of money?"

I sniffed. "No idea, but I don't have a plan B. I'll probably freeze to death outside before we can get anywhere."

Aaron bit his bottom lip before he slipped off his socks and handed them to me. I blinked at the multi-colored, frog-decorated socks.

"I am not wearing those."

"Yes, you are. And, here—" Aaron dropped the socks onto the floor in front of me. He pulled off his T-shirt and tossed it on top of my head. I plucked it off, scowling up at him. "You're going to wear that, too, and my jacket."

"So, what are you going to do?" My scowl deepened.

"Shift to wolf form, duh. I'll be twice as warm in a thick fur coat than wearing any human clothes."

My scowl turned into a glare, but I did pull his shirt on, which, for the record, was a size too small for me, and the socks, sighing in relief as my toes began to warm. His back was facing me, and he was hunched down, pulling the jacket from the backpack. Without looking back, he chucked it at me and I caught it midair.

Aaron waited a few minutes before he sat next to me, already starting to tremble from the cold. He held out the key.

"C-can you w-wear it f-for me? It'll g-g-get caught on a b-branch or something," he chattered.

"No problem. I'm practically one of those guys in the magazine who wear a ton of jewelry," I said sarcastically.

"You mean a model."

"Whatever." The chain was long and bulky enough that all I had to do was wear it and drop it between the layers of clothing so it lay against my chest.

Aaron gave me a thumbs-up before he shifted into his wolf form and shook his fur, including his tail, letting out a sigh of relief. He sat next to me.

"Any idea where to go?"

Aaron nosed my arm in response.

"Right." I sighed, pushing off the floor. I donned my boots, zipped up my jacket, and shouldered the backpack. "Let's try following the ravine down the river. Hopefully it'll lead somewhere."

Aaron woofed and waited patiently for me to force open the door. I gave the skeleton one last glance before I shut the door behind us, leaving it and its wealth to a world long gone.

Chapter Fourteen

IT HAD SNOWED a lot during the night, up to Aaron's furry shoulders. He had tried to lead the way, but he wasn't that big of a wolf to begin with, so I ended up making a path for him to follow. I didn't mind. We usually wound up doing this in Quebec, except Fern would force his way through the snow, and I would follow behind him with the others.

I hoped they were okay.

Except for Rock.

Rock could burn in hell.

I sniffed and grabbed a handful of snow. I brought it to my mouth and instantly spat it out as a heavy metallic tinge flooded my mouth. God, what was in the snow? Why did it taste so awful? Evidently, Aaron had the same reaction because he was gagging behind me.

Great, we couldn't eat the snow, there didn't seem to be anything to hunt, it was getting dark, the sky was overcast, and the wind was picking up. I scowled, looking toward the faint bright point above us as we walked along the ravine.

I was going to kill each and every Hunter for attacking the pack, stealing away Fern, and the others, placing the godawful collar around my neck and—*why was the wind picking up?*

I raised my arms in a pathetic attempt to shield my face from the blizzard that hit us like a rock wall. I stumbled to my side, Aaron yipping behind me, startled, and we both almost tumbled into the ravine. He pressed his body against my legs, hiding his face in the material of my jeans. Gritting my teeth, I grabbed him by the scruff of his neck and hauled us toward what I hoped was safety. My hand and part of my arm sank into the deep snow as I moved on my hands and knees.

We did this for what felt like an eternity, but, eventually, I spied a tree that cut through the blizzard and allowed me to catch my bearings. There was a group of them and I let go of Aaron's neck, pressing my back against the rough bark. Aaron crawled onto my lap and I held him close, burrowing my hands into his thick fur. He ducked his head against my throat, his wet nose almost icy against my flesh.

I barked out a laugh. "Aaron, your nose is fucking cold!" I shouted into the blizzard.

Aaron pawed at my jacket and I held him tighter, almost crushing him against my chest in a vain attempt to keep warm. I hauled myself to my feet and carried Aaron so he wouldn't get blown away.

I walked further and further into the forest and occasionally tripped over a snow-covered root. I almost bit my tongue as the weather shifted and the sun disappeared in the middle of the day—I was damn certain it was the middle of the day—and the storm turned into one of the worst blizzards I had ever experienced in my life. I couldn't see a foot in front of my face, I couldn't feel my toes or my nose. Why did this feel somehow familiar?

"Here kitty...kitty."

I froze, my breath a ghost in the snow. Aaron raised his head, his eyes meeting mine, confusion clear in those golden orbs. He'd heard it too, right? It wasn't just the wind mimicking a pup's voice?

"Please...home...not...safe!"

"Oh, my God," I whispered. Aaron hopped out of my arms, trying desperately to scent the air, while I stumbled forward, blinking into the white. I tried to focus on the sound and, through the rising scream of hail and wind, Aaron and I heard the pleading voice again.

"Please! Please come home!"

Not a pup, a Den daughter.

I tore after the voice, Aaron leaping through the thigh deep snow beside me, his ears forward, his eyes trained ahead of us. Young ones couldn't survive in this type of weather, they weren't strong enough, so why was one out by herself?

The voice came clearer, closer. I gritted my teeth, putting every ounce of energy I had into following her pleading voice.

"Here, kitty, kitty. Please, please, it's too cold out here."

A cat? Some of the Den Mothers in Quebec had cats and small yappy dogs, but I couldn't remember the last time I had seen one in the wild. I focused again when the daughter coughed.

She was sick.

We followed the voice in the storm, even as it got weaker and weaker. Aaron's frantic whines filled the air as he turned his head left and right, clawing his way through the snow. I wanted to yell, to ask where she was, but that might scare her. She might think I was a People Eater or a Hunter, but then I heard her voice much closer than before.

"Mommy, I want to go home. Mommy, it's cold out here," the girl's voice pleaded into the white.

Not a Den daughter. A human child. My heart sank, and we raced toward where the voice was coming from. Through the wind and snow, we found a great big oak tree, far older than any of the other trees. It had fallen some time ago, and its roots created a small shelter. As we got closer, the crying grew louder. When I crept around the other side of the tree, I found her.

Hiding in the arched roots of the oak was a young girl with no shoes. She wore a faded pink jacket far too big for her, her face was covered in dirt, and her lips, nose, fingers, and toes were turning the color of frostbite. Her blonde hair was almost as white as the snow, and when she saw me, her eyes grew wide in terror before her lids started to close.

I dropped to my knees and tossed aside my backpack. I pulled off my jacket and reached for her. She struggled, weakly, but I pulled her out of her jacket. She was only wearing shorts and a knitted shirt underneath. I dressed her in my jacket, and she started to tremble. I needed shelter, I needed someplace to keep her warm, but there was none.

I picked her up, startled by how light she was, and placed my back against the oak's upturned roots. I sat her on my lap and took the jacket that was too big for her, beckoning Aaron close. Without a word, he huddled next to the girl and I wrapped her jacket around the three of us, treating it as a blanket.

Her tiny frozen fingers dug into my T-shirt, and her frozen nose burrowed in the fabric shirt. I rubbed her back and breathed hot air onto the top of her head while Aaron pressed closer, his feet digging against my thighs and legs as he tried to warm her. His panicked eyes met mine. We had to keep her warm.

Eventually, her trembling gave way to small shivers, and she relaxed between us. Aaron pressed the side of his muzzle next to my face. I curled my hands over him, breathing in the air trapped between the three of us. Even when the wind blew harder, and the snow started to accumulate, I didn't let go. Not even when the girl fell asleep, her breath quiet, nor when I started to drift to sleep.

At some point, the storm broke. I groggily awoke to the girl struggling in my arms. I lessened my grip and opened my eyes, astonished to find that we were almost buried underneath the snow. Aaron's eyes rolled open and he blinked, his ears perked forward as he looked at the white powder that reached my neck. The girl pushed against my arms and I lifted the top of the jacket, peering down at the little hollow we'd made for her. Wide brown eyes stared back. Blonde hair and brown eyes, an odd combination.

She glanced at Aaron, then me.

"Are you going to eat me?" The girl's voice was small and scared.

That was straightforward. "I hadn't planned on it. What's your name?" I asked.

She chewed on her bottom lip before she answered, "Nevaeh."

"I'm Burner, and this is my friend, Aaron." I gave her a small smile while Aaron gently *woo*-ed at her. "Are your people here, Nevaeh?"

When she didn't respond, I looked back to her. She had fallen asleep again, so I gently shook her. Her eyes opened once more.

"Nevaeh? Where are your people?"

"By the lake," Nevaeh mumbled. She wrapped her arms around my neck and burrowed back into the warmth. She glued herself to me like a mollusk to a boat, and her breathing slowed. She was trying to fall asleep again.

Aaron shifted on my legs and tiny painful pinpricks danced along every nerve. I grimaced as he wormed himself back into the snow. Carefully, I held Neveah and the jacket in place, standing up and biting back the groan as the cold air hit my back and my legs felt like they were shocked by lightning. Aaron dug into the snow surrounding us, grabbed the backpack with his mouth, and pulled it free. Awkwardly, I picked it up and shook off the snow before I slung it onto my back.

Our chase in the snowstorm to find Nevaeh had completely ruined any sense of direction I'd had, my muscles ached, and I had no idea where the ravine was. Nevaeh must have read my mind because she wiggled in my arms and her head popped out from underneath the jacket. She looked around until she spotted something that must have been familiar to her. She pointed toward a grove of trees before she hid under the jacket once more.

"That way, Burner."

"Thanks, Nevaeh." We headed toward the grove. In the back of my mind, I hoped beyond hope that this wasn't some twisted People Eater trap.

Chapter Fifteen

THE RAVINE SPILLED into a massive freshwater lake which, in turn, spilled outward into several smaller rivers. Beyond that, who knows, but I suspected they might make it all the way to the ocean. As we walked, I caught a breeze of hazy smoke and Aaron and I followed it until we found an old farmhouse with poorly boarded windows alone near the lake. The smoke drifted up from a small chimney, lazy and slow, and I hesitated.

Fern once told me to avoid people at all costs, except for women with children, and even then, I was to be wary and make sure they were alone before approaching. Maybe it was because of the threat posed by the Hunters or Deadwalkers, but I brushed off the thought of the Deadwalkers. I had seen one Deadwalker, September, and she had left the night I'd met her. The Hunters were the greater threat.

Nevaeh peeked out from under the jackets. When she saw the house, she could barely contain her excitement. "That's home!" She squeaked and tried to squirm out of my arms.

If they were People Eaters, then I could take them out like the last group, but if they had weapons, then I would have to be careful, or if they had traps—

"Burner?" Nevaeh looked up at me.

Aaron was watching me. His golden eyes critical of what I did next.

"You'll get cold," I muttered and stalked toward the house.

Aaron followed without a word.

If there was trouble, well, there's a good chance they would be too weak to fight back. I glanced down at Nevaeh. She studied my face. I wasn't sure how I could keep her alive in this world, given how Aaron and I were barely surviving as it was, not to mention, we were trying to get to Boston, but I swore I would try.

As we got closer, I noticed the house and the small shed next to it were in rough shape. It was a two-story house with several broken windows on the bottom floor, and a shingled roof with holes in it. The windows had cloth shoved in the holes to block out the cold wind.

The little shed looked as if it had been attacked at some point. The door was gone and the roof collapsed. The faint wisps of an outhouse were nearby, but I wasn't certain where. What I found to be the oddest was the trees closest to the house were stripped of their bark. Steps away from the front door, I spied a little black cat pressed against the faded doorframe, huddled as it tried to keep warm while it mewled pathetically.

"Blackie!" Nevaeh shrieked.

She pushed herself free from my arms and helped her to the ground. My jacket, technically Aaron's, was huge on her tiny frame. She almost tripped in the deep snow as she raced to the cat. Blackie greeted her with another low cry, his tail rising as he danced on the tips of his toes. She picked him up and hugged him close, kissing his little furry head. Cat in hand, Nevaeh opened up the door. She flashed me a smile before she raced inside.

"Burner! Aaron!" she called from inside the house.

I picked up the other jacket, glancing at Aaron. Puffs of white drifted from his nose and when I didn't move, he looked up at me.

We couldn't survive another cold night outside. It was a damn miracle we'd survived the blizzard with Neveah, but I couldn't do that again, and judging by Aaron's tired eyes, he couldn't either. Not to mention, the hunger was growing to be too much, and the back of my jaws ached.

"If they attack us, you take Neveah, and I'll kill the others. Then we rip the house apart for food. Do you understand?" I broke the silence.

Aaron nodded his head. Together we walked inside.

I shut the door behind us. My mind twisted into some sort of hyper mode that made my collar buzz faintly and I grimaced as the sounds reverberated in my ears. Several pairs of old, cracked gumboots lined the door, and the walls were covered with images drawn by children. The scent of mold and dust was heavy.

"Burner! Come here!" Nevaeh called.

Fern's words echoed in my head, but we followed Nevaeh's voice into the living room. When I entered, I almost gagged at the stench of unwashed flesh. I covered my mouth and nose with my hand. Aaron sneezed, shaking his head. There were piles of filthy and rotted pants and sweaters next to the fireplace that hadn't been used for weeks.

"Burner?"

Nevaeh called yet again from another room, and I came to a poorly candlelit kitchen. Inside, people sat at the kitchen table completely wrapped in blankets and shivering in the cold. Their eyes were shrunken in and they all looked like hungry owls, but I wasn't sure if they were afraid of me. It was hard to smell anything over the nearly overwhelming aroma of mold, and dirt, and wood smoke. A balding elderly man at the kitchen stove stirred a large pot.

Nevaeh held Blackie in her arms as she was picked up by a woman at the end of the table and placed on her lap. The woman wore a thick gray blanket, but a shock of gray hair peeked out from the fabric. Nevaeh whispered into the woman's ear.

"Food," the man at the stove suddenly wheezed. He picked up the pot, his arms shaking with the weight of it as he moved it from the stove to the middle of the table. He had to have been in his seventies, and he had a limp. He wore a patched knitted sweater and faded jeans. He left the pot on the table and limped over to the cupboard above the dish-filled sink.

The woman who held Nevaeh spoke, her voice short of breath, her words slurred. "You...saved Nevaeh?" The people at the table finally noticed me, noticed Aaron who hid behind my legs.

"Yes." I shifted on my feet. Aaron bowed his head, his ears forward, eyeing the group.

"Will you...?" The woman shut her eyes before she opened them again. Her cloudy eyes were faded with age and exhaustion. "Will you kill us?"

Yes. "No." I kept careful watch of the man who pulled bowls from the cupboard, the movement seeming to take every bit of energy he had.

"Then, will you eat with us?" The woman's voice was hopeful.

Aaron nosed my hand. I glanced at him from the corner of my eyes, a silent message passing between us. These people would die soon. They were no threat.

"Yes."

The man turned away from the cupboard with another two bowls in hand. He limped back to the table and placed it with a pile of other cracked and mismatched bowls. The woman pointed to a seat at the end of the table. I pulled it out, scraping the wooden feet against the floor.

I dropped the backpack to the floor while Aaron sat next to me, his head resting on the edge of the table, watching the group curiously. Nevaeh stroked Blackie and scratched him behind the ear. A warm purr filled the small kitchen.

The woman pointed at herself. "Abbey." She pointed to her throat. "Sick." She waved her hand at everyone in the room. "All sick," Nevaeh whispered into her ear and Abbey gave me a confused look. "Burner?"

"Burner, and this is Aaron." I patted Aaron's head. He blinked his large golden eyes up at me.

The man with the limp poured some type of soup into the bowls. Abbey pointed to him before she covered her mouth and coughed; her slim frame shook with the force. When she could speak, she pointed at the man again, her voice rough. "Cook, my husband."

Cook placed the bowls around the table with some spoons, and gave me my soup, hesitating before trying to bend down to give Aaron some too. I took it from him, my hands brushing his burned hands and arm. He grunted as I placed the bowl in front of Aaron on the floor and Aaron sniffed it. Cook stood by my side, watching Aaron intently as the people around the table started to eat.

Abbey fed Nevaeh from her own bowl first. The others gathered as much energy as they could muster to eat. I picked up my spoon and swirled it through the bowl, keeping an eye on Cook. The soup looked, well, woody. Solid chunks of pale white floated at the top. I fished out one of the pieces and held it up to my eye.

"Bark soup," Cook rumbled.

I dropped the piece of bark back into the bowl. That explained the stripped trees outside the house. My stomach growled. I risked a quick glance at Aaron only to find him laying down, his face buried in the bowl. I waited a few minutes, just to see if he died, but when he lifted his head and spat out a piece of tree bark, then nosed it across the floor, I figured it was safe. I sipped my soup, wincing as the heat rushed past my throat and to my stomach. I sipped it slowly, but my back teeth throbbed, and my hands started to clench. My muscles ached.

I was so hungry. I needed meat, but this would have to do. I closed my eyes and savored every spoonful. Even though it was thin and weak, and I think the soup had been re-boiled for several days, it was warm, and it was food—sort of.

Cook made a gruff sound before he took his own seat at the table, sighing tiredly, and picked up his own spoon.

When I finished, Nevaeh crawled off Abbey's lap and raced over to me, crawling onto my lap. Well, she would have had Blackie not growled and howled at Aaron. Blackie jumped out of Nevaeh's arms and ran into the house and out of sight.

"Blackie!" Nevaeh cried as she raced off after the cat.

"She loves that cat." Abbey's voice was less rough. "Burner, was it? Will you stay the night? It's the least we can offer. We've been so sick, I didn't even notice Nevaeh wander off yesterday." Regret was thick in her voice. "If not for you, she would have..." Abbey covered her mouth when she coughed again.

The rest of the group listened. Their heads turned just slightly, but not one of them spoke.

"Of course, thank you," I said.

These people didn't act, or behave, as People Eaters or Hunters did. These people, for the moment at least, seemed to be like a small wolf pack. Abbey turned to one of the blanket-wrapped people.

"Nathan? Can you show Burner to the room upstairs? The clean one?"

Nathan, who resembled a mummy from an old black-and-white magazine, nodded and stood up from the table. His back was hunched over and he walked slowly. I stood up from the table, grabbing the backpack off the floor. Aaron instantly fell into step with me. I followed Nathan through the back of the kitchen, past a door I assumed led outside, and up the wooden stairs to the second floor.

The layout of the house was similar to the Maine pack house, but it was bigger, older, and smelled worse. The retro flower print wallpaper on the walls was peeled, and the walls were covered with pictures of people, faded sunflowers, and more child's artwork. There must have been eight rooms on the second floor with closed doors. A lone window illuminated the end of the hallway, casting shadows along the walls.

Nathan didn't speak as he walked to a room near the back of the second floor. He opened the door for me, and before I could thank him, he started back toward the staircase. He struggled down the stairs and held tight to the rail. I kept the door open for Aaron to enter before I followed him. I closed the bedroom door.

It was cold inside the room, really cold, and I missed my jacket, but Nevaeh seemed happy with it. I spied the bed with the thick mattress, blankets, and pillows. My back ached at the thought of sinking into a bed that wasn't rotting or steel-framed or hard ground. The window was closed, its lock long rusted shut, and the drapes were gone, giving a striking view of the lake. There was a little desk with a mirror against the wall, and a bookcase with just a handful of books left in it.

I placed the backpack on the table and ran my hand through my hair before I tugged off my shirt, boots, and pants, along with my socks. I shivered and pulled back the covers of the bed. When I slid underneath the thick comforter, I sighed, contented, as the mattress dipped under my weight. We could do this. Just rest here for a little bit. The people downstairs were no threat.

"Aaron." My teeth chattered. He was sniffing along the floor, his ears perking up at my voice. "W-will you please shift and g-get in here already? I'm fuck-fucking freezing!"

Wordlessly, Aaron padded around the bed and shifted as he reached the other side. He slipped underneath the comforter, his own teeth chattering at the contact of cold, but within moments our combined heat sunk into the fabric and mattress. We both gave small, happy sighs. It was just like being in Quebec. Several guys to a bed in order to keep warm during the cold nights in the barns while the Den daughters, pups, Elders, Den Mothers, Aunts, and Alphas got to stay inside the warm houses.

I wrinkled my nose while Aaron dragged the blanket to cover his own nose.

"What'd you think of the soup?" I broke the quiet silence. Aaron shifted underneath the blankets, shrugging.

"It had more bark than bite," was his dry reply.

I grinned before rubbing my eyes, sighing. "They're all sick."

Aaron hummed in agreement.

"But they didn't try and kill you and eat you, not like that last group." I dropped my arms to my side, glancing at him.

Aaron hummed again, his eyes starting to droop closed.

I grabbed the moldy pillow from under my head and whacked him with it. He jolted away, blinking rapidly and glaring hard at me.

"I was almost asleep," he hissed.

"I was talking," I snapped.

Aaron sighed heavily before he rolled onto his side, pulling the blanket up to cover his ears. "You have my complete and utter undivided attention."

"They're starving, and they haven't eaten the cat," I said.

Aaron's brows furrowed. "So?"

"If these people are starving, then why haven't they killed him? Boiled its bones?" I pushed. "Hell, they gave *you* a bowl of soup."

Aaron worried his bottom lip before he sighed, pressing half of his face against the pillow. "What do you want to do?"

"Huh?"

"Don't 'huh' me, Burner. You want to help them; it's that damn Alpha impulse Fern ground into you to make sure weaker members of the pack don't die. So, what do you want to do?"

My mouth parted, then closed and I flushed, bringing the blanket close to my face, tugging on the patched material. "I have no idea what you're talking about."

Aaron snorted. "Right. Who's the wolf that ends up teaching the pups to swim their first few days with us during the summer so they don't end up drowning?"

"That's just because Fern's busy helping Den Mother and the daughters with the house."

"And who's the wolf that stayed out in the woods hunting for a week when the primary storehouse was flooded in Quebec and all the packs almost starved?"

"All the Alphas were out hunting that week."

"And who's the wolf that's gotten between Rock and me when he's been drinking?"

I paused, flickering my gaze toward him.

There was a sadness in his eyes, and his smile was bittersweet before he rolled over onto his other side, his back to me. He pulled the blankets up over his head, completely covering himself. "Just do as you want, Burner. You'll do it regardless of whatever I have to say."

I huffed and rolled onto my side, staring at the door. I pulled the blanket over my ears.

What the hell did Aaron know anyway?

Chapter Sixteen

I COULDN'T SLEEP.

Aaron was deep asleep. His chest rising and falling with each breath, his face relaxed.

I sniffed and rubbed my nose. I think it was sometime before dawn because the moon was starting to dip beyond the horizon and the room was dark. Well, for people, I suppose. I could see fairly well.

I sat on the edge of the bed, pulling on my T-shirt, fighting back the shiver of cool material against my warm skin. I'd already dressed in my pants and socks. I bent and grabbed my boots, casting Aaron one last glance before I slipped out of the room and shut the door behind me.

The other doors upstairs were all closed. I padded downstairs and headed to the kitchen. Cook was asleep at the table, his head resting on his crossed arms. An old crossbow with bolts loaded next to him. He was doing what Fern always did: staying on the bottom floor to guard the pack while the rest of us slept.

I whetted my lips, quietly creeping around him, and deftly plucked the crossbow from the table, taking the other unloaded four bolts. Carefully, I made my way back to the front door, cracked it open, and slipped outside. I rested the crossbow against the door while I pulled on my boots. I tied the laces before I picked up the crossbow once more and took off toward the woods.

I knew how to use a crossbow. Andre, the pack Alpha in Quebec, taught me when I was nine. When you were out hunting and didn't want to startle a stag, or a deer, boar, whatever, it was the ideal weapon. If I focused too much, the muscles in my shoulder still ached from where I'd been shot by those damn Hunters, but I pushed it aside and listened to the woods as soft pale pink streaks filled the sky, chasing away the dark night's grip.

I walked until the house was out of eyesight, until the lake broke off into trickles, the water warming the ground it coursed through, exposing the tiny sprigs of grass struggling to survive against the cold.

I stopped next to a skinny tree and waited, white clouds of breath drifting from my mouth. The sky was properly warming up now, the pink hues giving way to an almost powerful gray that made everything darker, colder, even while the sun struggled to shine through the weight of the storm clouds. I sniffed the air, tasting the trees, the clean snow, Aaron's faint scent on my clothes, and...

My lips curled. I raised the crossbow with both hands. I pressed my back against the tree to steady myself as I took aim, waiting for the movement by the stream of soft brown fur against the white snow. I squeezed the trigger and the rabbit fell dead. Another flash of movement and I quickly reloaded the crossbow, taking aim and firing with a breath.

Silence.

I lowered the crossbow and pushed away from the tree. I grabbed the two rabbits lying dead in the snow, examining them carefully. They were fat and their fur was soft. I pulled out the bolts and scanned the horizon for any more movement. In the distance, I saw something digging into the snow, kicking up white powder. I marked a nearby tree with one of the bolts before I turned around and started back toward the house.

By the time I arrived back, the sun was high in the sky. At least I think it was high. One part of the sky was brighter than the rest. As I approached the front door, it was pulled open and Cook stood there, armed with a rifle in his shaking grip. Nathan from yesterday stood next to him, holding a fireplace poker. He wasn't dressed as a mummy, but in green and black pants and jacket, with a great red beard and red hair tied back into a frizzy, rough ponytail.

"You stole our crossbow!" Nathan croaked.

Wordlessly, I raised the rabbits. Cook blinked, squinting his eyes at the sight before he shook his head. "You found rabbits?"

"I'm a good tracker." I shrugged.

"Burner!" Neveah squeezed between Cook and Nathan and raced toward me. She stopped in the snow as her eyes grew wide at the sight of the rabbits. "Wh-whoa! Can I touch them?"

I held them out to Neveah and she stroked the fur, her eyes meeting mine. "They're so soft."

"They are, aren't they," I said.

Cook lowered the rifle and Nathan glanced at him. "Get in here before you get any colder," Cook said. I unloaded the crossbow. I handed it to Nathan who took it with both hands, grunting at the weight of it as I passed him in the doorway. I followed Cook into the kitchen and he placed the rifle on the table. I offered the rabbits to him again and he took them with reverence.

"Where did you find them?" Cook whispered, stroking the soft fur and squeezing their sides.

"A few hours away from here. I marked a trail," I said, craning my neck to look around the kitchen. Only Nathan and Cook were with us, Neveah had disappeared too. "Aaron—"

"Your dog?" Nathan's frowned. "Still upstairs. Abbey tried to go in there when we didn't see you at breakfast and the crossbow was missing. Anyway, she got a peek inside and saw him all by himself. She tried to give him some more soup and check on him, but he barked like crazy and clawed at the door."

I flinched. Shit. "Thanks, I'll go check on him."

"He sounded angry!" Nathan called as I left the kitchen and rounded the stairs. I walked up, my feet heavy on the creaking steps. At the top, I found Abbey and another woman with bobbed blonde hair sitting on the floor against the wall and wrapped up in blankets. The blonde-haired woman watched me with a mixture of curiosity and apprehension. Abbey gave me a tired smile. Neveah was between them, snuggling underneath the blankets with Blackie in her arms.

"You came back," Abbey said.

"I told you he would. He wouldn't just leave Aaron." Neveah rolled her eyes.

"You could have left a note," the blonde woman said, her tone short.

"Ashley!" Abbey hissed.

"I can't write." I ignored the startled look on Ashley's face. I scratched at the door, just below the handle. There was a responding growl from within. "Thanks for trying to feed him."

Abbey nodded. I turned the handle and slipped into the room. I closed the door behind me and twisted the lock shut before I turned to Aaron.

Aaron was on all fours, his hackles raised, his copper eyes glowing with a wild ferocity. He looked menacing, he looked dangerous, but he reeked of *fear*. I raised my hands, side-stepping the overturned bowl of cold soup, carefully approaching him.

Aaron growled low in his throat, anger and betrayal filling my nose. I locked my eyes on his, shaking my head slowly.

"*No,*" I ground out. Aaron paused, his eyes flickering to mine. "Don't make me say it, Aaron."

Aaron stepped back, his head dipping downward, looking away, looking for an escape route. The only way out was the window and I don't think he wanted that. I took another step toward him and Aaron's lips peeled back, the betrayal clear on his face.

"Aaron," I warned.

Aaron snapped at me, sharp teeth and snarls.

I took two steps closer to him and he cowered against the corner, barking frantically.

"*Shift,*" I snarled, "*now.*"

Aaron's amber eyes widened for a second before they squeezed shut. Moments later he was human, sitting on the floor and glaring murderously at me. I dragged the comforter off the bed and wrapped him in it. He hit my arms, growling low in his throat.

"You fucking left!" he hissed.

"I did."

Aaron grabbed my shirt, pulling me close. "You *left* me without saying a fucking thing! They tried to get in here. They almost saw me, Burner!"

"But they didn't," I said slowly. I grabbed his wrists, watching his eyes. "I had to go and find them something to eat."

"Of course, you did," Aaron sneered.

I squeezed his wrists warningly. Aaron bit his bottom lip. "I *had* to do it. Do you understand? These people are dying. They aren't Hunters. They aren't Deadwalkers. Hell, they fed us, Aaron."

"Wow," Aaron breathed, "if all anybody had to do was feed you to get them on your side, maybe September should have fed you like a pet dog."

Ice cold water rushed down my spine. Aaron looked away, shame burning its way across his face. "I-I didn't mean…" Aaron stuttered.

I dropped his wrists and stood up, then headed back for the door.

"Burner?" Aaron whispered, worry tinging his voice.

I didn't respond. I unlocked the door and slid outside, pulling it closed behind me.

Ashley, Neveah, and Abbey were absent from the spot they'd been, and I was glad. It meant I didn't have to explain why I hit the wall, putting my fist through the wood and wallpaper.

I gave myself the count of ten before I calmed and pulled my hand out, noting the small bloodied wounds along my knuckles were already healing. I dragged my tongue over the traces of blood and headed downstairs to where everybody was gathering in the kitchen, watching Cook as he carefully skinned the rabbits, and prepared them to be cooked.

I pulled out a chair from the table and placed it against the wall. I crossed my arms over my chest, my eyes starting to fall shut as the heat of the room sunk into my clothing, seeping through the fabric and spreading across my skin. The last thing I remembered was seeing Cook cut off a piece of meat and hand it to Blackie who grabbed it and dashed off into the house, Neveah hot on his heels, laughing.

Chapter Seventeen

COOK WOKE ME with a bowl of soup and a pleased as punch expression on his face. It took me a few minutes to realize that I was in the kitchen, that'd I'd fallen asleep in the chair, and everybody was eating soup loaded with tantalizing chunks of meat.

I straightened, taking the bowl with my hands, revealing in the heat. I inhaled deeply, the aroma so delicious that I didn't bother with the spoon. I brought the bowl to my lips, greedily slurping up the hot liquid, my eyes fluttering shut as it burned my throat and the heat worked its way to my belly, warming me from the inside out. When I finished, all that was left were chunks of meat. I pulled them out and carefully chewed each piece.

Neveah smacked her lips, humming in her chair. Ashley's face was inches from her own bowl, savoring each spoonful. Nathan was in a similar position, but he had one hand to his beard, keeping it out of the bowl. Abbey and Cook were holding hands, side by side, as they ate.

I noted the one bowl on the table, the heat climbing into the room. I finished my bowl and picked it up.

"That's for Aaron," Cook said. "Nathan tried to take it up to him, but Aaron wouldn't let him in."

"I'll do it, don't worry," I said. "Thank you for the soup."

Cook grabbed my arm, stopping me. "No, thank *you*, Burner."

I gave him a crooked grin and nodded, leaving the table and heading back upstairs. When I got to the door, I scratched again and entered, not bothering to lock the door behind me. Aaron was curled up on the bed underneath the blankets. I set the bowl on the bedside table before placing my hand on the piled fabric.

"Aaron, food."

The bed shifted, and Aaron stuck his head out, his eyes red and his cheeks blotchy. I opened my mouth, suddenly feeling horrible, but he shook his head frantically, sat up, and silently reached for the bowl. I handed it to him. Aaron brought it to his lips. He tentatively sipped the hot liquid before blowing cool air across the top.

I sat on the edge of the bed, rubbing the comforter, occasionally glancing at him.

"Aaron, I'm sorry—"

"We can't stay here."

I paused, tilting my head and meeting his gaze. He was staring at the soup, his eyes half-lidded.

"What do you mean?"

"We can't stay here, Burner. We don't have the time to play winter pack." Aaron's voice was soft. I sighed and ran a hand through my hair.

"I know. We need to save the others."

"I overheard the two women talking outside earlier." Aaron shifted in the bed, trying to keep the blanket tucked underneath his armpits and move at the same time. "They said we were going to be hit by a big snowstorm tomorrow night."

"Ashley and Abbey." I nodded to the door. "Those are their names."

Aaron brought the bowl to his lips and drank slowly, his Adam's apple bobbing as he tilted his head back. When he finished, I looked back to the blanket, plucking the stray threads.

"We'll die in the storm," I murmured.

"Yes, but we'll need to leave the day after that. And hope we don't miss the pack." Aaron handed me the empty bowl.

"Come downstairs with me?" I blurted out.

Aaron slowly blinked. "What?"

"Please?"

Aaron opened his mouth, confused, before he bowed his head and nodded reluctantly. I squeezed his cool exposed shoulder. He trembled at the touch. "Thank you."

Aaron handed me the bowl. I stood up from the bed as he slid out of the other side. He took a moment before he rolled his shoulders and shifted into his wolf form. We went to the door and I picked up the bowl from the floor, noting the cleaned spot. I opened the bedroom door and together we walked down the stairs toward the sound of laughter and talking in the kitchen.

Neveah gasped when she saw Aaron and rushed over to him. She wrapped her arms around his neck. He blinked, looking up at me worriedly, and I rubbed his furry ear, mouthing *it's okay* to him. Aaron didn't look relieved but let Neveah cuddle him regardless.

Nathan patted the table and I took my seat while Cook took a kettle off the stove and poured hot water into a teapot, soon followed by some ancient dried green leaves.

"Nettle tea," Abbey explained, placing mugs around the table. I nodded, waiting for Cook to fill mine before bringing it close.

It was fascinating to watch these people, who only yesterday were at death's door. A little bit of food, and they all looked like they just might survive to the spring.

"Is there a big storm coming?" I asked Abbey.

Abbey picked up her own cup, leaning back in her chair. "Yes. Ashley's got some of her father's meteorological tools. That's how we knew this winter would be bad."

"So far, from what we can tell, tomorrow night will be the worst, but from my data, it should even out after that." Ashley shrugged.

"It was hot and sunny not long ago," I mused.

"Where?" Ashley perched an elbow on the table, leaning onto her hand.

"On the coast," I answered.

"You've been to the ocean?" Neveah whispered in awe.

I froze. Aaron froze in Neveah's arms.

"Uh, I, yes." I cleared my throat.

"Forgive me for asking, son." Cook settled in a chair across from me. "But...are there any people looking for you?"

I frowned. *Looking for me? Why...Oh.*

"No," I said, "no, nobody is looking for me. I'm, well, Aaron and I are looking for some friends of mine. They're headed to Boston?"

Ashley paled and looked away while Cook shot Nathan a worried glance. Abbey leaned across the table, placing her wrinkled hand on mine. "There is nothing in Boston for a young man like yourself, Burner."

Did they mean wolves? Did they understand what Aaron and I were?

"I...don't really have much of a choice." I cleared my throat.

"There's always a choice," Abbey said.

I opened my mouth to speak, but Ashley cut me off, "Don't go to Boston. Don't go to New York. Don't go to Texas."

I frowned, my back straightening. "What are you talking about?"

"Son, I don't know where you've been living, but if you're healthy and you have Aaron as your friend... There are monsters in those cities." Cook's voice dropped to a whisper. "Monsters that'll take your blood and turn you into one of them."

"They're called Deadwalkers," Nathan murmured next to me. He was staring into his cup. His lips twisted into a curl as he raised it in a toast-like motion. "But as one said to me when I was a child while they loaded the people of my village onto a train: 'We're not all monsters.'"

My mouth parted, my eyes widening. That's what September had said. Those exact words.

"Those aren't even the real monsters. At least they have a mind," Ashley muttered in a low voice. She flashed a glance at me. "The real monsters are the wolfmen."

"Wait, what?" I leaned across the table, grabbing her arm. "What did you just say?"

The room fell silent.

Ashley glared at my hand and I let go of her, easing back in the seat. Abbey cleared her throat, standing up. "Neveah, honey, let's get you tucked into bed."

"But I want to hear the story!" Neveah complained.

"When you're older." Abbey gently shooed Neveah out of the room, giving Cook a knowing look. We listened as they climbed the stairs and disappeared out of earshot.

I focused on Ashley. She held her cup with both hands, she chewed her bottom lip red before she drew in a shuddering breath and let it out.

"My stepdad was a doctor, military doctor, actually. We came from Fort Worth, Texas. One of the safe places in the States, and there was a lot of weird shit down there. Medical experiments, doctors trying to build super soldiers..." Ashley looked away, staring at the kitchen door like it would answer all of her questions before she shook her head, clearing her throat.

"My brother was picked to be a soldier. He was older than me, twenty-one, and they took him into this white room, and after about an hour, he came out. He looked fine. He had this bandage on his left arm." She placed the mug back on the table and tapped her left arm, her brows drawing up in confusion.

"But he had this horrible fever after about three days. He was vomiting on the fourth, and by the fifth, he seemed okay, weak, but okay. My dad was ordered to be sent out with a search crew to look for food supplies, but I volunteered instead. It was a routine mission. It would be good for me to get some field experience as the medic. Besides, he could keep an eye on Jake—that's my brother's name, Jake." She waved her hands, avoiding looking any of us in the eyes as she spoke.

"So, you can imagine my surprise when we get back to the fort four days later, and all hell has broken loose. Let me tell you, Fort Worth has a shitload of guns and trained personnel who know how to use them. But that didn't stop Jake. Oh no, nor did it stop any of the other 'soldiers' who looked like monsters out of nightmares. Jake and the others, that is."

Ashely squeezed her eyes shut, her jaw tight. She drew in a shuddering breath and Cook leaned over to rub her back. She shook her head and Cook pulled his hand away, worry etched on his face. Ashley let out the breath before she cleared her throat.

"One even tried to come at me, but Dad shot 'em, right in the head—" she tapped her forehead "—and when they were all dead, out of two-thousand people, there were only thirty left, those thirty people were turning into monsters and attacking us. By us, I mean my dad, and me, because Jake was right there with them, literally clawing on the other side of the door, howling, like a fucking *wolf*."

I sucked in a gasp. Aaron's head snapped up, staring at her in shock.

Ashley leaned across the table, waving her hands. "My stepdad told me he loved me, told me to make my mother proud, told me to head as far north as possible, to get away from the monsters and told me to run." Ashley's fingers twitched. She looked away, shifting on the chair, squirming before she shot out of the room and raced upstairs, her feet hitting hard on the wooden steps before a door upstairs was slammed shut.

"I found her on the road about a month later with a twisted ankle." Nathan cleared his throat before a smile tugged at his lips. "She threatened to shoot me, but I wrapped her ankle. Together we left the road behind and eventually we found this place. Cook and Abbey saved us, but that was before Martha and Eddy went missing." He sighed.

"Martha and Eddy?" I frowned, trying to focus. It was a lot of information to take in.

"Neveah's parents," Cook offered. "You'd have liked Eddy, Burner. The man was a fantastic trapper. Martha, well, she had this talent with plants. Could grow anything and everything." He drank from his mug before setting it down, his shoulders sagging as if the world weighed upon them. "They went off in the summer to chase an elk. Eddy tracked it and Martha went with him because there'd been traces of wild blackberry in the elk's shit, and Martha wanted to grow some nearby." Cook glanced at the covered windows. "They left Neveah here."

"What do you think happened?" I frowned.

Cook shook his head. "I don't know. They never came back. They wouldn't have abandoned Neveah, she was the whole world to them."

"It was Eddy that trapped the cat." Nathan smiled, the corners of his eyes crinkling.

"He did, didn't he? Angry little thing." Cook sighed and patted the table. "Anyway, Burner, could you show Nathan tomorrow where you found the rabbits? I'm thinking we could catch some more and we might have a chance of surviving the winter."

"You can't live off of rabbits forever," I warned.

Cook nodded. "True. But it's better than nothing. Anyway, everyone, to bed."

Nathan rapped his knuckles against the table and stood up. I stood up as well, watching Cook. "What about you?"

"Me?"

"Aren't you going to bed?"

"Nah, I'll stay here and keep the fire going. Make sure we don't all freeze to death." Cook winked. Reluctantly I left the kitchen. I headed upstairs and back to the bedroom. Aaron's nails clicked on the hardwood surface as he followed. I was about to close the door when I noticed the door across from ours was opened, and Neveah was peeking through the cracks. I knelt and waved her over.

Hesitantly, she crept across the floor. She was wearing slightly thicker clothing with home-knitted socks and her hair was braided.

"What is it, Neveah?"

"Have you seen my mommy?" Neveah whispered.

"No, I'm sorry."

"Oh." Neveah's face fell. "It's just that sometimes at night she stands by the kitchen window, or by the edge of the lake, but she always stares at my window."

"Neveah?" I whispered. "What are you talking about?"

"Grandpa Cookie says she's not allowed inside anymore because she's sick, and he doesn't want me to get sick, too, but if you see my mommy outside, can you tell her I love her?" Neveah pleaded.

I nodded, and Neveah smiled brightly. "Okay, goodnight, Burner! Goodnight, Aaron!" she sang before dashing back into the bedroom and closing the door.

Slowly, I stood up and turned to Aaron to ask if he'd heard what Neveah had just said, but he was staring outside the window. I walked across the room to join him. My breath caught in my throat at the black, human-shaped figure wobbling from the edge of the forest, its arms spread at its side as it came to stand by the edge of the lake. It seemed to pause, to consider for a moment before it tipped its head upward and stared back at Aaron and me.

I flattened myself against the wall, my eyes wide. Aaron was pressed against the floor below the window. I held my palm out, slowly curling my hand closed one finger at a time. Aaron nodded. When my hand was a fist, we both peeked through the window once more.

The figure was gone.

I sunk to the floor, my legs stretched out before me, dumbly staring at the shut bedroom door.

"Was that...?"

"A Deadwalker? Did September... Was she like that?" Aaron whispered, once more human and wrapped up in the comforter.

"No." I swallowed. "No, she wasn't. She moved like you and me. Did you hear what Neveah said?"

"I heard what Ashley said." Aaron turned his head. "She was talking about Hounds. Someone was making Hounds on purpose."

I grunted and rubbed my hands together before bringing them to my mouth and blowing hot air onto my knuckles. "We can't tell any of them what we are."

"You'll need to be careful," Aaron answered.

I glanced at him, surprised. "What do you mean?"

"Your canine teeth," Aaron huffed. "They're too sharp to be human, especially when you're pissed off. Your eyes too; I'm actually surprised none of them have mentioned it. Blue and green aren't normal."

I rolled my eyes. "Okay, okay, I get it. I'm special," I dragged out the word. Aaron snorted, his lips twitching.

"Such a special boy."

"You know it." I flashed him a grin with too-sharp teeth.

We sat in silence until Aaron sighed, scratching his neck. "Tomorrow, you go with Nathan and find the rabbits. I'll stay here and keep an eye on things."

"You're not going to come with me?"

"God, no. Do you realize how cold it is outside? No, I'm going to go downstairs and stay next to the stove. Besides—" Aaron crossed his arms "—Neveah wanted to brush my fur."

I bit my bottom lip, desperately trying to stifle the laughter that was bubbling up, but I couldn't, and I roared, falling to my side while Aaron tried to cover my mouth with his hands, hissing that I needed to shut up, that I needed to be quiet or else I'd wake up the house.

Chapter Eighteen

"HE'S PRETTY SPOILED."

"Who?"

"Your dog, Aaron," Nathan breathed, stumbling in the snow. I grabbed his arm, steadying him. He breathed a soft word of thanks and I let go, continuing onward.

"Not really," I said. I readjusted the crossbow, taking one step at a time. "He...hasn't had the best of lives."

"Did you steal him?"

"No. He came with me willingly."

"That dog must love you," Nathan mused. "When I was a kid, my family lived next to this farm. This guy had this dog he'd stake out and just leave for days. My sisters and I would give it water and whatever scraps we could, the poor thing was desperate for affection, but one day the guy found out and just beat the creature. You could hear the screaming and howling for miles and miles. I wanted to save it, but..."

"But?" I glanced at Nathan. He shrugged his shoulders.

"My parents wouldn't let me, told me not to interfere. It died that night. Two days later, the guy had a new puppy tied to a post with a heavy chain." Nathan's eyes softened. "Course, the next day, the Deadwalkers came with their train and everybody but my family left. The guy took the puppy with him. I hope it got away." The words were small. I tried to focus on the path, focus on where I'd left the marks on the trees.

Would Rock have killed Aaron? I didn't want to think about that or think about all the times I'd put myself between Rock and Aaron, or the days when Aaron would disappear into the woods and I'd eventually find him curled in a ball staring at nothing.

I swallowed hard, shaking my head.

"Deadwalkers?" I asked. "You mentioned them last night."

"I did," Nathan said. He sniffed, rubbing his cold, red nose. "I'll never forget them."

"What did they do?"

Nathan shrugged. "Took the people of my village away, well, except for my family. My parents didn't want to leave, but they were offering everybody new housing with electricity and safety. Said it would be like before the two years of darkness. One of them came to my house and spoke to my parents. She warned my parents not to go with them and promised to help them, but they had to hide and pretend they weren't there." Nathan sighed, kicking the snow around his feet. "We hid in the root cellar until the whole town had gone. When she came back, she told us to head North and as far from New York as possible."

"That when she told you 'we're not all monsters'?" I asked.

"Pretty much. I mean, we managed to survive a month, but my family got sick and died. I was left on my own until I found Ashley."

"Wow."

"Yeah, sometimes I wonder what happened to them. The people from my village? Sometimes I wonder if September realized something was wrong, or told my parents something that spooked them—hey, why'd you stop?"

I glanced at him over my shoulder, my eyes wide. "September?"

"That was her name. Why?" Nathan's eyebrows pulled together.

"September 24th Amon?" I said.

Nathan's eyes glazed over. He cleared his throat, looking around the forest as if he thought we were being watched before stepping closer to me. "You've met her."

I nodded slowly.

"Shit," Nathan breathed. "Is that why you're running?"

"My people were taken. I have to get them back," I said.

"That's why you need to get to Boston?"

"Yes."

Nathan eyed me critically. "Are you sure they're worth it?"

I frowned. "What do you mean?"

"Never mind." He shook his head and flashed me a wide smile. "Come on, let's go find those rabbits."

Wordlessly, I turned and started walking again, Nathan falling in step behind me. We didn't speak again until we came to the stream and I found the tree I'd used as support last time. We waited in silence for hours until I spied the barest of movement and fired the crossbow. I quickly reloaded as a twenty-something group of rabbits suddenly shot out from the snow and raced off in various directions.

Nathan fired his rifle, missed, and cursed loudly. I brought the crossbow to my shoulder and took aim, letting out a breath before squeezing the trigger. The rabbit fell to the snow, dead.

I lowered the crossbow while Nathan raced over to it and held it up, then another, a grin on his face. "Supper! We found supper!" he cried.

I sniffled, rubbing my nose, grinning. "Yeah, we did, didn't we? Come on, let's head back."

Nathan whooped again, and I laughed, resting the crossbow on my shoulder, letting him lead us back toward the house.

"Damn, Burner, you are a fine hunter," Nathan said.

I shrugged. Maybe, maybe not. "You should give them a few days before coming back, or else they'll scatter for good," I said.

"Gotcha."

"Can I ask something?"

"Whatever you want." Nathan flashed me a grin.

"Cook doesn't stay in the kitchen at night to keep the stove fires going, does he?"

The grin slowly slipped from Nathan's face and he cleared his throat. "You saw Martha?"

"Last night, standing by the lake."

"Shit," Nathan breathed, eyes troubled. "Goddamn it."

"She doesn't move like September," I said carefully.

"No, she doesn't." Nathan's voice was grim. "It's only happened a few times, but she comes at night. Cook's shot her twice so far." Nathan shook his head. "She still keeps coming back."

"Can't you kill her?"

Nathan lifted his head, his eyes wide. "How the hell do you kill something already dead?" He gazed up at the sky and cleared his throat. "Anyway, come on. I don't want to be out after dark."

"Because of Martha?" I asked.

"Yes."

I grunted and nodded toward the path. "Let's get going."

Nathan led the way, his pace a bit quicker. Occasionally, he cast worried glances at the surrounding woods. I listened, sniffing the air for anything other than the mold that clung to Nathan's clothing, or the heavy sweat that wafted off him. But I didn't smell anything.

The house came into view, and I caught sight of Neveah in the upstairs window, looking toward the lake.

"Did you find anything belonging to her and Eddy?" I asked quietly.

Nathan swallowed. "There's an old shed not too far from here. It's loaded with old hay. It's where Eddy trapped Blackie, and it was where I found Eddy's jacket. Why?"

I didn't say anything, just grunted in response. Nathan stared at me before he looked toward the kitchen door and the coal oil lamps illuminating the kitchen. We entered the house and Cook took the rabbits from us, grinning, and immediately went to work on them. I hesitated, looking to the door then back to Nathan who was pulling off his bear fur jacket.

"Where's Aaron?" I licked my lips.

"Upstairs with Neveah." Cook waved his hand.

I perched the crossbow against the corner and left the kitchen. When I passed through the living room, I noted Ashley and Abbey were sitting together in front of the fireplace. I climbed the stairs, skipping the creaking step. Neveah raced past me, her arm full of crayons, and colored paper. She disappeared downstairs, shouting for Abbey about something she'd drawn.

I headed for the bedroom and found the door partially opened. I pressed my hand against the wood and paused, listening as Aaron shifted around inside, before soft humming greeted my ears. He only hummed when he was in his human form. I pushed open the door to find him wrapped up in the comforter, sitting on the floor and holding a black leather book, his fingers slowly turning the pages.

September's journal.

Aaron had September's journal.

I pushed the door open and slammed it shut behind me. Aaron jumped, panic momentarily filling his eyes before they widened and he tucked the book behind his back.

"Why do you have September's journal?"

Chapter Nineteen

"WHY DO YOU have September's journal?"

Aaron licked his lips. "I...I don't."

"Don't lie to me!" I hissed.

Aaron blanched before he held it out, looking away. I snatched it from his hand and opened it to where he'd marked it with his fingers. Spread across two pages were lines and symbols of skulls, mantraps, red crosses, and poorly drawn illustrations of wolf heads with a knife through them.

"What is this?"

Aaron shuffled on the floor, drawing the comforter around his shoulders.

"Aaron?"

"It's a map," he mumbled. "It's September's map to Boston."

"You..."

"Yes! All right. I had her map. I used it with the other one that we lost because hers shows where we need to go, where to avoid the Hunters and traps." Aaron stood up. "Burner, this is a gift—"

"Why didn't you tell me?"

Aaron slowly blinked. "What?"

"Why didn't you tell me you had her map? Why didn't you tell me that we were never truly lost?"

Aaron swallowed, stepping back. "Burner—"

"Shift. Right now. We need to talk, and we can't fucking do it *here*," I growled, teeth too sharp, and my collar faintly burning against my neck.

Aaron's eyes fluttered, but he nodded and shifted into wolf form, the comforter dropping to the ground. I turned and stalked out of the room, Aaron quietly following. Downstairs, Nathan was sitting in front of the fire, warming his hands while Neveah drew on sheets of paper. Ashley glanced at me, but Abbey was focused on her sewing, mumbling about the poor light.

"That shed, where is it?" I bit out.

"To the west of here. You can't miss it. Why?" Nathan said.

I left the living room and entered the kitchen. I grabbed the crossbow and the cleaned bolts.

"I'm going to see if I can round up some more rabbits," I lied.

Cook nodded. "Sounds good, just don't be gone too long. Ashley says tonight will be the coldest night yet, but it should warm up in the next few days."

"Right. We'll be back soon. C'mon, Aaron." I opened the door. Aaron slunk out first, his ears flat against his head, his tail tucked between his legs. I gave Cook a thin-lipped smile before I followed him out, shouldering the crossbow and starting along the trek.

Aaron didn't speak, nor did I. Not until the farmhouse was well out of sight, and nobody would question why I was talking to thin air.

"You lied to me."

Aaron bowed his head, several steps behind me.

I spun on my heel, fury starting to build.

"You fucking lied to my *face*, Aaron! You had her goddamn journal all this time, and you *knew* there was a map inside and you didn't say *shit!*"

Aaron flinched, pawing at the snow.

"Will you fucking shift already!" I snapped.

Aaron shook his head, refusing to meet my eyes, so I turned around, growling low in my throat. I marched on, heading toward what I thought was the shed Nathan had talked about.

Fine. If the little shit doesn't want to talk. Fine.

He had September's book and her map inside. We could have been in Boston by now and not lost in the middle of fucking nowhere. How could he have lied to me? How could he have not told *me!*

I stomped through the snow, my lips twisted downward as something dark and vicious and bitter built in my gut, my mind burning with anger. Aaron's steps grew slower. I was furious; it was making my vision blur as we passed countless trees until we reached the shed. It was about ten feet high with peeling red paint, but the windows weren't broken, and the door was partially opened. I slipped inside, noting the heavy scent of old hay and the birds' nests in the rafters. There were some hay bales stacked against one wall, and a small bench pressed against the other.

Aaron hesitated outside the open door.

"Get in here and shift!" I dropped the crossbow to the floor.

Aaron entered, shifting with each step until he was human. He opened his mouth, but I grabbed him by his shoulders, shoved him against the hay, and straddled his waist. He yelped, pushing at my shoulders while I grabbed a handful of his hair, my other hand curling tight around his throat. I brought our faces close until we were inches apart.

"You. Fucking. Lied. To. Me," I spat, my canines sharpening, the collar buzzing angrily in my ears. It only made things worse.

"You don't understand!" Aaron desperately clawed at the wrist around his throat, while the other tried to push my face away. I snapped at his fingers, nicking one, and hot copper flooded my mouth. Aaron cried out in pain, trying to buck me off him.

"Don't you want to save Fern? Save Albe and Danbe and Eric? God*damn it,* Aaron, they have Rock! Or what is it?" I sneered. "Just because I can't fucking read, you think I wouldn't figure it out? You think I'm an idiot, Aaron?"

"No!" Aaron's eyes snapped open, wide with panic and hurt. "No, Burner, I—you—no," he stuttered.

"Spit it out!" I roared. I let go of his hair and raised my hand, curling it into a fist. A light, a panicky, terror-stricken light, flashed in Aaron's eyes before he squeezed them closed and lifted his arms to cover his face.

"Dad, no!"

I froze.

"Please, *no.*" Aaron's voice carried something, something that overrode the anger that shot through the bitterness and left me rolling with horror and nausea. I scrambled off him, onto my ass, my hands trembling while Aaron curled into a ball, covering his head with his arms. "Dad, no, no, no, *please.* I'm sorry. *I'm sorry!*"

What have I done?

Without thinking, I grabbed the crossbow and fled the barn, Aaron's sobbing voice echoing in my ears. But no matter the distance I put between myself and him, all I saw was that light in his eyes and the realization I was no better than Rock.

I sagged against a tree, hiccupping and out of breath. I dropped to my knees, staring at my hands. How could I? How could I hurt him?

I was just the same as Rock. I was a monster.

Aaron would never forgive me.

I pressed my back against the tree, the rough bark digging into the fabric, and desperately tried to fight back the panicky breaths that were tightening my throat far worse than the collar, cutting off the sobs.

Chapter Twenty

THE WIND WAS picking up, and with it, the temperature dropped dramatically. I stood up, rubbing my hands on my numb thighs. I let out a shaky breath and turned around, wrapping my arms around myself and following my tracks back toward the shed. The sun was barely overhead now, and with the rising storm, it was hard to see. My teeth chattered as I fumbled through the snow. After too long walking I saw it; the shed.

I hesitated, but I shook my head. I needed to make amends, I needed to apologize to Aaron, to beg his forgiveness for what I'd done. I squeezed through the opened door and ruffled my hair, shaking out the fat snowflakes.

"Aaron?" I called.

Silence.

I blinked, checking the hay piles.

"Aaron?" My voice cracked, even as the wind picked up outside and the shed shuddered. I was met with silence. I searched again, checking the rafters and only finding cold birds snuggled deep into their nests. I hopped off the hay, fighting the rising panic.

"Aaron!"

"*Bad.*"

The hair on my neck rose at the hissed sound; my nose flooded with the scent of rot. Slowly, cautiously, I turned around.

The figure from the lake stood before me, blocking the door. Its head was bowed, long dirty hair covered its face, its clothing was stained red, and its skin...its skin...pulled taut and tight, its hands turned to claws. Slowly the figure lifted its head, its mouth full of sharp teeth, its eyes black pits.

Martha. It was Martha.

"*Baaaad,*" she hissed, her head swiveling like a snake. I swallowed hard, stepping back.

I glanced past her at the crossbow just behind her feet.

Shit. I couldn't shift. I couldn't fight back with teeth and claws. *Goddamn it!*

"Martha?" I tested the words. She froze, her head twitching to the side, listening to my voice. "Can you hear me?"

Her mouth parted, and she screamed, lunging at me. I yelped, raising my arms and yelling as she bit into the flesh, her head shaking rapidly. I snarled, grabbed her hair, and yanked her head back. She flailed in my arms and I threw her toward the hay and scrambled for the crossbow. I rolled to the ground and grabbed it. I tried to load it while she spun around and ran toward me with her claws out, screeching.

And then Aaron threw himself at her.

Stunned, I could only watch as Martha focused on Aaron. She swiped at him, screaming. Aaron was barking, snapping viciously at her, ducking each blow she gave. She got his nose and I snapped out of it. I tossed aside the crossbow and tackled Martha from behind.

Aaron jumped out of the way, barking frantically as I jerked Martha's head back and sank my sharpened teeth into her throat, my eyes watering at the horrific taste of her flesh and blood. I spat it out and bit into her throat again while Martha gurgled, clawing uselessly at the ground.

I did this again and again until she stopped moving. I stilled, my eyes wide, then jumped as her body liquefied into brown goo beneath me.

"Jesus Christ." I gasped for breath, my stomach rolling. I turned and vomited every drop of blood and bit of flesh I'd consumed. My body racked, my hands digging into the soil as I gagged and threw up, spitting whatever I could out of my mouth.

Dimly, I felt warm hands running through my hair, rubbing my back, as I heaved and passed out.

WHEN I WOKE up, the door to the shed had been shut tight and the goo that had been Martha and my vomit was cleaned up. A lit oil lamp hung from the ceiling and it rocked slightly as the wind blew against the shed. I was lying on a pile of hay, and Aaron was sitting at the small table, wearing old, dusty clothes, too big for his skinny frame. An empty rucksack was on the floor next to his chair. He must have cleaned everything up, lit the lamp, and moved me.

I swallowed, hard.

"Aaron?"

His back stiffened at the sound of my voice, a tremor running through his thin frame, but he didn't turn around.

"What is it, Burner?" His voice was hollow, distant, the same voice he used to talk with Rock. I flinched at the sound of it. I crept toward him, kneeling behind him.

"I'm..." The words hung on my tongue. I ran my hand through my hair. "I'm sorry."

Aaron didn't respond. The air was heavy. I opened my mouth, to say something, to apologize again, but Aaron cleared his throat. "We should move tomorrow at dawn. There's an old dirt road that leads to the main highway. We should be in Boston within the next few days, sooner if we don't stop."

"No, Aaron." I grabbed his arm and he froze. "Please, I'm sorry. I shouldn't have hurt you."

"Okay."

I blinked slowly, my eyebrows climbing upward in confusion. "What?"

Aaron turned to me, looked at me with that flat expression he saved for Rock. "I said okay. I heard you."

My lips parted. I let go of him. "But..."

He tilted his head. "But... What? What else do you want, Burner?"

"No, Aaron, listen." My voice was rising. Aaron abruptly turned away, his back once more to me.

"We don't have time for this. We have to plan for tomorrow." Aaron continued with that same tone. "It might be our only chance to save the pack."

I swallowed, my Adam's apple bobbing against the collar. "*Aaron.*"

Aaron spun around, his lips twisted into an ugly grimace. "What is it, Burner? What do you want?" He shoved me against the wall, his eyes searching mine. "What do you want me to do to make *you* feel better? Huh? 'Cause I feel like shit!"

"I'm *sorry.*" The words bubbled up from my throat. Aaron looked away, his frame starting to tremble, his hands curled at his sides. He sucked in a deep breath and raised his eyes to mine. The betrayal, the hurt, the anguish I saw inside felt like a punch to the gut, like someone had shoved a dying wolf deep in my belly and it was desperately trying to crawl its way out.

"You *hurt* me," he whispered. "You hurt me, Burner, just like *he* does."

I swallowed hard, my fingers twitching uselessly at my side. I wanted to say something, to make what happened between us better, but the words weren't right, nothing was right, and all I could say was a croaked-out, "I'm sorry."

Aaron bowed his head. He rubbed the tears from his cheek with the wrist of his sleeve, sniffing. Hesitantly, cautious, I touched his arm. He froze once more, but he wasn't pushing me back, wasn't pushing me away.

Gingerly, I curled my hand around his wrist and stepped closer to him. I put my other arm around his back and pulled him close. He resisted, squeezing his eyes shut before he sobbed, and his hand flew to his mouth. I hugged him tightly, rubbing his back as his sobs turned hysterical and he clung to me, hiding his face in my neck.

I don't know how long we stood together, but eventually, we settled amongst the hay with Aaron's back pressed against my chest. I kept my arms wrapped around him, holding him close, resting my head against his. Aaron cleared his throat, but I didn't move, just hugged him tighter before slightly easing my grip.

"I... I didn't lie to you." His voice was soft. "September's map has symbols that mark where Hunters look for wolves, where Deadwalkers hunt, leftover traces of People Eater groups, Burner." He craned his neck, his eyes stained red with tears and worry, his cheeks still carrying that blotchy red from crying. "There are traps everywhere, Burner. Any other road, any other path, we... It's too dangerous." He looked away, studying the fabric of his sweater. "I'm sorry."

"Don't say that."

"What?"

"I was a complete and utter bastard." I pressed the side of my face against his. "I'm sorry for acting like that. Like *him*. The last thing I want in this world is to see you look at me like you look at him."

A hesitant nod against my cheek before Aaron spoke again, his voice even softer. I strained to hear him. "I don't want Rock to come back with the pack."

He won't.

I won't let him.

I'd kill him before he can hurt Aaron again.

I didn't voice these thoughts. I closed my eyes and dropped my head to rest on Aaron's shoulder, my body relaxing as he ran his hands through my hair, soothing me.

Rock will die by my hands. I swear it.

"Are you okay?"

I nuzzled his shoulder. "Hmm?"

"Your arm, where she bit you. Are you okay?" Aaron tilted his head back. I raised my arm, showing the healing flesh. It was already dark purple, the teeth marks fading.

"I think so. If you hadn't come, I'd be dead," I said, wrapping my arm around his waist.

"I was going to leave, to go back to the farmhouse, but then I figured you'd probably come back here, so... I waited outside." Aaron stroked my arm. "I saw you enter, and I hesitated, and then I saw her clawing along the ground, following your scent."

I shuddered at the image.

"When I saw you trying to fight her off, I had to help."

"Thank you." I squeezed him tight then loosened my grip. He hummed in response. I tilted my head, watching the door rattle as the wind pounded against it. "Did September's book say anything about melting people?"

"Not that I've read yet. I haven't really been reading it a whole lot," Aaron admitted.

"You should. Read all of it, I mean. It'll probably hold the key to saving everyone." I flashed a wolfish smile. Aaron bit his bottom lip, his eyes shyly meeting mine.

"Okay."

"And Aaron?"

He frowned. "Yes?"

"The next time I act like a complete and utter bastard, tell me. Don't keep everything bottled up. You know I can be as dense as a brick."

Aaron tilted his head back, laughing. I squeezed him tight, grinning too. Relief swept through my body. We were okay. We were going to be okay.

Chapter Twenty-One

BY THE TIME the sun began to rise, the storm had ended. Aaron and I'd kept warm, burrowed into a makeshift nest of stacked hay. I woke a few times when the shed creaked and I was sure the roof would fall on us, but it didn't, and I'd gone back to sleep, keeping Aaron close even when the oil lamp extinguished itself and we were cast into complete darkness.

Aaron didn't want to leave the hay. I had to drag him up to stand on his own two feet, chiding him for sleeping so late. He'd yawned in response, rubbing his eyes. I cracked open the shed door, squinting into the white and giving a quick glance toward the sky.

It was a soft blue and I sighed with relief. Hopefully, Ashley was right, and the worst was over. I left the door and turned to Aaron. He was absently rubbing his shoulder, his hair messy and pieces of hay stuck to the baggy sweater, large jeans, and old, cracked gumboots that came to just below his knees.

"Do you want to go out on foot?" I offered.

Aaron paused. "You mean as human?"

"Yeah, if the clothing's warm enough."

Aaron plucked off some of the hay, noticing it on his clothing. "It would be nice not to have my feet *and* hands be freezing cold," he admitted.

"Then come on, you can shift once we get closer to the house."

I grabbed the crossbow off the floor, slid the strap over my shoulder, and followed him out of the shed. He took a deep breath and let it out, almost relaxing as he saw the clear sky. "This is a good sign."

"It is." I nudged his back and together we started walking through the snow. It hadn't really built up during the storm, and that in of itself was a miracle.

Aaron crossed his arms over his chest, hiding his hands from the cold. When he didn't say anything, I nudged his side.

"What is it?"

"When will we leave?"

"Probably as soon as we get back. I'll grab the backpack and we'll go," I said.

Aaron looked ahead, his gaze taking in the woods. "How will you explain to them why you're going?"

"Well, about that... I told Nathan about September."

Aaron's head snapped toward me, his eyes wide. "You *what*?"

"Turns out he met her too," I went on, only for Aaron's eyes to grow wider. Hurriedly, I explained to him about Nathan's experience with September, with the Deadwalkers and his village, but I left out the detail of the dog chained in the yard.

"So... he knows you're going to Boston to try and save your people," Aaron said.

"Exactly."

"Do you think he'll have told the others?"

"Probably, especially since we didn't come back yesterday," I said, looking down to watch where I stepped, not even noticing Aaron come to a halt. I took two more steps forward and stopped when Aaron grabbed my arm. I frowned, but he was pointing away from the trail and east toward a grove of trees and...

An elk.

A big, fat-ass, male elk, roughly fifteen feet high, and almost as big as the living room. Its antlers were wide and pointed. It stood, head bowed as it pushed away the snow and ate the frozen grass.

"So," I murmured, "think the storm drove it toward here?"

"Yes, I do." Aaron's eyes were locked on it.

"Think we could take it?"

Aaron licked his lips. "I can try and herd it toward you, or have it charge me, either or," he offered.

I sniffed, finally catching a glimmer of the beast's scent, and it was *good*. I lowered the crossbow to count the bolts. Five. I had five shots. Not nearly enough to take it down. I chewed on my bottom lip. It would have been a lot easier to shift. Usually took three or four wolves to take down a single elk, but we didn't have that luxury, not unless we had help...

I grabbed Aaron's shirt and dragged him close, whispering into his ear. "Okay, new plan. We're going to herd it toward the house, I'll chase it from behind while it charges after you; if it starts drifting or turns around, draw its attention back to you. Hopefully, Nathan or Cook is awake and has the rifle ready."

Aaron nodded and took off his shirt. I held out my arm and he grabbed hold of it as he pulled off his gumboots and pants, momentarily shivering in the cold before he shifted into wolf form. Stealthily, he crept away into the woods, his eyes focused on the elk.

I took two steps toward it, the snow crunching beneath my feet. The elk raised its head, great tendrils of steam erupting from its nose as it inhaled deeply and exhaled. It stared at me, distracted, and not paying any attention to Aaron, who crept behind it, getting into position.

Good.

Slowly, I raised my hand, my signal to Aaron. The elk raised its head before lowering its rack and digging at the snow, snorting, preparing to charge.

I dropped my arm and Aaron barked at the elk from behind. Panicked, the creature suddenly tore away from him and toward the path leading back to the farmhouse. Its antlers banged against the low tree branches as it fled, the muscles beneath its skin shivered and rippled. I couldn't hold back the whimper as the succulent fat on its ass jiggled when it leaped over a fallen tree.

Aaron howled as he chased after it through the woods and I followed, hot on their trail, panting and desperately trying to keep up. The plan seemed to be working, we were getting closer and closer to the house, and as soon as we rounded the next grove, it should be within eyesight.

That was when the plan went south.

The elk turned suddenly and lowered its antlers, jerking with a wide sweep, trying to hook Aaron on them. Aaron dove out of the way just in time and the elk noticed me. Again, it lowered his rack and charged at me. I ducked behind a tree.

Aaron sprinted through the snow from behind me, snapping and barking at the elk's heels. Saliva and foam flew from his mouth through the icy air. The elk snorted deep in his throat and started running again toward the house.

Staggering to my feet, I yelled, out of breath and hoping someone inside could hear us and see us coming. Aaron's voice was loud, booming. My jaws ached. The collar sparked, and electrical currents pulsed through my skin, forcing me to stumble into the snow. I fell face first, skidding the last few feet, and reached up to claw at my neck, wheezing as the world spun around me in a daze of agony and lack of oxygen.

Not now, please, *not now!*

Boom

I froze, Aaron's barking ending abruptly.

Boom

Sucking in a deep breath, my muscles trembling, the world spinning just so slightly, I climbed to my hands and knees, to where the sound had come from.

The elk lay on the ground dead. Nathan stood outside the house barefoot without a shirt on, holding the smoking rifle in his hands.

Aaron stared at the elk before he tipped his head back and *howled,* dancing around the downed creature, tail up. A grin split across my face and I collapsed back into the snow, letting it cool my feverish skin.

What a hunt.

Chapter Twenty-Two

THE LAST TIME I had roast elk was two winters earlier in Quebec. It'd been covered in spices and herbs, baked with potatoes, carrots, rutabagas, turnips, and oats that soaked up the fat. I'd devoured my large slice within minutes and dreamed of it for days afterward.

There were no spices this time, or vegetables, or oats, for that matter. Nor was it a roast. After Ashley, Cook, and myself had butchered it, Cook had fried pieces cut into steaks on the pan and I'd gorged on the meat. For the first time in what had to have been weeks, I was satisfied, as was that hunger I'd been doing my best to ignore. Even Aaron was pleased, laying underneath the table, still in his wolf form, his eyes glazed over as he lovingly chewed on his portion.

"We'll survive," Cook announced, banging his fist on the table, catching everybody's attention. "We're going to survive this winter. And we wouldn't have been able to do it without you, Burner."

I shook my head. "No, it was Aaron. He was able to herd it toward here. I almost missed it, wouldn't have seen it if he hadn't told me. If you can, smoke it, and it should see you through to the spring," I explained.

"Does this mean you're going to leave us?" Nathan shoved a forkful of meat into his mouth.

"You're leaving?" Neveah gasped from her place on Abbey's lap.

"Um," I cleared my throat. "Yeah. I—I have to get to Boston."

"Boston is a death trap," Ashley blurted out. "You can't go there. You're not allowed to leave."

"Ash." Nathan placed his hand on hers, swallowing the meat before he spoke again. "He saw her, he saw September."

Ashley straightened in her seat, shooting a panicked look between Nathan and myself. "What?"

"She saved me," I said. "But she wasn't able to save my people, so..."

"Are they in Boston?" Abbey frowned.

"Yes. At least, that's where I think they are."

"Do you have a map? To get there?" Cook said.

"I do, actually," I said.

"No!" Neveah yelled. She crawled off Abbey's lap and grabbed me, hugging my leg tight. "Don't go! Don't leave us!"

"Neveah," I sighed, stroking her hair. "I have to."

"No, I don't want you to become like Mom or Dad!" Tears welled up in her eyes and my mouth fell open. Neveah shook her head and bolted from the room, crying hysterically.

"I'll go take care of her." Ashley pushed her chair out. She squeezed my shoulder as she passed by.

"When will you go?" Abbey put down her fork and knife.

"Probably tomorrow at dawn. I'll need the light," I explained. I glanced over my shoulder, toward the living room, before I rested both arms on the table and lowered my voice, my gaze on Cook. "You don't need to worry about keeping the stove fire going at night anymore."

Confusion filtered across Cook's face before realization dawned and he leaned back in his chair. Abbey's hands flew to her mouth. Nathan coughed. He hit his chest until he finished.

"You saw her?" Nathan hissed.

"Yes."

"And you, you…" Abbey swallowed.

"You freed her?" Cook finished.

I shifted in my seat, felt Aaron move underneath the table. "She attacked me, attacked us. I didn't have a choice, but she won't come back."

The kitchen was silent for a while after that until Cook reached over and squeezed my shoulder. "Thank you, Burner, and you, too, Aaron."

Aaron softly *woo*-ed underneath the table in response.

"At least she's finally in peace." Abbey breathed a sigh of relief.

After we finished, and Ashley rejoined us to tell us that Neveah was busy drawing upstairs with one of the oil lamps, we said our goodbyes over hot mugs of nettle tea. Aaron and I would leave before they awoke, and I don't think they wanted the night to end.

Abbey and Ashley each hugged me before they left for bed. Nathan slapped my back, whispering a thousand *thank-yous* before he followed Ashley out of the kitchen. Cook stayed at the table while I grabbed the backpack upstairs. When I came back down, Cook had prepared several pieces of elk meat into strips and was wrapping them in paper. He placed them outside in the cold snow to freeze so they would last.

"For you and Aaron," he'd explained

"Thank you." I smiled. At least we'd have something to eat on our way there.

Cook looked around the kitchen, while I sat back down, Aaron leaping up into a chair. I poured him a cup of the nettle tea and Aaron sniffed it curiously. Cook, brushing imaginary dirt off his pants, cleared his throat. "You never mentioned that collar around your throat."

"No, I didn't," I said quietly.

Cook nodded, looking toward the kitchen door then back to me. "Before me and Abbey moved here, we lived on the West Coast. I, uh, I grew up in a small town, middle of nowhere, called Moonlight Bay." He cleared his throat. "It wasn't unlike other towns. It had its secrets, of course, but...it was different. Mainly because of the number of wolves that lived nearby."

I stilled. Aaron raised his head a fraction.

"Strong creatures. Always traveled in packs. Always took care of their own, helped others when they could." Cook's eyes softened. "Well, I reckon if my folks had moved to town when I'd been younger I could have...could have joined them. What do you think?"

"You'd have to have been really young. Younger than eight, I would think," I said slowly.

Cook nodded. He reached up to rub his jaw, the corners of his eyes crinkling. "That's what I reckoned. Anyway—" he cleared his throat again "—when you find your people...you make sure to come back our way. Our door's always open, and whatever we have, we'll be more than happy to share. Anyway, I'd better go join Abbey in bed. Those old bones of mine will enjoy sleeping on something soft."

I tilted my head and rested it on my palm, my elbow perched on the table. "How long did you know?"

Cook paused in the doorway.

"Was it me? My eyes? My teeth?" I frowned.

Cook chuckled, shaking his head. "No. It was Aaron."

Aaron sat straight up, panic in his golden eyes.

"What?" My jaw dropped.

"When I was growing up, I had two friends just like you two." Cook grinned. "It's easy to put the pieces together when you know where to look. His barking, the fact that he listens like a human, his eyes—most dog's eyes don't look gold like his—and the way you two talk together. I hope when you guys make it back, I'll be able to meet you in person, Aaron." Cook waved and left the kitchen, leaving Aaron and me in silence.

"Wow." I rolled the word in my mouth, my lips twitching as Aaron growled low in his throat, only for it to increase as I covered my mouth with my hand and crossed my arms on the table. I buried my face in my arms, my shoulders shaking with laughter while Aaron snarled at me.

Eventually, I peeked out. Aaron had his back to me, his tail twitching in annoyance. I yawned and let my eyes shut, falling asleep within moments.

"BURNER?"

Blearily, I opened my eyes. Neveah was standing next to me, her small hand clutching my sweater. She held a piece of paper against her chest, her worried eyes staring into mine.

"Neveah? What are you doing?" I yawned, cracking my jaw.

"For you." Neveah pushed the paper against my chest and I took it, flipping it over. I rubbed my eyes with one hand before I stopped, blinking at the drawing. It was a crayon picture of the farmhouse with Ashley, Abbey, Cook, Neveah, Nathan, and myself drawn as stick figures. Aaron was a crudely drawn dog, but he was holding hands too. The upper corner had a brilliant yellow sun smiling down at us and the rest of the picture was covered with happy plants and trees.

"Wow, Neveah, you do this?"

"Uh-huh. I wanted you to have this, so you'd never forget us." Neveah suddenly sniffled. I sighed.

"Neveah, no way in a thousand years could I forget you, or anybody else here for that matter," I said.

"Please don't go," Neveah whimpered. I rubbed her back.

"I have to, Neveah. But this picture?" I leaned back. She rubbed her eyes, shaking her head. I patted the picture on the table. "Every time I feel sad, or lonely, or I miss you guys, I'll look at that and know that you're safe and sound."

"Yeah?" Neveah hiccupped.

"Yeah." I smiled. "And you know what?"

Neveah shook her head.

"When I have my people back, we'll come back here for a little bit and visit before we go home, okay? And when I do, I'm going to bring my best friend. I think you'll like him."

"I thought Aaron was your best friend." Neveah glanced at Aaron. He was curled up next to the stove, his back to the heat, his eyes closed, but his ear was ticked toward us. He was listening to our every word.

"He is, but my other best friend can be pretty funny sometimes, and he can read too."

Neveah bit her bottom lip before she squeezed my neck tight, avoiding the collar. "I'll miss you, Burner."

"I'll miss you, too, Neveah," I whispered. I set her back on the floor and ruffled her hair. "Now, you need to go back to sleep, okay?"

"Come back soon." Neveah padded toward the hallway. She gave us one last look before creeping out of the room and up the stairs.

I sighed, rubbing my eyes. I picked up the letter and folded it in half, then in half again. I pulled September's book out and carefully tucked it in the front, safe and sound, before shoving it back into the bag. I glanced out the glass of the kitchen door and saw dawn was rising.

"Aaron," I whispered.

Aaron lifted his head, watching me curiously.

"Let's go."

Chapter Twenty-Three

"ARE YOU SERIOUSLY going to carry that all the way to Boston?"

A grumbled, garbled *woo* was the only response. My lips twitched. Aaron carried a sawed-off piece of the Elk's antler in his mouth, growling each time I made a move for it.

It'd been part of Cook's farewell gift, something we'd found when we unpacked the meat on the dusk of the first night. We didn't bother with a fire; we didn't have any matches and the wood we did find was damp with snow or too wet. It would've been nice to eat it cooked; the smoke always gave the meat an extra flavor, but raw had its perks too, as long as it was fairly fresh.

It was the middle of day three. According to Aaron, we should reach the outskirts of central Boston by nightfall if we followed Highway 93 then 28. Evidently, we'd gotten lost in some place called White Mountain National Park. When Aaron showed me September's map to prove it, I'd been stunned both by the distance we'd crossed in the time we'd had on foot, and the fact we were nowhere near the coast.

Already, there were burned and wrecked cars pushed to the side of the road, and dilapidated buildings made of red brick. Power poles and collapsed signs dotted the rocky landscape and old makeshift barriers were scattered here and there. The streets blurred in a mixture of various stores, homes, and factories. I lost count of the street numbers, focusing on what was coming.

We had to find the pack, save Fern and everyone else, and I had to kill Rock in a cityscape I had no reference to, with Hunters and Deadwalkers potentially lurking around every corner. Simple, right?

I rubbed my neck, absently pulling at the collar, grateful Aaron was with me. The number of side streets and roads was confusing as it was, but at least he could read the signs, and September's map, which proved to be a godsend. I was so caught up in my thoughts I didn't realize Aaron had stopped and was staring into the distance. I followed his gaze and spied a group of people wearing black slowly walking toward us from further down the street.

Without a word, we tore down a side street, putting a block between them and us. Cautiously, we crept in the shadows until I guessed we were on a similar street and only then did I look around the corner.

Two Hunters wearing those long coats with the pierced wolf's head symbol on their shoulders. With them were three individuals wearing the same black clothing and mask that September wore. I swallowed hard. Aaron nosed my palm, and I squatted low to him.

"Deadwalkers," I mouthed. His gold eyes widened. Belly to the ground, he slunk to the corner and peered around the edge before backing away. We waited until they were gone and then, just for extra security, crossed down another street and into an alley.

Kneeling between two dumpsters, I pulled out September's book from the jacket's inner pocket and flipped through it until we came to one of the many maps she'd drawn. Aaron eyed it critically before he flicked his ears and I turned the pages until he leaned closer, examining the lines and details.

"Did you find a place?" I whispered.

Aaron nodded and waited until I pocketed it before he started down the street, looking both ways before he swished his fluffy tail. I followed.

The sky was darkening, the air drastically cooling, and I swear I felt rain starting to fall among the sheets of snow as we raced into some park. I wasn't sure if it was a park, or just more housing because the area was scattered with gothic-style mansions that looked like they'd seen better years. Many of their roofs had collapsed, while others were just burned frames of once great homes.

Aaron led me deeper into the park until we found one mansion that didn't look like it'd been touched in decades. I tried the front door only to discover it locked. We walked around the outside and the back door was also locked, but I jimmied open a window and held it up while Aaron slipped inside. I squeezed in after him.

I dropped the backpack to the floor and looked around in the dim light, squinting into the darkness until I found an old oil lamp on a desk against a wall. I fidgeted with it, pulling off the glass topper. I padded at the desk, tugging open a drawer, and lucked out when I felt a hand-sized cardboard box. I took it out and shook it, grinning at the familiar rattle of matches.

Carefully, I lit the wick of the lamp and turned it down when it flared up into a brilliant flame, illuminating the room. I capped it with the glass tapper and lifted it, then turned to Aaron who'd already pulled on his pants and was currently struggling with the sweater. The flames cast light on his narrow, pale stomach and I swallowed, looking away.

I'd seen Aaron naked a thousand times. Seen him shift from wolf to human far too many times to count. He'd seen me naked too. So, what the hell was the problem? I rubbed my eyes and pinched the bridge of my nose.

"You okay, Burner?"

I dropped my hand, meeting Aaron's confused gaze. He was rolling up the sweater's long sleeves to his elbows, but he paused as the oil lamp illuminated the room, sending shadows dancing.

"Wow," he breathed, slowly turning around, and I understood why he'd forgotten about the sleeves.

The room was like nothing I'd ever seen.

It was two stories tall and jammed packed with thousands of books. There were ladders in various places and more piles of books that couldn't be crammed into the shelves on the walls. A large wooden desk faced a tall window that was covered with thick, dust-covered curtains and a fireplace with two overstuffed chairs in front of it. Above the fireplace was a giant oil painting of a wealthy family, a man and woman smiling brilliantly as they held a little girl in a red dress between them.

"I've never seen so many books," Aaron whispered in awe. "Get over here so I have some light."

I sniffed but did as he asked, holding the oil lamp while Aaron perused the books, his eyes roving along the titles.

"This is a neat room," Aaron murmured. He was dragging his fingers along the old books, head slightly tilted to read the titles. "*Pathogenesis and Gene Memory, String Theory and the Question of Souls, Cloning from Zero, The Real Eve Code* and *Mitochondria: An Exploration of Genetic Fact and Fiction...*" He paused, fingering the rough text of the last one. He pulled it out of the bookcase. He flipped it open and his eyes skimmed the pages.

We stood in silence until I cleared my throat. Aaron didn't respond. Instead, he slowly turned the page, a small frown dotting his forehead.

"So, you're going to just stay here?" I raised an eyebrow.

"Mmm?" Aaron barely responded.

"Right. I'll just go lay siege to Boston on my own. Maybe join the Hunters."

"Okay, don't be too long."

I rolled my eyes. After a few more minutes of looking, I spied another lamp near the fireplace, so I placed the oil lamp on a stack of books, which Aaron automatically sat next to. I lit the other and left the library to explore the house on my own.

I highly doubted a Hunters attack, let alone a Deadwalker attack, on the house would stir him from that room. I'd be lucky to even be able to drag him away when we *would* need to leave. There were two rooms on the bottom floor with carpeted stairs going upward and a locked door in the kitchen across from the library.

At least, I think it was a kitchen.

There was a table in the middle. It was white and cool with slightly raised sides, but there were red stains along the end of the table with the hole. The whole room carried a faint aroma of old chemicals, like in a school, and there were round lights with three bulbs in each one.

The stove was old, probably didn't work anymore, and when I opened the fridge, I was met with jars filled with...things. Long-dead things in various liquids. I closed the fridge door and checked the cupboards for any food to go alongside the remains of our elk. All I found were bottles with symbols of skulls on the front and more books. I rubbed my arms, goosebumps crawling across my skin as I eyed the kitchen.

I don't think this was a kitchen, at least not in the technical sense. It was nothing like any I'd seen in my magazines. I went to the door in the corner and turned the copper handle, but it didn't budge. I shrugged. If it was locked, fine. Probably more creepy stuff behind it. I abandoned the kitchen and followed the narrow wooden staircase upstairs, alert for any sort of sound, but for all my worry, I found two bedrooms and a bathroom at the end of the hall.

Everything was dusty and moldy. My nose wrinkled in distaste as I entered the first bedroom, holding the oil lamp up. The bed had a partially stuffed briefcase on it, but it looked untouched, the sheets neatly folded on top. The closet was open and there was clothing scattered everywhere too like someone was trying to leave in a hurry. I saw two picture frames near the bed and I held the lamp closer to them. It was the same man and woman from the oil painting below. The other picture was of the same little girl from the painting. She was smiling brightly.

I left the room and opened the door to what I assumed was the daughter's bedroom. It was untouched, her bed made like she would return any moment. There was a picture tacked to the doorframe and I pulled it loose, frowning at the man and wife, and the little girl, and a man wearing vaguely familiar clothing. They were all sitting in front of a lake. I turned it around and saw writing.

I left the bedroom, picture in hand, and padded downstairs. Aaron called me, his voice excited. I followed it into the library where he beckoned me close.

"Burner, look at this." Aaron waved the sheet of paper in front of my face. I placed my oil lamp on the floor and plucked the paper from his hands. I shoved the picture into a back pocket with a mental reminder to show it to Aaron later.

"I'm looking?" I scowled at the page. Aaron huffed.

"It's a bit long, but let me read it all, okay? It's really important."

I sighed. "Fine, fine. Go ahead, oh wordy one."

Aaron cleared his throat. He stood next to me, tracing his fingers along the text as he spoke so I could follow with him.

From Dominic Lewis, Assistant Director of the Center for Disease Control and Emergency Services in Atlanta, to all surviving laboratories:

At exactly 10:43 p.m., just four days after Halloween, an asteroid the size of Manhattan entered Earth's atmosphere and crashed in the Middle East. The last information received from Israel pinpointed its final location as the Dead Sea, but after that, no other information was received. Furthermore, there was no information sent either.

I shot him a confused look, but Aaron shook his head, so I kept my mouth shut and focused on the sheet again.

According to Doctors Evens and Kirk, astrophysics with NASA's asteroid research team, had the asteroid traveled at a faster rate, it would have triggered a planet-wide extinction event not seen since the end of the Jurassic period. Thankfully, the weight of the asteroid, combined with the gravitational mass from Jupiter, was able to slow it to a speed that resulted in a planet-wide electronic magnetic destruction event similar to the one that occurred in the early 1900s, known as the Tunguska event. The result, however, was the use of longwave radios, GPS, and satellite communication was devastated. Plans were put into place by the

UN and various worldwide government agencies that would focus solely on the realignment of satellites, and the rebuilding of the planetary worldwide information infrastructure, with landline communication being the first primary focus.

"Why does this sound like one of those spaceship books you're always reading that doesn't make any sense?" I groaned.

"Please, just be patient," Aaron begged. I rubbed my forehead, staring at the meaningless text.

However, another result of the asteroid crashing into Earth was the amount of particulate matter sent into the atmosphere which covered the Earth and effectively blocked out all sunlight. In order to avoid mass crop failures and starvation, impromptu tests and agriculture reforms were instituted that followed in the styles of Korean and Japanese breakthroughs for hydroponic towers and ensured the production of stock animal feed. Cattle, pigs, and chicken production remained much the same. Nuclear reactors were reactivated as solar power could no longer be used. Military, and in America's case, Homeland Security set up community measures to dispense food, water, and healthcare requirements.

"None of this means anything." I sniffed.

Aaron bit back a groan of frustration. "Just let me finish, okay?"

"Fine, fine."

Unfortunately, due to the particulate matter, planes could no longer fly, and freighters were employed to move mass populations of people back to their home nations at the cost of their own government. While long-range radio, wireless communication, and the internet were disabled, shortwave radio was still usable and accessible. There were community and countrywide efforts to establish local radio stations where people produced stories, shared news, and provided tips on how to survive the blackout.

At the emergency UN meeting, the available world leaders gathered and were informed that the darkness caused by the asteroid would last for roughly two years. Martial law and curfews were instigated in order to keep populations safe and secure during normal night hours. Drug use increased drastically, as did the use of other black-market items and illegal intoxicants. Prostitution, abuse, theft, and murder did see a marked increase after the second month, but military force ensured that these issues were kept to a minimum in towns, cities, and other communities.

However, and for reasons that are as yet unclear, a new disease emerged that decimated the population in less than twenty-four hours. Its spread was random; children, the elderly, and adults were all affected. Information gathered from sites of the infection provided little to no evidence for where it had come from. Victims bled from the eyes and mouth, as well as exhibiting rabidity and aversion to sunlight. The UN health agency issued a global alert for this new disease that was comparable to a strain of Ebola that had mutated with the rabies virus.

Whole cities, towns, and neighborhoods were destroyed by those infected, and what bodies remained to be buried were bloodless corpses. People were warned to avoid contact with anybody who was sick or showed signs of being ill. But the disease spread undeterred amongst the population, and people began to whisper stories of monsters from the dark, of "Deadwalkers" amongst the survivors. Some groups chose to leave towns and cities, and went off the grid, disappearing into small communities that quickly, and effectively, cut off all contact with the outside world. It was also around this time that gossip began to circulate of large vicious dogs that were seen to attack these "Deadwalkers". These sightings have not been verified.

I stared at Aaron, my eyes wide. "Deadwalkers? They saw Deadwalkers?" I breathed.

"Apparently, they didn't exist before the Two Years, or if they did, then in much smaller numbers. They said it's a disease, but they... I think they mentioned wolves, Burner." Aaron's voice was hushed. I swallowed, turning back to the page.

On the advice of Doctors Cho and Malkovich, experts in their field of disaster relief, local military forces evacuated people into stadiums, arenas, local churches, and military posts for protection. Within hours, many of these locations went dark.

At exactly the two-year mark, the heavy clouds that had darkened the sky lifted and cities began to burn as people who were infected with this disease burst into flames. Research by surviving members of this medical personnel into the cause of this outbreak determined that there is a parasite in each blood cell of every victim causing an insatiable desire for iron.

New York City has fallen. Boston has fallen. Los Angeles still stands, as does Las Vegas. This is the final entry from the CDC in Atlanta, there will be no other. May God help us.

Aaron finished, his voice cracking. He rubbed his throat, starting to rock on the heels of his feet.

"So... that's..." I frowned, trying to comprehend everything Aaron had just said. "What is it?"

"This is what happened." Smugness danced on his lips. "This is how the world fell into darkness. This is how it *happened!*"

"And it'll help us...how?"

"Los Angeles and Las Vegas might be free of Deadwalkers, Burner. They could be an oasis. They could be safe zones!" Aaron's voice was practically giddy, almost relieved and yet...

"Why would we need to go there?" I asked.

Aaron paused. "What?"

"I said, why would we need to go there? We're going to get the others and head back." Aaron eased the paper away from my hands and turned away. "Aren't we?"

Aaron cleared his throat, pacing back and forth. "I, um, well..."

"Aaron?"

He stilled and cast a bitter, sorrowful smile in my direction. He wouldn't meet my gaze. "I... I'm not going back."

"Why not?" I demanded.

He stared down at the page, carefully folding it into a square, and then a smaller square. "I can't go back to the way I lived, Burner." He let loose a shaky breath. "I can't live with Rock again. This whole experience...you and I, Neveah, Cook, Abbey, Nathan and Ashley, heck, even the Deadwalkers and Hunters...I was so scared of being on my own. Rock had me convinced that I was weak and useless. That I wouldn't survive a day, let alone weeks, outside of his control."

"But now?"

Aaron smiled at me, brilliant and wide. His blue eyes were filled with warmth and hope. "I've never been so happy before, Burner. I'm free."

I couldn't respond. There was an ache in my chest, squeezing my heart in a steel grip, making it impossible to speak, to respond, to scream at Aaron that he couldn't leave.

The smile on his face melted away to one of worry. "Are you okay?"

My tongue felt too fat for my mouth and dumbly I looked away. His worried tone echoed behind me as I left the library, heading to the kitchen and into the darkness it offered. The roof there was starting to leak. I grabbed the edge of the white porcelain table, digging blunt nails into it. I ignored how it started to crack under the pressure and sucked in deep breaths, fighting the desperate panic crawling up my spine.

Aaron was going to leave. He was going to abandon the pack—no, not the pack, *me*. He was going to leave *me*. Me. We'd been bitten under the same moon together. We'd played as pups together. We grew up together.

"Are you okay? What's wrong?" Aaron stood behind me. I spun on my heel, my eyes flashing to his before I looked away.

"You're going to leave."

Aaron blinked, his lips parted, confusion dotting his forehead. "I—I *can't* go back, Burner. Rock will kill me one day."

"I won't let him. I'll kill him before he touches you again."

"You can't do that, Burner." Aaron sighed. "His connection with my mom was the only reason why the Quebec pack allowed the Maine pack to winter with them. Even if he did treat her as he did," Aaron whispered the last part. He cleared his throat, looking at the floor. "If you did that, you would risk banishment, you would risk the name of Lee. That's a death sentence, Burner, you know that."

"I would rather wear the name of Lee than lose you," I blurted out the words before I thought about them, thought about a smarter response.

The silence was deafening.

"That isn't funny." Aaron's voice was low, dangerous. I grabbed his wrist.

"I'm not joking," I rasped, eyes searching his. "*I* can't go back without you. Without you, there's nothing there." I rambled.

"There's everything for *you!*" Aaron snapped. I swallowed, letting go of his wrist as if I'd been struck by lightning. "Goddamn it, Burner." Aaron set the lamp on the porcelain table and turned to me. "You're going to be the next Alpha of the pack once Fern passes on. You will lead it, you will protect it, you will teach the pups how to hunt and fish and fight. You have a future there, I don't."

"That's not true," I said. Aaron snorted in response, crossing his arms.

"Really? And what do I have to look forward to? Aside from Rock's ultimate death from liver failure except I'm pretty damn sure the fact he heals so quick that won't happen any time soon which means he'll live to be a hundred!"

"You could marry one of the daughters?" I cringed as I said the words, felt uncomfortable heat dig in my belly at the very thought of it.

"Wow," Aaron breathed. "I know you're dense, but you cannot be *that* dense."

I turned away and clawed uselessly at the white porcelain, my blood pounding in my ears. Aaron grabbed the oil lamp from beside me.

"I'm going back to the library. After we get the pack back, I'm leaving." Aaron's feet were carrying him away and I didn't think. I grabbed the table, the collar buzzing my neck like a thousand jolts of electricity were coursing through my veins. Before I realized it, the table had shattered against the door with the copper handle and the door popped open, revealing a stairwell illuminated by a pale white lightbulb.

"Holy crap, Burner, what have you done?"

Chapter Twenty-Four

"HOLY CRAP, BURNER, what have you done?"

I stared at my hands, then at the door. I took two steps toward it before Aaron grabbed my arm. I shot him a look, which he returned. Without a word, we entered the doorway and started down the long staircase, following the lights.

The wooden stairs creaked under our weight, but I was alert, waiting for something to leap out and attack us, but there was nothing except for a faint, quiet hum further down the stairs.

"Do you smell anything?" Aaron whispered to me. I shook my head.

"Nothing," I confirmed, reaching the bottom step. I peeked around the corner, preparing for the worst, but all I was met with was a room roughly the size of the library except half the height. Aaron's hand rested on my shoulder, his finger curling into the fabric of my shirt. I tapped his knuckles and he let go. Our silent communication for him telling me to be careful and I got the message.

On silent feet, I entered the room, taking in the thick curtains against the far wall, the desks of flat black mirrors that, were, um...

"Aaron, word?" I waved at them.

"Computer screens," he answered from behind me.

I nodded, stepping further into the room. There was a red blanket covering a curved table in the middle. A symbol of a gold bird was spread on the blanket. Aaron walked around the room, his eyes wide and drinking in everything he could see. I went over to one of the desks and flipped through a pile of papers until I came across one with a picture of the same gold bird. I held it up.

"Aaron," I said. His ears perked up and he examined the pages, frowning. "What is it?"

"It's a report about something called the *Robin Project.* Something about..." He flicked through several pages, chewing on his bottom lip. "Life after death? And lawsuits? There's a mention here of unethical treatment and experimentation upon corpses...yuck."

I ran my hands over the curved table, dug my fingers into the blanket and ripped it off. My jaw dropped.

Aaron glanced over my shoulder and jumped at the sight of a little girl in a white dress asleep in a glass coffin. She wore a wreath of brightly colored flowers atop her head and held a small stuffed rabbit in her arms. "Holy *shit*. Is she dead?"

I looked at the fabric in my hands and dropped it to the floor.

"I, ah, I think so?" I offered.

Aaron bit his bottom lip and leaned closer to the glass, his eyes searching her small frame. "She looks so peaceful, like she's sleeping."

I examined the case, running my fingers along the sealed edge and the silver underbelly. There were a series of wires, and tubes, attached underneath that disappeared behind the curtain. I grabbed a handful of the material and yanked it down, revealing a wall of machinery as tall as the ceiling. Some of the machines were on, and others were flashing words with a red warning light.

I swallowed. "What does it say?"

When Aaron didn't respond, I checked to see if he'd run, but he was standing there, slack-jawed, staring at the wall of screens and machines.

"Aaron?"

He shook his head before he started pointing at the different screens. "Um, they say 'warning: solar panels corrupted, activate alternative energy source,' 'warning: memory files corrupted,' 'danger: subject at loss of life, open pod.'" He turned his gaze to the little girl. "I don't think she's dead," he whispered, pressing his hand against the glass.

The little girl's eyes opened wide, revealing cerulean green. Her mouth parted, gasping fruitlessly. Aaron leaped back with a startled yelp while I tried to pry open the sides. The little girl beat her curled hands into fists against the glass, shaking her head.

"Aaron, give me a hand here!" I shouted. When the edges wouldn't budge, I settled for punching the glass and only resulted in hurting my knuckles. I ground my teeth together while Aaron dug into his pocket and pulled out the keychain. He shoved it into the lock on the right side and turned it. The glass dome opened with a loud *hiss*. The little girl gasped for air and broke down into a coughing fit. I picked her up. She wrapped her arms around my neck, coughing onto my shoulder, and I rubbed her back, casting Aaron a worried look.

"There we go, little one, there we go," I soothed.

Aaron brushed away my hand. The back of her dress was opened and all along her spine were a series of tiny holes that healed within seconds. He shot me a confused look and zipped up her dress. I shrugged. How would I know what was going on?

Just as sudden as the coughing fit started, it stopped. She rubbed her eyes with her small fists before she sagged in my arms.

"Hello?" Aaron whispered. "Little girl?"

The little girl's mouth opened and a weird, static-like child's voice spoke. "Systems sixty-five percent operational. Last update over seven thousand days ago. Unable to connect to the cloud for a system update. Please ensure internet connectivity. System analysis detects abnormal programming. Warning, continued usage of third-party software can lead to irreparable corruption of Robin program. Warning, Robin is not applicable to Axton designs. Warning, stolen property detected, please return to Dr. Mirim and Kyle Broderack of the University of Boston advanced robots department, Warning—"

"What the hell is wrong with her?" I snapped. Aaron's eyes seemed to grow and grow in size as the little girl continued speaking. "Hey, honey, you need to stop! Can you hear me?"

The little girl raised her head, her green eyes staring at mine. "Unknown facial mapping detected—"

"Aaron, give me a hand here!"

Aaron lifted her hair again, trailing his fingers along her hairline before they slipped behind her ear and suddenly the girl fell against me like a broken doll.

"What. The. Hell," I growled.

"Please don't ask me." Aaron raised his hands. I gently shook her.

"Little girl? Little girl, can you hear me? Shit, Aaron, what did you do?"

Aaron ran his fingers to behind the little girl's ear again and, as if she'd been startled, she sat up in my arms, blinking sleepily and yawning widely. She stretched her arms above her head before she rubbed her eyes again.

"Five more minutes," she whined. She dropped her arms, blinking between Aaron and myself, her eyes shimmering iridescent green. "Are you my daddies?"

Aaron practically squawked and my jaw dropped. "*What?*"

The little girl blinked several times before she nodded. "Please hold. Restoring previous family data." She squeezed her eyes shut before they opened wide again. "Have you seen my mommy and daddy? They promised they'd be here when I woke up."

"Uhh," *Okay, smart words, Burner, good job.*

"I-I don't know, sweetie, what do they look like?" Aaron soothed.

I had to applaud Aaron. At least he was trying.

The little girl tilted her head to the left, then the right, her eyebrows coming together in confusion. "I-I don't remember."

I cleared my throat and rubbed her back. "That's okay. Can you remember your name?"

"Robin," she chirped.

"Right, well, I'm Burner. And that's Aaron." I nodded with my chin. "Do, ah, do you know what you were doing in there?"

Robin blinked. She squirmed in my arms, staring at the glass casket for a few seconds before she smiled brilliantly. "I was sleeping. It's the special bed my mommy and daddy made for me so I could sleep for as long as I needed."

"Why?" Aaron dragged out the word.

"Oh, um, because I was really sick, but now I'm not, but..." Her forehead wrinkled.

"But?" I frowned.

"But I'm really cold and hungry, can you feed me?" Robin pleaded.

"Yeah, we'll start a fire upstairs, and we've got some food," I said. Robin smiled at Aaron and me again.

"Um, where are we going to get the kindling?" Aaron scowled.

Chapter Twenty-Five

"NO!" AARON THREW himself against the library wall, spreading his arms protectively across the numerous texts. "You are *not* burning any of these!"

"Aaron, we need kindling. It's pouring rain outside and it's freezing in here. We need warmth, Robin needs warmth *and* food." I pointed at the little girl sitting in the threadbare chair, wrapped tightly in the white jacket I'd found her. Aaron bit his bottom lip, his eyes dancing between the wall of books and the girl. He sighed, sagging against the wall.

"Fine. Just, let me pick the books?"

"Get picking." I walked back to the little girl and the cast-iron stove nestled into the other wall. I knelt next to her, smiling. "Hey, sweetie, we'll get you warmed up in no time, okay?"

Robin rubbed her iridescent green eyes. "Why can't I connect to the cloud?"

"Because you're indoors and it's raining outside?" I offered. Robin seemed to consider my words before she nodded.

"Answer accepted." Her tone was crisp until she coughed, her small frame shaking with the movement.

"Here." I wrapped her tighter in the jacket, brushing back the hair from her forehead. "We'll get the stove up and working in no time."

"Internal thermal temperatures too low, outward thermal increase needed to reestablish proper channels." Robin sighed, her shivering worsening.

Aaron joined us moments later, his arms full of books that he dumped on the floor. I opened the gate and filled the stove with the tomes. I pulled the packet of matches from my pocket, lit one, and held it to the paper until it caught. I took a few of the small pieces of firewood and carefully layered the books, and the wood, together.

"There we go." I let out a breath, closing the gate. I reached back and opened the damper to let in air from the chimney, which I sincerely hoped was empty, until a faint roar reached my ears. I pulled on the chain, closing it and keeping the fire contained. We didn't need a chimney fire, especially right now.

It took moments for the room to warm with the heat, and when it did, I physically relaxed. It was nice to be warm. Aaron picked up Robin and brought her closer to the stove. We sat in a semi-circle around it.

"So nice." I sighed. Robin raised her hands to the stove, her palms outward as her eyes seemed to shiver in the fire's orange light from the glass door. Her eyes shifted from iridescent green to a pale blue before they turned green once more. Aaron hummed in agreement before he grabbed one of the books off the floor and flipped it open.

I rolled my eyes and dug into the backpack to pull out a slice of elk. I shoved a poker through it and held it in the fire. It cooked quickly, and I blew on it, making sure it wasn't too hot for Robin before I handed it to her. Robin sniffed it and took a bite, her eyes widening before she ate it, humming happily to herself.

I waited for her to finish before I grabbed a curtain and wiped her hands and face clean, smiling as she yawned and stretched before curling up in front of the fire. I mimicked her, glancing at Aaron who was putting down one book, a sour wrinkle on his face.

"You finally find a bad book?"

"It's about traditions from the Isle of Man," Aaron sighed, reading the spine of another. "It talked about this practice where, when their dogs died, they'd turn them into floaters and the fishermen would set them out into the bay so that when the tide came in, the dogs would bob up and down. The fishermen called it 'all the dogs are dancing.'"

"That's horrible," I said. Aaron snorted in agreement. "So, what's that one about?" I rested my arms behind me, stretching out my legs.

"This one is called *Frankenstein; or, The Modern Prometheus*. I've heard it mentioned in a few other books and some of your magazines." Aaron said.

"So..."

"So?" Aaron raised an eyebrow.

"Which is it? *Frankenstein* or *The Modern Prometheus*?" I frowned.

It took Aaron a few minutes before his lips curled and he turned away, hiding his face in the book, his shoulders starting to shake.

I smacked him on the back and he burst out laughing. "Oh, come on, just shut up and start reading," I grumbled, settling back into position.

Aaron cleared his throat, swiveling his body around as he shot me a smile. "Okay, Letter 1, St. Petersburg, December 11th, 17-something-something..." Aaron began to read. I laid back on the floor, resting my head on my hands, staring up at the ceiling and finding myself disappearing into Aaron's voice.

When I awoke, it was still dark outside, and the fire was warm against my face. Aaron was asleep next to me, stretched out on the old rug. Robin was curled protectively in his arms. His face was relaxed, his eyes tracking something behind his shut lids. He opened his mouth, mumbling under a breath before pulling Robin closer and falling still once more.

I couldn't let him leave.

It was a fact. A statement of intent, of determination and fate. He didn't want to come back with the pack, because he didn't want to live with Rock anymore. Fine. If that was the reason, then I knew in my gut I had a solution. Kill Rock.

The only question was how.

He was with the pack, the Hunters had the pack, then I could free the pack and kill Rock before Fern or the others could stop me, but I sure as hell couldn't let Aaron or anybody else *know* it was me. You never kill one of your own. Pack rules.

I sat up and ran a hand through my hair, watching him and Robin. She seemed happy, and honestly, I thought she'd fit in well with the Den daughters. Jessica would probably love her, and Robin was still young enough to be turned. But what would we do with her while we were freeing the pack? I dropped my hands to my side and dug my palms into the fabric. She couldn't fight, and I doubted Aaron would let her stay by herself. We could be captured and then she'd be all alone.

Honestly, it was better that Aaron stayed with her, given that there could be fighting and killing, and Aaron couldn't kill...so...Aaron would stay with Robin, keep her safe, while I went and freed the pack, killed Rock, and we could all escape back home. We'd all get what we wanted, we'd all be safe, and Aaron wouldn't have to leave.

It made perfect sense.

I just needed September's map of Boston to get into the city and not trigger any of the traps, avoid the barricades, or whatever else awaited naïve travelers. Said map was in her book, and her book was in Aaron's backpack, which was beneath his head, acting as a pillow.

Carefully, I shuffled on my knees closer to him and placed my hand on his head. He didn't move. Holding my breath, I sunk my fingers into his loose hair and around his skull and lifted his head just enough to tease open the zipper of the backpack with my other hand. I wiggled out September's leather-bound book and eased Aaron's head back onto the pillow. I let out my breath and flipped open the book, using the stove's light as a guide until I came across the page Aaron had said was a map of Boston.

As quietly as I could, I tore the page out and silently grimaced at the sharp tearing sound. When it was done, I folded up the page and pocketed it. I placed September's journal just out of the way and went to leave when Aaron's eyelids fluttered open. Exhausted blue eyes with flecks of gold stared up at me.

"Burner?" Aaron murmured.

"I need to go outside and take a piss. Go back to sleep," I whispered.

Aaron nodded, his eyes falling shut, and buried his face in Robin's pale blonde hair.

I waited with bated breath a few seconds longer before I stood up and padded to the door. I pulled my windbreaker off the edge of the stairs and glanced back at them.

It was the only way.

I slipped out of the house, pulling the hood of my jacket over my head to cut off the rain and wind, and took off running toward the city.

Chapter Twenty-Six

BOSTON WAS *HUGE*. Whatever it looked like before must have been jaw-dropping, because it was full of charred buildings with broken windows, torn-up concrete roads, and barricades everywhere. As I slunk through the city, I'd press my back against one of the red brick walls and pull out the map, raising it to whatever street sign still stood, matching the symbols.

So far, I'd avoided a street laid with mines and a couple of trip lines, but I wasn't anywhere near close to the Hunters' Lair that September had angrily circled with a red pen amongst the scribbled green and blue ink.

I pocketed the map, grateful and cursing the wind and rain. Yes, it hid my footsteps and covered my scent, but goddamn it was cold. I pressed my palms against the bricks and darted down the side street, pausing momentarily when I found an open intersection before continuing down another and slipping through a toy store with open doors.

Thankfully I hadn't encountered anybody yet. Maybe it was because it was still nighttime and rainy, I wasn't sure, but I wasn't about to curse away my luck as I raced down another alleyway and turned right, only to come face first with a barricade.

I frowned, stepping back and eyeing the structure. It was tall, about fifteen feet high, and the metal looked brand new. I ducked beneath an eave, pulled out the map, and traced my finger along the path I had taken to where I thought I was now.

There was no sign of a barricade.

"Damn it," I hissed. I left the alleyway, looking at my options and comparing my surroundings with the map. I'd need to race back at least four streets, and even then, I'd have to hopscotch across a street laid with mines. I really didn't want to do that.

My eyes drifted down to the sewer lid.

I knelt and curled my fingers into the metal lid, grunting as I lifted it and pulled it to the side. There was a ladder going down but the stench? Good God.

I covered my nose with the collar of my shirt and started down the ladder, giving the sky one last, longing, look before I grabbed the sewer lid and dragged it back on top, casting myself and the world into darkness.

When I reached the bottom, my feet landed in water and I grimaced, bracing my hand against the wall. I tried to follow the curved halls of the sewer, listening to rats squealing underneath me and scurrying over my feet as I walked, the water sloshing with my every step.

Eventually, I passed the barricade and started looking for another ladder up, only to pause when a light flashed through the lid's circular holes. For a moment, it illuminated my face and I froze mid-step.

"Lucky doesn't want them," a man growled above me. "Said they're 'too feral' for his pits and too much trouble. People want a show, not a bloodbath."

"Well, shit," another man sighed, the light moving away.

Cautiously, I stepped onto the ladder and climbed up as the men above me spoke.

"We could always sell 'em off to auction. Those twins should fetch a pretty penny."

My ears perked up. Twins? Were they talking about Albe and Danbe?

"Yeah, but one's a deaf-mute. Richard said they'd tried to separate 'em but the healthy one actually half-shifted, shock collar and all, when they tried to force them apart."

They *were* talking about Albe and Danbe! And they were together!

"What about that other young one? The one with the broken leg? He's already damaged goods." The second man walked overhead, his boots clinking along the sewer lid. I ducked my head, blinking into the dark.

"Might be able to sell him off to the dog house. He's got the looks—not that I'd know what one of those filthy fucking animals find attractive," the first man hastily corrected.

I frowned. Eric? Were they talking about Eric?

"And...what about Him?"

"You mean the Alpha? He's a smart one. Doesn't speak much, but Kevin overheard him talking to the one with the broken leg, said he's got a Texan accent. 'Course, what an Alpha with a Texan accent's doing all the way up there is anyone's guess. Agatha says that as long as we don't try and hurt the others, he won't fight back. Shock collar or not."

Fern. My heart did a double thump. I pressed my forehead against the ladder's cool steps, unable to fight the grin crawling across my face. They were alive.

"Still...damn shame the others didn't make it back."

"Yeah. I hate to imagine the windfall we'd have gotten had we bagged a Den Mother. The King of New York would have set us up for life."

"You ever meet him?"

"Nah, you?"

"Creepy bastard. Reminds me of the guy who was president, but competent."

There was a rough laugh between the two men.

"Anyway, shift's almost up. Can't wait to get out of the cold and get some sleep."

"I hear you. Come on, it's dead out here, let's hit the kitchen."

I waited for the two men to be far enough away before I pushed open the sewer lid and peeked out. They were wearing long coats and heading toward a building illuminated by strings of light bulbs flickering like dim stars in the cold night. Faintly, I heard the muted roar of a generator nearby. I glanced around the area. There was nobody nearby, no one in the windows. I crawled out, holding my breath, and slid the sewer lid shut.

God, I wished I could shift.

I raced toward the darkness of the buildings, giving myself and the men a wide berth. I pulled out September's map and found I was one block away from the Hunter's Lair. I shoved it back into the pocket and ducked behind a dumpster as two women wearing long coats walked past.

Shit.

Silently, I ran down the alleyway they had walked up, the scent of ocean air filling my nostrils and getting rid of the scent of shit and rot from the sewers. I turned right on another street and stopped behind a collapsed billboard as two more people walked past. I waited, my heart thundering in my ears, before I bolted and turned left, almost tripping over my feet at the sight that greeted me.

An old tugboat was in the dock. A string of lights stretching from its chimney to the tail of it gave a soft light. The flag that flapped in the breeze at the top was the same symbol from the armbands: a wolf's head with a dagger through it. Behind it was a barge stacked with empty cages.

I swallowed hard and twisted in position, realizing that I was in the middle of the Hunters' lair, and just four blocks down was a building lit up with laughter and music spilling out. A giant four-leaf clover flashed above the entrance.

Where the hell were they?

I bit my bottom lip, racing toward the tugboat and along the pier, desperately trying to listen for any sounds until, by a chance breeze that wasn't drowned out by the taste of salt water, I smelled them.

I. Smelled. Them.

I bolted toward the direction, almost delirious as I found a building that I think was once a fish market with wide open doors. I heard a cough and ducked against the doors outside, holding my breath tight.

"Stupid fucking mongrels," a man wheezed. "You'd think they'd be grateful for anything to eat."

"Yeah, well, they're dogs, what can you say?" a woman sneered as they walked out the door, not realizing they'd walked past me.

"Come on, let's go to Lucky's. I need a drink before the sun rises."

As soon as I dared, I slipped into the building, noting the small room by the front, and the rows and rows of cages filled with...with...

"Wolves." The cold air pulled the breath from me. In a daze, I walked down the lines of cages. The vast majority of the wolves were asleep in collected piles, trying to keep warm. Most of them were in their human forms and wearing badly sewn together rags, others wore expensive-looking clothing and ignored the filthy ones in the cages.

I swallowed hard, walking past a cage filled with Den daughters not much older than me. One with strawberry-colored hair lifted her head, a gold shock collar around her throat. She eyed me, sniffing me in disdain before rolling over and curling into the others.

What the hell was going on? Where did they all come from? Did they belong to other wolf packs? But they wore collars, too, and their clothing was so different. What was happening?

I shook my head, fighting back the hysteria that wanted to bubble out, and focused on my goal, on my nose. I was close. I was close to my pack. *Focus, Burner. Focus.*

It took what felt like forever, but against the back wall, hidden away in a corner, I found my pack in a cage, and I wanted to scream.

Albe was sitting against the wall, cradling Danbe's head on his shoulder, asleep. Their bodies were covered with dirt and mud. Albe's neck was badly burned from the collar. Eric was asleep on his side, his broken leg discolored, and Fern... Fern was sitting cross-legged between the three of them, resting his head on his propped-up arm, his eyes shut in sleep. They all wore the same poorly sewed together clothing of pants and shirts. I peered at the other cages, but I didn't see Rock anywhere.

Had he not made it? Did he die on the way here?

A small giddy feeling of victory flooded my chest and I immediately squashed it down. Until I was certain, I wouldn't celebrate. Besides, I had to free my pack.

I knelt, my mouth dry as I gripped the bars of the cage.

"Fern?" I whispered.

No response. I glanced over my shoulder to make sure nobody had heard me, that nobody was coming. I turned back to Fern.

"Fern." My voice was just a bit louder. Fern's brows tugged together in sleep. "Fern, wake up."

Gold eyes slowly opened, exhaustion clear in them. He blinked, staring at me blankly before his eyes widened and his mouth parted.

I raised my hands, shushing him.

"No time to explain, I'm here to get you out," I whispered.

Fern glanced at Albe and Danbe and Eric before he crept toward the bars. "Burner? You're alive? What are you doing here? Where's the daughters?" he hissed.

"Safe. Den Mother survived." I kept my voice above a breath. "Aaron and I are here to get you out. I mean, Aaron's at a safe place. Where's Rock?"

Fern's lips thinned and his eyes narrowed. He took in a ragged breath before he shook his head. Whatever he was fighting internally, he didn't share. "They keep the keys to the cells in that office by the front. You need to get it before they come back. I'll wake the others. We'll need to hurry."

Without a word, I turned and padded back to the office, keeping low and hoping I was quiet enough not to wake the others. I twisted the door's handle, praying it was unlocked, and let out a small sigh of relief as the door popped open. I stepped inside, momentarily stumped by the key ring with the dozen or so keys on it perched on a desk, but on the wall, next to a shock collar, was a long, pencil-thick key. I grabbed it and dashed back to the pack's cells just as Fern was awakening Eric. Albe and Danbe were awake but looking stunned as I handed Fern the long key through the cell's door.

"Here, I think this is for the collars." I fidgeted with the keyring, trying each and every one on the lock. Fern examined the long key and ran it along his collar first until it snapped open and dropped to his feet. He let out a ragged breath, a grin forming on his face. He did the same to Eric's and it popped open too. He handed the device to Albe and Danbe.

I was on my twelfth key, quietly cursing, when I heard people speaking near the entrance of the building. I froze.

"Goddamn it, he took the keys! Shit. Now I have to go all the way back to Lucky's," a man grumbled. He walked out of sight and I let out the breath I'd been holding. Finally finding the right key. I turned the key twice in the lock and the door clicked. I pulled the door open while Fern gently shook Eric's shoulder.

"You need to shift, you can heal once you shift," Fern murmured. Eric weakly shook his head. Fern leaned down, baring his teeth, and growled low. "I said *shift*."

Eric froze and before a cry could escape his lips, Fern slammed his hand over his mouth as Eric's skin shifted and moved, his bones breaking apart and re-fusing until a solid black wolf was lying on the ground. He panted in pain, but at least his leg looked right.

"Burner, here." Albe handed me the pen key as Fern carried Eric out of the cell and stood at his full height, eyes taking in the other cells. Albe and Danbe scurried after him. I ran the pen along my collar.

Fern eyed the other cages, even as I pressed the pen to my neck just a bit harder. Why wasn't it unlocking?

"Burner?" Fern tilted his head, confused, and I shook my head. I'd figure out what was wrong later.

"Come on, follow me. But you have to be quiet," I whispered.

They nodded and, as a group, we crept through the warehouse, past the other cages. A few times Fern faltered when he saw the wolves, his jaw clenching at the sight. Fern wanted to free them, wanted to rip open the cages and let the wolves out, but that would attract too much attention, and none of us would make it out alive. We left the factory as the sun blossomed over the water, filling the sky with a pinkish hue. Just as we were about to turn the corner, I spied a group of Hunters coming toward us.

Frantic, I took the keys and threw them at the tugboat. It broke through one of the windows and the group immediately armed themselves and approached the ship. I waved at Albe and Danbe, and we crept past the group around the corner. We were headed back to the sewer lid, back down beneath the streets. It was the only way.

At least that's what I told Fern, who carefully listened to my instructions.

"And Aaron is back at the mansion on the edge of town?"

"Yes. He's with this girl we found. Fern, where is Rock? I need to know where he is."

"He's not with us." Fern's voice held barely contained anger and I hesitated.

"What do you mean? Fern?" I grabbed his arm, stopping him.

Fern's eyes were a dark shade of amber. He cleared his throat, shaking his head. "Once we're somewhere safe, I'll tell you."

"But I..." I needed to kill Rock or else Aaron wouldn't come home.

"We're close, right? To the sewer entrance?" Fern pushed ahead.

I nodded, mindful of the people I'd seen patrolling earlier. It was odd, but the streets and little alleyways we crossed were empty now. Whatever, I was grateful.

When I saw the manhole, I raced over and, with Albe's help, pulled it open.

"Okay," I breathed. We were going to make it. "Fern, you go down first, Albe and I will help Eric down. Then Danbe, then Albe, then me."

Fern nodded, reluctant, and with his first step, he grabbed my arm, his eyes searching mine.

"Someday, you will be a great Alpha, Burner. Never forget that."

My throat tightened. I nodded stiffly, turning to help carry Eric when a high-pitched siren filled the air, making the hair on my arms rise, and all five of us froze.

"What is that?" Albe looked to the sky in confusion.

"*Danger, wild wolves are loose. Danger, wild wolves are loose.*" A voice from a speaker hugging one of the high corners of the buildings spoke.

"We need to move. Now!"

Fern made it to the bottom and Albe and I carefully lowered Eric into Fern's arms. Albe waved for Danbe who climbed down the steps. Shouting down the street caught my attention and I glanced past Albe to see Hunters chasing after us.

"Burner!" Albe gasped.

"Down, down, down!" I shoved him toward the opening and he climbed down, the water splashing as Fern tried to catch my gaze.

"Burner, come on!"

"There's no time." Arrows sailed past my ear, nicking the flesh. I grabbed the manhole cover.

"Burner! No!" Albe cried.

"Run! Find Aaron! He has a map that'll lead you home." The words were choking me, tight in my throat, but I squashed it down and shoved the sewer lid back into place. Defiantly, I hopped to my feet and stood over it, baring my teeth as I was surrounded by a hundred Hunters, all of them armed with those damn poisoned arrows.

I had to give them a head start, I had to try to give them *something*.

"Shoot the fucking dog!" A Hunter in the back yelled and, like a thunderous echo in the air, or the roar of a distant forest fire devouring everything in its path on a too-hot summer's night, they fired.

Chapter Twenty-Seven

I DON'T KNOW why I didn't die, why the Hunters didn't kill me, and it scared me. I'd only been scared once in my life, and that moment haunted my dreams on hot summer nights when I couldn't sleep. But those were dreams. I could wake up from them. Wherever I was, I'd been in and out of consciousness for what had to be days. Not that I could tell what day it was. The only light was the skinny bulb hanging overhead.

My body was covered in dozens of wounds where I'd been shot with the crossbow bolts. I raised my hand; my fingers webbed together while the bones and ligaments inside worked overtime as they tried to heal. They'd beaten me while I'd been unconscious, and I could still feel the pressure of the boot against my throat. At least I didn't remember that.

I shifted against my place on the wall and winced as the second rib on my right side struggled against the bruised muscles before it finally popped back into its rightful place. I let out a ragged breath and gazed up at the bare lightbulb, then at the thick steel bars that even I couldn't bend. I turned to the other prisoners who were lying in their cells either dead or near death.

From what I could tell, they were wolves shifted to humans too. They didn't carry that wild smell I did, but their scent, it was...human? Was that the word? I sighed. My bones felt like weak lead.

But it didn't matter because the pack was safe. They'd escaped. I made sure of that. Aaron would help them. My lips curled into a smile. Aaron wouldn't leave. Rock wasn't there, Fern had said so. Aaron could go home. He'd be safe, and he'd protect Robin too. They'd head North and join the Quebec pack. They'd have everything they needed there; shelter, food, friends.

Everything would be safe. The pack would be safe. Aaron would be safe.

I didn't kill Rock.

My lips soured at that, and I scowled at the wall. Hopefully he was dead, tossed into some side road, never to trouble Aaron again.

The door at the far end of the hall opened. I rolled my head to the side, curious as a tall, skinny man with dirty blond hair and rumpled clothes walked along the cells until he reached mine. He was roughly one or two years older than me.

"This one," the man yelled. He pointed at me and five more men, all wearing identical green and black uniforms with masks that only showed their copper eyes, joined him in front of my cell. They were armed with metal batons and a catch pole.

I eyed them, my bruised muscles tensing as the men in masks glanced at each other.

The man slowly opened the door.

"Are you going to come willingly?" His yellow eyes focused on mine. I realized with a jolt he was a wolf in human form. The guards were wolves too.

I wetted my dry lips, tilting my head to the side. They weren't with the Hunters?

"Who are you?" I murmured, my voice croaky.

The blond-haired man stared at me before he sniffed. "Sam. Who are you?"

"Burner."

"Are you going to come easily, Burner?" Sam's eyes watched me like a hawk and I sighed.

"Give me a minute." On limbs that felt too much like jelly, I crawled to my feet, using the wall for support. I took one step toward Sam and the guards growled in warning.

"Serga's waiting for you." Sam backed out of the cell and I obediently followed.

Chapter Twenty-Eight

SERGA WAS AS tall as Fern, and probably as strong. He was like Rock, too, but Serga's anger and his strength was controlled and collected. He had that look in his eye, that god-awful gleam of a person who took pleasure not in the hunt, but in killing the prey slowly and listening to its death cries.

I was strapped to an X-cross in the middle of a white room where the light hurt my eyes and the scrubbed-at bloodstains on the walls spoke of what Serga had done to past prisoners. Serga towered over me. Curiosity, and that horrific gleam, shone in his yellow eyes. Sam was behind him, nervous as he shifted from one foot to the other.

"Sammy says you put up quite a fight when he caught you in Boston." Serga stroked his black goatee slowly.

"He did—" Sam spoke up.

"Quiet," Serga ordered. Sam bowed his head and stepped back into the corner. Serga began again, as he slowly walked around my cross, "Sammy told me you got shot with dozens and dozens of arrows, didn't die, even with the shock collar on."

I craned my neck, even though the muscles ached.

"Where is your pack?" Serga walked full circle.

I kept my mouth shut.

"Can he talk? You didn't rip out his tongue, did you?" He didn't bother to look back to Sam.

"He can. Told me his name," Sam answered.

"Then he can tell me." Serga crossed his arms.

I remained silent.

Serga narrowed his gaze. He grabbed my hair and dug his fingers against my jaw with his other hand. He looked in my eyes. His breath was horrible.

"Mismatched eyes. My, my. You're two steps away from being a half-breed, aren't you?" He pried open my jaw and examined my teeth while I gagged on his fat fingers. "All the proper teeth. Canine's a bit longer than normal." He opened my mouth wider and I struggled against the frame. "You have two wisdom teeth just emerging in the back, so, younger than the Two Years, but not born during it...maybe...eighteen? Nineteen?" He let go of my jaw and looked down.

He grabbed my arm and examined it carefully, his calloused fingers running up and down my tanned flesh until he saw the fang mark on my arm. "You've been bitten the old-fashioned way, but..." Serga turned my arm. I grunted as the restraints dug into the flesh of my wrists and ankles while I tried to turn with my arm. He stopped when he caught sight of my lower back.

"You're covered in burns, from a fire, was it? Before you were bitten?" He let go of my hips and I sagged against the frame. "So, burns, and bitten the old-fashioned way, I'm going to guess your name is...Burner." Serga snapped his fingers.

I swallowed.

"Which means that whoever bit you, taught you how to fight, and that person is an old bastard of an Alpha. Which means he survived the Two Years of Darkness, so that means there's a werewolf pack out there that hasn't been shattered and a Den Mother thrives." Serga paused. "What pack are you from?"

I didn't answer.

Serga tsked and, faster than I could comprehend, he punched me hard in the stomach. I gagged, and my muscles screamed as I fought for breath.

"What pack are you from?" Serga demanded. His next hit was aimed directly at the ribs that had just healed.

Two of them broke.

"Speak up, Burner," Serga ordered. He drove his fist into my stomach and I swear I saw stars.

I coughed, and blood spattered my lips. He stepped back and crossed his arms again. When I could breathe, and the stars were gone, I met his yellow eyes and I growled. That gleam in his eyes darkened. "Get my kit. We'll trigger the collar. A few hours of electricity will make him talk."

Sam, who stared at the floor, meekly nodded, and went to the door.

"W-wait!" I yelled, panicked. I had to think fast because I sure as hell did not want to spend *hours* being shocked!

Sam paused. Serga grinned, triumphant.

"Why are you working for the Hunters?" I gasped. "Why are wolves working for them? They hunt us!"

Serga tilted his head, curiosity lighting a fire in those damned eyes of his. "Tell me your name, and I'll tell you what you want to know."

I swallowed, trying to shift against the restraints, but I couldn't move, and I couldn't fight back. "My name...is Burner Lee," I rasped.

The grin slipped from Serga's face momentarily. If Serga knew as much about wolf pack ways as he claimed, then he sure as hell understood what the name of Lee meant, and I might be able to buy some time.

"Which pack did you betray?" Serga quietly asked.

"New Hampshire."

I caught a glimpse of his fist before I saw the stars once more. I'm not sure what happened next, but I awoke face down in the prison cell, with my head throbbing in agony.

How the hell was I supposed to survive this?

Chapter Twenty-Nine

A WOLF IN the cell next to mine, a man painted in bruises who didn't speak, died during the night. Sam's guards came to get him and dragged him out by his ankles. The only proof he'd ever existed was the trail of blood on the floor.

The room, this cell, this godforsaken city, was no place for wolves.

"You okay?"

I glanced over my shoulder at the man in the cell across from us. His forehead was tattooed in letters I didn't understand, and he had a concerned look on his aged face. Forties, fifties, I wasn't sure. He was bald and skinny, but I think everybody in the place was skinny, except for the dogs that obeyed Serga and Sam's orders.

"Fine," I murmured.

"You don't look like you belong here," the tattooed man suggested.

I paused, uncertain, before I glanced at him again. My eyes meet his. Full yellow. A true Wolf. "What gave it away?" I covered his eyes with my hand to block out the dim light of the naked light bulbs that hung from the cells.

"For one, you don't stink like someone who's grown up in one of the cities." He leaned against the bars.

I snorted in response. Another wolf a few cells down coughed and muttered to themselves before silence echoed amongst the cells.

"My name's Bear."

"Burner," I sighed.

Bear smiled and sat forward. He held onto the bars. "I hope you don't mind, but uh, can I ask you something?"

"I don't know. Are you going to punch me afterward?" I rolled my head against the wall, eyeing him.

"No, God, no." Bear flinched.

"Go ahead, ask away."

"Where are you from?"

The uncertainty, the quiet nervousness attached to those words made me pause. I frowned at him, catching the movement of some of the others hesitantly raising their heads, holding their breaths to listen.

"Somewhere far away," I answered.

Bear nodded as if he expected that answer, but then he asked, "What's it like to grow wild?"

I slowly blinked.

"I mean, not working under a Deadwalker King or Queen? Not—not being sold by the Hunters while you're still a pup to some farm, or factory, or dog house? What's it like to grow up free with no master?" Bear breathed, his dirt-covered hands clinging to the bars of his cell, his gold eyes wide, and the room flooding with his panicked, hysterical scent.

"I..." The words died on my tongue. How was I supposed to answer that?

"Does the air taste different?" another man whispered from a cell further down.

"I mean—" I stumbled, sitting up.

"Is there always food?" a different man asked, somewhere on Bear's side of the cages.

"Um," I faltered.

"Are you with a pack? A Den Mother? Den daughters?" a faint voice called, somewhere near the door, and the cells exploded in murmurs of "Den Mother."

I shifted, rubbing the tight muscles in the back of my neck, my fingers curling around the cool steel of the collar as a thousand-pound brick began to settle in my stomach, the realization of staying while the pack fled slowly dawning on me.

"Burner? Tell us, please," Bear begged.

I curled onto my side, my hands covering my ears as the voices picked up, desperate to know what my life was like, what'd I'd done before, how I'd lived free.

What have I done?

Chapter Thirty

I LOST TRACK of time.

There was no sunlight, no moonlight, no windows, or a fresh breeze. The air that did come in and momentarily flooded away the stench of unclean flesh, piss, and shit was when Sam and the guards came to get a prisoner. Sam's dogs, the only way I could describe them as they all wore those black masks which only revealed their eyes, had taken the man from the cell next to Bear's some time ago. I think his name was Bernie. He was a pale bag of bones of a creature who'd begged for his life when the guards dragged him out of the room.

After that, another one of Sam's dogs came in with the water ladle and bucket. If I didn't get to the bars fast enough, he would just dump the water on the floor.

The only way I could tell when it was night was the temperature in the cells dropped and the floors and bars became ice cold. I spent hours wishing I could turn wolf to try to keep warm, but I couldn't, not with the damn collar around my neck.

Why Sam and the others hadn't removed it yet boggled the mind. The lack of warmth combined with no food was turning painful, and my stomach grumbled in distress. I couldn't remember the last time I'd eaten anything. Across the room, Bear's stomach rumbled, too, but he had a distant look in his eyes as he gazed at the ceiling of his cell. Mind over matter, I supposed.

The door at the end of the hallway opened. I glanced over, confused. The faceless man with the water had already visited us, but when I caught a new scent, I almost fell over. I climbed to my feet and went to the cell door. I gripped the metal tight and tried to peek down the hall, past the others who suddenly moved, or awoke from their sleep as a petite form appeared. My breath caught in my throat.

Den daughter.

She was almost as tall as my shoulders, and her pale face was not marked with the letter of a pack's tattoo. One of her eyes was milky white, and the other golden. She walked with a limp, and her nibbled wolf ears peeked between her short, black curls. She wore a dirty knee-length black dress. She carried a pile of metal dishes that resembled curved plates.

Behind her was one of Sam's guard dogs. He carried a large cooking pot stained black with soot on the bottom. The Den daughter stopped at the first cell. She scooped one of the dishes into the pot and placed it on the floor of the cell.

The man inside, already in his wolf form, barked at her happily before he tipped the contents of the dish over and started to eat. I couldn't see the contents, but I thought it smelled like fish and milk. It was hard to tell over the stench of death, rot, blood, piss, and shit.

The daughter did this for every cell, and soon the sound of excited barks and pathetic puppy-like yips filled the room. When she limped to my cell, she paused when she saw me at the bars. Her gold eye betrayed her nervousness, and this close, I caught her scent.

"Den daughter?" I whispered.

Her brows furrowed, as if she didn't recognize the term. She turned away from me, scooped into the pot with the metal dish, and placed it on the ground in front of the cell.

I didn't look at it. I kept my gaze fixed on her.

"Where's your Den Mother?" I said.

The daughter stepped away from my cell. She looked to the guard behind her and he motioned for her to continue. She walked past me, past the empty cell next to mine, and stopped at the next cell further down where a prisoner in wolf form spun in a circle, excited to see her.

"Where is your Den Mother?" I yelled.

She froze again, but then relaxed and fed the Wolf who danced on all four legs.

"Shh, or else they'll take your food," Bear hissed from his cell. I swallowed, looking at the meal in question.

In the dish, half a fish floated in milk-soaked oatmeal, along with half a sliced apple, and a piece of stale bread. I gave the Den daughter one last glance before I sat down. I picked up the fish, checking its scales; it looked like a striped bass.

I peeled the skin off the fish and ate it, grimacing at the bitter taste of metal. Nobody should eat fish that tastes like that, but I didn't have much choice. I leaned my back against the wall, watching the daughter as she made her rounds amongst the cells until she came to Bear's. A faint smile danced on her lips, and Bear looked close to tears.

"You being good for Serga, Melody?" Bear whispered.

"Yes, Daddy." Melody nodded.

"He's not making you work too hard, is he?" The words were oddly weighed, as if he was asking something completely different, and Melody paused.

"All she does is cook and clean," the guard answered for her, his voice gruff.

Relief swept across Bear's face. "Good girl. Have you, ah, have you heard from your sister?"

Melody shook her head. "No, but Mister Sam says he'll ask around for me. He doesn't want me walking around Midtown by myself."

Bear let out a relieved shuddering breath. "You do as Mister Sam and Serga ask, yes?"

"Yes, Daddy."

"Melly, we don't have all day," the guard said, shifting his grip on the pot.

Melody poured the contents of the pot into a plate and placed it on the ground before pushing it through the opening at the bottom. Bear took it reverently, giving her a tight-lipped smile as she moved on to the next cell and continued on until she finished. She and the guard left the cells.

I dragged the bit of bread crust that was too hard on its own through the dregs of the dish, catching Bear's gaze as he ran his finger through his food slowly then brought the digit to his lips, savoring every bite. I glanced at the other cells. The other prisoners were still eating. That heavy brick came back, making it hard to eat, hard to focus. A small voice chirped in the back of my head and I ignored it, blocking it because I didn't want to hear whatever it had to say.

The door at the end of the prison hall opened, but I focused on eating, picking the bones from the fish, putting everything I had into ignoring the rising voice.

"Burner."

Startled, I looked up and found Sam was standing at the door of the cell. The guards were with him again. "Serga wants you."

I swallowed nervously, glancing to Bear who watched us.

I licked my finger clean, popping the last piece of bread in my mouth as I got to my feet. The door opened, and I approached Sam, chewing quickly and swallowing before the catch pole caught my neck and the black hood covered my head.

Chapter Thirty-One

"WHY DOES IT smell like paint?" My nose wrinkled at the fresh chemical odor. The room was brilliant white, spotless, except for the steel chair in the middle of the room and the clear plastic that crinkled under my toes. Sam made me sit on the chair while he wrapped the metal wire tightly around my ankles and wrists, the hood on the floor next to him. The wires didn't cut into the skin, but I couldn't move.

"Because I painted it this morning." Sam tested the wires, his eyebrows pulling together in a frown.

I blinked at him. I hadn't expected an answer, but I couldn't stop myself from asking why he'd painted it.

"Serga says the paint hides the stench of death," Sam mumbled, avoiding my gaze.

"You...you killed the wolf next to Bear's cell?" Ice dug deep into my gut and Sam paused, before he glanced up and met my gaze.

"Serga did."

"Why?"

Something akin to uncertainty flickered in Sam's eyes. He shifted on his knees. "Because."

"Because why?" I tilted my head.

He pursed his lips together, his frown digging deeper into his forehead. "What...what the hell are you? You don't act like the others. They just tell Serga whatever he wants, usually after the first couple of hits."

I leaned forward, as best I could as I sat in the chair, baring my canines. My voice dropped to a growl. I ignored Sam's questions. "Why did Serga kill the wolf?"

Sam's hands stilled, gold flickering in the blue of his eyes for a second, and he slapped his hands over his mouth. I growled again, and he jumped to his feet and backed toward the door. He gave me one last look before he almost ripped the door off its hinges and fled the room, leaving the door to close shut on its own. I craned my neck, glimpsing the hallway and the numerous doors along the long corridor. I caught a slight scent of a breeze and, beneath that, dead blood and rot.

Deadwalkers. There were Deadwalkers outside.

I swallowed, checking the room for something I could use to make my escape, even testing the restraints once more and grateful I wasn't attached to that god-awful cross, but there wasn't anything. Just the light bulb dangling above my head, the plastic under my dirty feet, and the steel chair.

I needed a plan, an escape route. If what Sam said was true, and I didn't think he was lying, I didn't have much time left. I pulled at the wires around my wrists, hissing as they started to cut into the flesh. *Damn it*. I huffed, fighting back that wave of panic that wanted to spread from my chest outward. Panicking would get me nowhere. Literally. The thought of never seeing Fern, Eric, Albe and Danbe, and Aaron ever again, that I'd never see the stars overhead, or hunt with them... I swallowed hard.

No matter what happened, I couldn't give up. I would die before that happened.

I straightened my back as the door cracked open and Serga entered, carrying a cup of something that smelled strongly of coffee. He was dressed in the black shirt and green pants with black boots that all the wolves here seemed to wear. He gave me a considering look before he closed the door behind him and leaned against it, lazily stirring a small flat stick in his cup.

"You scared him," Serga said simply.

I said nothing.

"Haven't seen him that scared since he was sixteen and I bought him at one of the auctions in New Vegas," Serga continued. He pushed off the door and walked around the room, examining the walls and ceiling. "You ever been to one? An auction, I mean?"

I kept my mouth shut, keeping a careful eye on Serga's slow, almost methodical movements. He chuckled and shook his head. "I doubt it, but that storage house you freed your pack from in Boston? That's just a holding place; they and the other wolves would be moved to an auction in just a few days."

My eyes widened, my breath suddenly caught in my throat. Boston? Wasn't I in Boston anymore? Where the hell was I?

A wild grin spread across Serga's face. "Ah, there we go! I knew that'd get your attention. See, the Hunters were going to kill you, but then when they searched you, they found this and thought my King would be particularly interested in talking to you." Serga reached into his back pocket with his free hand and pulled out a folded piece of paper. He unfolded it single-handed and held it in front of my face. My heart sank at the sight of September's map, the one I'd used to find the pack amongst the barricaded streets of the city, in his hands.

"So, Burner, where is the rest of it?"

Slowly, my eyes crawled up the image, up Serga's scar-covered arm, to his face. His eyes were hooded, his lips a thin line.

"I don't know."

"Where is September 24th Amon?"

"I don't know."

"Where is your pack?"

"I don't know."

Serga finally nodded, as if he expected me to give him those answers. He drank his coffee and tossed the empty cup into the corner of the room. He carefully folded the paper and pocketed it. Suddenly, his arms were gripping my shoulders, his face inches from mine. I pressed against the back of the chair, eyes wide.

"Who guided your pack home?" Serga hissed, his eyes solid gold. "And before I hear 'I don't know,' think carefully about your answer."

A growl crawled its way up from my throat, my lips peeling back and revealing too-sharp teeth. The collar started to spark against my skin and I thought I tasted ozone for a second before I sneered at him.

"I. Don't. Fucking. Know."

Whatever I expected Serga to do, it wasn't for his lips to pull back into a wide grin. He slapped my arms, laughing as he stepped back.

"The moment I saw you...I could tell you were another Alpha." Serga ran his hands through his black hair. "It's been way too long since I got to play with one." He walked around the chair. His hands gripped my shoulders from behind, his fingers digging into muscle and bone. I flinched at the touch.

"Do you know who I answer to?"

"Hunters." I gritted my teeth.

"Try again."

I scowled, craning my neck to look back at him but he dug his fingers into my hair and forced me to look forward, toward the door. He leaned over the chair, his chin resting on my shoulder.

"Come on, Burner." My name was a cruel purr in my ear. "Who do I answer to?"

"I don't know," I hissed.

Serga drew in a long deep breath and let it out. "September's got a soft spot for ferals, but you're really taking the cake."

I froze.

"Oh? You didn't know that? Well, I know everything, Burner." The words were a soft laugh and I struggled against the binds, growling low in my throat.

Serga patted my shoulders and stood once more as he walked around, a false smile on his face. "I know your little pack is from far up North, I know your pack was picked up by the Hunters—well, except you—" Serga tapped the collar. "And I know your Den Mother is dead." My fingers dug into the steel of the chair. "Now, personally, I would love to know where your Alpha, where Fern, is hiding."

The blood drained from my face, my pulse pounding.

"Oh, yes, I know you're Fern's chosen. You're supposed to lead your pack. But, unfortunately, there are more pressing matters to attend to." Serga crossed his arms as he stepped back, eyeing me with distaste. "The Deadwalker King of New York, King Daniel, my Master, wants to know where September 24th Amon is."

How did he know that? How did he put everything together? How did he know how Fern and I were connected? He'd need an insider, someone to tell him, but who? Who would betray the pack?

He snapped his fingers in front of my face and I swallowed, hard, before I bared my teeth at him.

"September left me to die after the Hunters attacked my pack, she led them to us," I spat, riling myself up. "I've been tracking her ever since, and when I find her? I'm going to rip out her fucking heart and eat it!" I roared.

Serga stared at me dumbly before he tipped back his head and laughed. The sound bounced off the drying white walls. He clutched his sides, almost doubling over in laughter.

"It's not funny!" I yelled.

"Oh, oh, no, no, that is priceless." Serga wiped away a tear, casting a wild grin at me. "You and me, Burner? We are going to have *so* much fun together." He straightened and opened the door wide to leave the room. "Sam, take Burner back to his cell."

Sam soon entered, his face masked with worry. He cleared his throat, rubbing his hands against his legs as he knelt before me and started on the metal wrap ties. "Don't fight me. It'll only make things worse," he whispered. This close, I could smell him over the paint, I could taste fear, worry, and...

I frowned and leaned closer to him when he untied the metal around my ankles. I breathed in his scent and sat back, startled. Sam looked up at me in alarm. We stared at each other for a long time before Sam looked away and freed my ankles and wrists and pulled the hood back over my head. Guards entered the room soon after and escorted me back to the cell.

I waited for the guards to leave before I collapsed onto the ground, my head pounding with the beginnings of a headache from being in the freshly painted room too long. But that wasn't all I was thinking about. The fact was that someone close to the pack had betrayed us. Serga seemed to know everything. He was working for *something* called a Deadwalker King, and Sam was covered with Serga's scent.

"You're still alive," Bear said, interrupting my thoughts.

I swallowed, slumping to the ground and rolling onto my back. "Lucky me," I breathed.

Chapter Thirty-Two

SEVERAL DAYS AFTER my session with Serga, one of the guards came into the prison hall and announced that we would all be moved. I was confused at first, but more guards entered and they escorted all of the prisoners out of the prison.

We walked up the flight of cement steps and I flinched at the hot sunlight that shone down on us. It took several moments for my eyes to get accustomed to the bright light, and a rough shove from one of the guards before I moved again.

We were in some type of barren field with a large lake near the middle. The buildings that surrounded the park were bigger than any mountain I had ever seen. Some of them were stained black from old fires, and many of the windows were broken. The whole place was disgusting and reeked of the miasma of old urine, shit, and rotting bodies.

I wasn't in Boston anymore, that was a fact, but how long had I been in the cells? The chill of winter was gone, the ground dusty beneath my bare feet. There wasn't even a cloud in the sky overhead.

We were made to stand in a line, twelve of us in total, and Bear stood next to me. He was only a few inches taller than me. Bear glanced at me, his shoulders hunched, his face gaunt, and I shrugged. I had no idea what was happening. Sam spoke with one of the guards before he strode across the dusty brown ground. He clutched a wooden clipboard with numerous sheets on it, flipping through the pages.

"All right, you miserable dogs," Sam's voice boomed across the field. "It's been decided that instead of wasting away down below, you are to earn your keep by working the fields." He pointed to a set of rusted farm tools piled on the ground. "You will be placed into teams. Charlie and Burner, step forward."

I stepped forward and glanced at the man named Charlie. His head shook from starvation, and his ribs and spine struck through his dirt-covered skin. I think he was one of the few who tried to stay in their wolf form as much as possible.

"You two are to pull the plows," Sam said.

I eyed the old-fashioned plow then Charlie. There was no way he could pull it, he'd be dead by the end of the day.

"Sebastian, Chris, Otter, step forward." Three skinny men roughly the same size, dressed in poorly sewn together rags, and covered in thin scars, stepped forward. "You three will be planting each seed by hand. No seed can go to waste. Each seed that is eaten by a bird will result in two lashes." Sam looked at a paper in his hands.

"Neil, Sinclair, Auther, Cameron, and Luke, you will be responsible for digging the fruit trees from here—" Sam dug his heel into the ground. "To there." He pointed at the lake. "Bear, you will be responsible for picking rocks and placing them into a pile every one hundred feet. Now, get to work!" he yelled.

Bear went to the equipment pile where he took a wheelbarrow. I glanced at Charlie, whose head started to shake worse before walking to the double harness plow. The plow itself was steel, and the harnesses carried the faint scent of old horses. It would be a thousand times easier to do this if I shifted and could wrap the straps across my chest and pull, but I couldn't because of the damn collar. I rubbed my neck, scowling at it when one of the guards struck my side with a baton and I yelped.

"Burner." Sam walked over to Charlie and me. "You'll be doing this in your human skin."

"If you've got the key, it's easier to do this on all fours." I tapped my collar.

Sam startled. "You've done this sort of work before?"

"Yeah, I have."

Sam didn't follow up, and I think he expected me to speak, to tell him more, but when I didn't, he turned to the guard with the baton. "If they don't start moving, beat them." Sam left us and marched over to check on the others struggling with the seed bags.

"Pick it up." The guard pointed at the double harness.

I grunted when I lifted half the harness, and my side ached. I eased it down over my head and let it come to rest on my shoulders. Charlie hesitantly lifted his half of the harness. He struggled under the weight until the guard placed it firmly on his weak shoulders and attached the lengths of rope to a steel plow.

"Now, get tilling!" the guard yelled at us.

I grunted, my toes digging into the warm earth. Charlie stood there, uncertain. "Just pull," I hissed. Charlie nodded meekly. The harness was heavy, and the steel plow was heavier. The places where the Hunters shot me ached.

I risked a glance over my shoulder. Bear was following a few paces behind us, picking up rocks Charlie and I overturned and tossing them into the wheelbarrow. I huffed, looking forward once more.

I needed to escape, but as we dragged the plow, I mentally counted the dozens of guards who watched our every move like hawks and realized it would be next to impossible to run.

That didn't mean none of us tried.

Sebastian, I think his name was, threw a bag of seeds at one of the guards and bolted. A crack of thunder filled the air and Sebastian collapsed to the ground with the grace of a pup's ragdoll. I held my breath, my eyes wide. I looked up to the tallest building and saw the glint of a rifle scope from an open window.

"If any of you think about escaping, you will be shot." Sam's voice drifted across the landscape and I swallowed. Hard. How the hell was I going to get out of here?

Chapter Thirty-Three

IT WAS HIGH noon and I could barely move. My shoulders were the color of rotten eggplant, my fingers were covered with scratches, and my feet were blistered. We were taken from our cells as dawn was breaking and labored in the field until the sun was at its peak when Sam made us kneel in a row, most of the group half-asleep, or staring vacantly into the distance. After Sebastian's escape attempt, the others simply gave up.

I sunk my hand into the dirt and rubbed the dry soil between my fingers; summer was already here. I don't think Sam and his dogs understood how farming worked. They should have turned the soil last fall and started to plant pre-seeded sprouts after the last freeze. That's what Andre always instructed us when we worked the Quebec fields to prepare the strawberries.

Andre.

The pack.

Aaron.

I shook my head, focusing on the present.

Charlie, much to my amazement, was still alive, but in his head, I think he was gone. While we dragged the plow, he muttered to himself about Texas, about monsters in old government vaults and laboratories that should have never been opened. I tried to ask him what he was talking about one day, but he ignored me. I raised the topic with Bear one night when the others were asleep, and he shrugged. He had no idea either.

I craned my neck when a high-pitched bell rang behind us. Melody approached with two of Sam's guards close behind her. One of them carried the heavy, stained food pot in his hands, and the other had a patched potato sack tossed over his shoulder.

I straightened my back and winced as the muscles in my shoulder pulled. I absently rubbed it, trying to ease the ache, while Bear came to life at the sight of her. All of us waited while she scooped out our food onto metal dishes and placed them in front of us. Otter grabbed her ankle, and Bear drew in a sudden breath, his hands clenching at his side. The guard carrying the bag backhanded Otter, sending him flying, while the other kicked his dish over into the dirt.

When Melody approached Bear and me, she placed his dish on the ground and filled it with thick milky barley, and another piece of stale bread. Bear whispered a soft "thank you," and Melody nodded. She was nervous filling my plate, but I bowed my head, averting my gaze. She placed my dish by my knees.

When all the dishes were served, Melody turned to the guard with the sack. She stepped next to him, and he dropped it onto the ground. He turned it upside down and shook it, letting a small, round, freshly cooked pork roast roll into the dirt. Cameron and Otter moved to grab it, and the guard snapped at them to stay.

Not that I blamed them. One whiff told me it was heavily seasoned, and my teeth ached at the sight of it. The very thought of digging my teeth into it danced on my tongue. I wanted to moan. I rubbed the dirt off my hands and focused on the others who stared back at me. If anybody was getting that pork, it was me and the others didn't stand a chance—

A sharp crack of thunder filled the air and I flattened myself to the ground. Otter fell next to the pork, his yellow eyes wide, his jaw slack, dead. Panicked, the others scrambled out of the way and away from the meat. I raised my head and looked up at the building again, the hair on the back of my neck rising. The same glint of steel from when Sebastian was shot reflected in the sun's light.

Sam approached us. He cleared his throat. "You're done for today. Take your dishes and follow me."

Cautiously, I stood up, staring at the building in question.

I turned to check on Bear, to see if he was all right, but Bear wasn't watching us, or Otter. His gaze was focused on Melody. She was squatting, her face buried in her hands, her terrified cries echoing across the field. The guard who brought the pork roast picked her up like she weighed nothing, cradling her in his arms, and carried her away, walking past the steel bars that lined the land and the curious gazes of Deadwalkers and people, and—

I froze.

Thick black hair cut short, an achingly familiar too-large sweater, and wide, sorrow-filled gold-flecked blue eyes stared at me from beyond the bars.

Aaron.

Aaron was there. But he couldn't be real. He had to be an illusion, something brought about by working in the heat without near enough food or water because Aaron couldn't be in this godforsaken city. He was supposed to be safe with the pack in Maine, not in hell with me.

"Aaron?" I mouthed the word, unable to stop myself. Aaron's hands clenched the bars tighter, his eyes widening, and I took a step toward him.

A loud shot echoed through the sky like lightning, the bullet striking the turned earth inches from my feet. I held my breath, staring at Aaron whose face morphed into panic. He looked up toward the building before looking back at me and frantically shaking his head, silently begging me to stop.

I took another step forward, my hands trembling at my side.

The second bullet grazed my shoulder. I stilled, my mouth opening as Aaron stepped away from the bars, glancing to his left and right desperately before he turned and fled into the crowd.

Something raw curled in the pit of my stomach as Bear laid a cautious hand on my shoulder, whispering that we had to leave and go back to our cells. I sucked in a deep breath and nodded, letting him pull me back to the lineup. The guards were strangely quiet. I glanced over my shoulder, my eyes scanning the crowd once more for any sign of him.

I hadn't imagined him...had I?

I must have. He couldn't be here. There was no way in a thousand years Aaron would have followed me to New York. He was smart. Far smarter than I ever had a chance of being. He knew to stay away...

Right?

Chapter Thirty-Four

AARON WASN'T REAL.

He couldn't be. He was an illusion, something my brain had dreamed up to keep hope alive that I might escape one day and not die in some hellhole city surrounded by Deadwalkers and traitorous wolves. But his eyes... those *eyes*...

"You okay, Burner?" Bear called out.

I rolled onto my back, staring at the dangling lightbulb. I never wanted to see that type of sorrow in those eyes of his. I never wanted to see those lips sour, or that desperate panic on his face. I wanted him laughing, smiling, rolling his eyes when I got my metaphors wrong.

I wanted to see him *happy*, surrounded by a pile of books, and *free*.

"Burner?"

I cleared my throat, blinking. I glanced at Bear. He waved his hand at my face and confused, I touched my cheek. It was wet. I sat up, staring at my hands.

I'd been crying. Why was I crying?

"Are you okay?"

I nodded, roughly scrubbing my cheeks. I let out a ragged breath and flashed Bear a weak grin.

"Fine, yeah, something in my eye," I sighed. I dragged my hands along my filthy jeans.

"I know it's been a few days since the shooting, but it's okay to be scared about what happened to Otter," Bear tried to soothe.

"I'm not crying about him," I snorted.

Bear frowned, leaning against the bars of his cell. "Then why?"

"I thought I saw a ghost," I murmured.

"Ah, I think I understand," Bear mused.

"You do?" I leaned against the concrete wall of my cell, grateful for the cool against my sunburned skin.

"When I first got here, I thought I saw my wife. Course, she left me with the girls when they were five and eight so...more of a nightmare, actually." Bear chuckled. The sound was cut off as the door at the end of the hall opened and Sam entered, alone. He walked down the hall of cells and stopped in front of mine. The other prisoners got to their feet and watched. Even Bear looked openly curious.

"Burner." Sam's voice was clipped.

"Sam." I nodded. "Serga want me?"

Sam seemed to hesitate before he cleared his throat. "You're to follow me. Any movement, any threats, any attacks, and you will be executed on the spot. Do you understand?" Sam warned.

"Will I be gone long?"

"That depends on you," Sam said.

I hesitated and shot a look at Bear over Sam's shoulder. He held up his hands, mouthing he had no idea what was going on. Sam followed my gaze and Bear quickly looked at the floor.

"All right."

Sam unlocked the cell door. He pulled it open and stepped aside. "Follow me."

Chapter Thirty-Five

SAM LED ME down an almost endless stream of busy, claustrophobic, streets. We passed wolves, Hunters, Den daughters, and Deadwalkers, many of whom stood outside in the sunshine in thick green and black clothes, their masks fixed to their faces. Some of the Deadwalkers had wolves in human form wearing collars and attached to chains that they gripped in their gloved hands, while others were in their wolf form, sitting at the Deadwalkers' feet like a trained dog from one of my old magazines.

The numbers of Deadwalkers and wolves was impossible to count, and there weren't any people, not like Martha, or Neveah, or Nathan, or Cook. Or even Robin, for that matter. If they were human, they were Hunters. Den daughters raced up and down the busy streets wearing dresses with designs of sewing needles, words, or cakes on armbands and aprons.

That same question I had since I first saw Melody giving out food in the prison rose again: where the hell were the Den Mothers?

Sam turned a corner, without a backward glance, and I obediently followed, casting longing looks up and down the streets, scanning for Aaron. None of the guards were with us. I thought of just bolting into the crowds, but judging by the endless streets of the city, I wasn't sure if I was still being watched from above and I would only end up lost and captured once more.

I rubbed my arm when we stopped at the large green door of an old dilapidated brick house. The windows were boarded shut. Sam knocked twice on the door and we waited for whatever to happen.

The green door cracked open and a Den daughter with too-long fingers greeted us. She wore a black dress that stopped at her ankles with a white apron on top. Her brown hair was cut short and she bore no pack tattoo. She looked at Sam, then me, and opened the door. She bowed her head as we entered.

The inside of the brick house was ominous. Faded brown wallpaper peeled on the walls and cracked glass picture frames hung on the wall of the stairwell to a second floor. There was a narrow corridor that led to the back of the house on the bottom floor; I think it was the kitchen, judging by the scent of coffee drifting from there.

The daughter closed the door behind us, and without a word, she led us up the stairs which creaked under our weight. I wiped my nose as the smell of rot and mold increased with each step. At the top, the daughter showed us to a beige door with a fuzzy glass window. She scratched on the glass.

"Enter!" a man called from the other side.

She turned the handle, pushed open the door, and waved for us to enter. Sam went in first and beckoned me to follow him. I covered my nose and mouth with my hand, fighting back the urge to gag at the taste of rot and mold. It was strongest in the room, but there was something behind it, something familiar. The small room was cramped with piles of papers and overstuffed cardboard boxes. The orange light from the gas lamp on the desk cast shadows on the walls and a man, I think early thirties, sat hunched over a desk scattered with documents. His brown hair was messy. He lifted his head and I froze.

Red eyes.

Deadwalker.

"July 9th Kren, I've brought you the Wolf, Burner." Sam jerked his thumb at me.

Puzzled, July sat back in his chair before his eyes widened, and he rose to his feet. I stepped back, eyeing him and Sam. What the hell was going on?

"Leave us," July ordered.

"You should know, this wolf isn't like the others."

July shook his head. "I said, leave us. Your payment is downstairs."

"I'll need the prisoner back. The King still wants answers from him."

"And he will, I promise." July trembled.

"You have three hours," Sam said. He went to follow the Den daughter out, but he grabbed my shoulder. "Remember: you fuck up, you're dead."

I didn't take my eyes off the Deadwalker as the door shut behind me and the lock was turned.

"Do you—?"

"Deadwalker!" I growled, my fingers curling sharp, the collar on my neck buzzing angrily.

July paled and raised his hands in self-defense. "No, no, no, it's not what you think." He reached into his pile of paperwork and dug out a folded piece of paper. His hands shook when he opened it. "You remember this, right? You've seen this before?" The piece of paper was a child's crayon-drawn image of a farmhouse surrounded by green grass and a sunny sky.

It was Neveah's drawing. The drawing I had tucked away safely inside September's notebook. The notebook I'd left behind with Aaron and Robin. Why...why did this Deadwalker have it?

"Where did you get that?" I whispered.

"You know what this is, don't you?"

"What did you *do* to them?" I roared, hands shifted to claws, my mouth full of fangs and my brain on fire. The collar went ballistic, electricity burning through my veins, making it hard to breathe and I choked, dropping to my knees, clawing at the floor, desperately trying to draw in a breath.

Goddamn it, no, no, no, not now!

Suddenly, July was at my side, his hands were on my shoulder. I snarled, feral and wild. I grabbed him and we tumbled to the floor. He cursed and kicked underneath me, biting my shoulder and sinking his fangs deep. I howled, punching him in the side until he gagged and released his hold. I rolled us, starving for breath and drowning in white-hot agony.

I straddled his waist and he reached up to claw at the bite mark on my shoulder. I fumbled to grab his wrists with my hands, the world tinging black at the edges. July hissed, thrashing like a trapped animal when I grabbed both wrists, and I smashed my head hard against his. That seemed to make the collar stop for a second. I sagged against July, gasping for breath, my nerves on fire. I squeezed my eyes shut, waiting for the world to just stop spinning.

July blinked rapidly, his red eyes focusing and unfocusing, as if he was fighting his own terrible internal war. He lay limp underneath me, swallowing hard.

"Why," I rasped, "why do you have that picture? Answer me!" I grabbed a handful of his shirt and shook him.

"Because it was a gift," July whispered.

I panted, my eyebrows coming together in confusion. "What do you mean 'a gift'? Tell me."

July's eyes fluttered closed for a second before he opened them once more.

"We are not all monsters."

I was across the room faster than July could blink, my eyes wide in panic, my back pressed against a pile of papers. "How...how do you know that?" I croaked.

July sat up, his moves slow and cautious as if afraid I would attack him at any second. "I know a lot," he whispered. "I know that you are a long way from home. I know that you didn't embark on your quest alone, and I know that you saved them—" He pointed at the paper on the floor. "You saved my little girl, you freed my wife."

"Who told you that?" I whispered.

July's forehead wrinkled. "He said you'd be cautious, that you wouldn't trust a Deadwalker."

"*Who told you?*" My voice was cracking, my skin prickling with goosebumps.

July's lips formed a thin line, and he wrung his hands, looking at the floor. "He told me to tell you that you're a stubborn, arrogant, Alpha idiot and he should leave you to rot but he won't, because you're an idiot, and he can't leave for Vegas, or Los Angeles, until he knows you're safe and free and eating inland oysters," July finished, his voice unsure.

I stared at him.

He ran a hand through his hair, sighing. "He was really upset when he left the message, but he said it'd get through your thick, annoying, id—"

"Idiot skull," I finished.

"Yes."

This wasn't real. I was hallucinating everything. I was still in the cold cell, soothing my wounds, listening to men cry. Aaron had been a heat-based illusion, July couldn't be here, passing on this message. It just wasn't possible. The only solution was I was going insane. Right? Right.

Laughter bubbled up from my chest. I slapped my hands over my mouth, my eyes suddenly wide and disbelieving, but I couldn't stop it. I couldn't stop the raucous laughter from spilling past my lips and filling the room. It soon turned hysterical, and I was clawing at the floor, tears rolling down my cheeks, my chest painfully tight.

July's face was a mixture of concern and confusion. "Are...are you okay?"

I nodded, unable to stop laughing, going light-headed. I collapsed onto my side, squeezing my eyes shut, trying to cover my mouth to stop the sound. Heck, the wooden floor felt like a real wooden floor!

A hesitant knock on the door, and the daughter slipped into the room with a tray of sandwiches, a glass of water, and a large ceramic cup. I was leaving claw marks on the floor, out of breath but unable to stop laughing. Without a single word, she placed the tray on the table and shot July a worried look before he shook his head and waved her out of the room.

"Burner?" July knelt next to me. I panicked, backing away from him on my hands and ass.

"No, no, no, no. This is all a dream." I waved my hand at him, shaking my head. "You're a dream. None of this is real." The last words were whimpers.

A strange, strangled sound left July's throat, and he bolted from the room and raced down the stairs.

It took me a while before I was able to catch my breath, but when I did, I was physically and emotionally exhausted. If I'd lost whatever grip I'd had with reality, then this was a dream I didn't want to wake up from. A smile drifted across my face. Aaron coming to rescue me, September somehow involved, and Neveah's father was alive, technically a Deadwalker, and thankful that I'd saved her.

Distantly, I heard hushed voices. I shut my eyes, listening as the staircase squeaked and warm summer and smoke filled my nostrils, drowning out the Deadwalker stench of mold and rot. I wrinkled my nose, refusing to open my eyes as feet stopped next to my head. Whoever it was, I didn't care. They could rot. Let me die in the fantasy my mind created.

"Oh, Burner. What have they done to you?"

Chapter Thirty-Six

"OH, BURNER. WHAT have they done to you?"

My eyes snapped open.

Aaron was kneeling next to me, his fingers trembling as they cupped my jaw, touching the steel of my shock collar. He was checking the bite mark on my shoulder, his hands drifting to touch the bruises on my shoulders from the weight of the plow harness. I swallowed, staring into his gold and blue eyes as they softened when they met mine.

We stared at each other for what seemed forever until I spoke, low and guttural, "You're not real."

"I'm not?" Aaron tried to smile. Instead, his lips turned downward and he bit his bottom lip. I raised a filthy hand, my fingers stained with dirt and mud, my arms a stark tanned contrast to his pale skin. I cupped his cheek, smiling.

"You're a dream," I whispered.

"I am?" Aaron's voice dropped.

"You're not here. You're safe back with the pack, and Robby too. You went home because you're smart." At the mention of the affectionate nickname I'd given Robin, Aaron rapidly blinked, his bottom lip trembling in his teeth. "You're not stupid like me. You're safe and free." I grinned, delirious. I brushed the white hair away from his forehead, tucking a strand behind his ear. "Serga probably has me strapped to his chair, ripping out my heart, but I'm in here—" I tapped my forehead with my other hand "—with you, safe and sound."

Aaron's lips twisted, his eyes wet, and he tried to rock back from my hand. I whined. "No, no, don't go, please, don't leave me," I begged, grabbing him with both hands, desperate to hold him. "I don't want to go back to the cells. I want to stay with you."

"*Burner.*" Aaron bowed and pressed his forehead to my shoulder. Hot tears fell onto my chest and left wet streaks in the thick layer of dirt covering my skin.

He felt so *real.*

I clung to him, digging my fingers into his sweater, hiding my face in his hair. I drowned myself in his scent of hot summer days and endless campfire nights.

"Aaron? Burner?" a voice called from the end of the hallway, but I ignored it.

Aaron shifted in my grasp, and I shook my head, pleading with him not to go. He sat back on his heels, briskly wiping his cheeks before he bumped his forehead against mine.

"I'm not going anywhere, Burner," Aaron promised, his eyes searching mine. "We're going home. Together."

My shoulders started shaking before hysterical laughter peeled from my throat. I thumped my head against the wall, my entire body trembling.

"Oh, God, this is too good to be true," I wheezed. "I never thought I was this creative."

"Aaron? What's going on?" Worry tinged the voice and boots fell on the wooden floorboard.

"September, they did something to him." Aaron's voice was panicked. I sighed, unable to stop the full-on grin from stretching across my face as I turned to the doorway.

September 24th Amon, Deadwalker, the obsession of the King of New York, entered the office, her mask attached to a strap at her hip. On her other hip, Robin was perched, her small arms wrapped around September's neck. She was wearing a new blue dress with swirled patterned leggings and gumboots. Her blonde hair was pulled back into a ponytail, and her eyes were a soft green. As soon as she saw me, she wiggled free of September's arms and raced over to Aaron and me.

"Burner!" Robin shrieked. She wrapped her arms around my neck, hugging me tightly, even as her nose wrinkled. "I missed you so much! Aaron tells me all the stories of things you've done, but...you smell really bad."

I wrapped an arm around her waist, pulling her close. "He did? I do?" I croaked.

"Yeah."

"He doesn't think we're real. He thinks we're a fragment of his imagination," Aaron explained to September.

"It Serga's method." September knelt next to me. She leaned close, her face right next to mine. I swallowed, trying to pull back. "He starves his prisoners of food, water, keeps them locked underground for months to avoid sensory stimulation, and then brings them out and makes them labor, between sessions of beatings. Most of your kind goes crazy, it's no wonder Burner's so close to the edge."

"How do we fix him?" Aaron stroked my hair, his gaze on September.

"We need to get him out of the city and get this collar off him so he can shift, that usually helps with the neuron plaque build-up..." September scowled at the collar around my neck. "Why is it...?" She pushed my head forward and ran her hands along the edges of steel. I blinked at Robin who watched me with curiosity. "Oh."

"Oh?" Aaron sounded worried. "Fern said he was able to remove the collars of the others when they escaped, but the key didn't work on Burner."

September's frown deepened before she let go of my neck. "I've never seen this type of collar before."

"What does that mean?"

"It means if I haven't seen it, then the Network hasn't, and the Hunters have been busy developing new tech," September explained. She drummed her hands on her black pants, eyeing me before she turned her gaze to Aaron. "I can't take you back to Boston, not while he's still got that collar on."

"He has to be free," Aaron whispered.

"The network has a safe house in Centralia."

"Centralia? Are you insane?"

"Centralia is in Pennsylvania, it's a mining town with a coal fire that never goes out," Robin offered.

"You're such a smart girl, aren't you?" I smiled.

"Uh-huh."

"I'm sorry, it's the best I can do." September sighed.

Aaron looked like he wanted to say something more, but he cleared his throat and nodded. "Fine. We'll head there, but how are we going to get Burner out of New York?"

September eyed Robin before covering her ears. She glanced at Aaron and me.

"Distraction."

"It'll have to be a pretty damn big one," Aaron growled.

"It will be," September promised. She let go of Robin's ears and stroked her hair, giving her a small smile. "July said Sam's coming in two hours to take Burner back. Jasmin, his maid, knows all the back alleys. She'll take you to a blind pig while I get everything prepared."

Robin perked up. "Oh! A blind pig sold alcoholic drinks to the lower classes during American prohibition."

Aaron opened his mouth then shook his head. "And Robby?"

"I'll take her with me." September squeezed Robin's shoulder. "It'll raise fewer questions if I have her than you two."

Aaron pulled Robin into a hug. "You be a good girl and do as September says?"

"Yes, Aaron," Robin whispered. She hid her face in his sweater. "And then we can go home?"

"Yes." Aaron kissed her forehead and gently pushed her back. He silently nodded toward me and Robin hugged me again. I held her tight, a knot forming at the base of my throat. I tried to swallow it down, but I couldn't so I gave her a weak smile.

"I'll see you soon, okay?"

"Yes, Burner," Robin said.

September stood up. She plucked her mask from its spot on her hip and pulled it back on. She gave Aaron a thumbs-up and picked Robin up before she left the office and disappeared down the hallway toward the stairs. When she was gone, I looked back to Aaron.

"Aaron?"

"Yeah?"

"This..." I tried to swallow again, but my mouth was dry and that damn knot was still there. "This isn't a dream...is it?"

Aaron shook his head. "No, Burner. This is reality."

"So." I waved my hand awkwardly between us. "You're really here?"

"I am."

"You came back for me?" My voice was starting to crack again.

"Yeah." Aaron looked toward the table and went to move. When I tackled him to the floor, he yelped in surprise.

"Don't go!" I wheezed.

"I—I'm not, Burner," Aaron said, his eyes wide. He pointed at the table. "There's some water and food. When was the last time you ate? Let alone had a bath?"

I hesitated. Those were really good questions. "Umm, well... I..."

Slowly, Aaron wiggled out from underneath me and, still clutching one of my hands, pulled the tray off July's desk and settled it onto the floor between us. A tall glass of water and a thick sandwich stuffed with two types of meat, lettuce, tomato slices.

"Here, just let me." He dipped a piece of clean cloth in the edge of the water, wetting it. He picked up the glass, offering it. "After you're done, we'll leave. I don't know when we'll be able to get something to eat, but you look starved."

I brought the glass to my lips, startled at how my hand shook. The water was cool on my tongue and I groaned, tipping my head back and drinking half of it before Aaron eased it out of my hands.

"Not so much, here, eat, but slowly," Aaron murmured, handing me half of the sandwich.

I sniffed the meat, my stomach gurgling at the thought, and took one small bite. The flavors flooded my mouth and I moaned, my eyes falling shut as I followed Aaron's advice and slowly chewed my piece.

Coolness against my forehead caught me off guard and my eyes snapped open. Aaron gave me an apologetic smile and focused on wiping away the layers of dirt from my skin with the moist cloth.

"I wonder what Den Mother would say if she saw us," Aaron mused, taking a wide sweep of my cheek and jaw.

"They got away?" I murmured.

Aaron focused on a spot at my neck, frowning as he scrubbed at it. "Yes. I tore out September's map and gave it to Fern. I told him to follow it and it'd lead him to a group of humans we'd saved. I also told him the bridge was out by the watchtower, so he'd need to figure out a longer way around."

I nodded absently. "Did they…um…"

"He wanted to come back for you." Aaron gave me a warm smile and focused the rapidly dirtying cloth on the other side of my jaw, careful with the bruises there. "He was prepared to send Albe and Danbe and Eric off and find you."

I stared at my partially eaten sandwich.

"I told him that if anything happened to him, you'd never forgive yourself," Aaron murmured. "I tried to get them to take Robby with them, but she threw a *massive* hissy fit, screaming so loud it hurt." His eyes were warm. "Actually, it was a good thing she came with me, she had the layout of the streets memorized like she was born with an internal map." He laughed.

The sound made my heart ache. I couldn't help but smile in response.

"How'd you find September?"

Aaron sighed, suddenly looking exhausted, his shoulders sagging. "They found me. I thought I'd done a good job of hiding Robin and me in the house while searching the streets of Boston. I spent weeks looking for clues about where you'd gone, but word had gotten out about a young, feral Alpha wolf with scars on his back and wearing a collar who'd freed his pack from one of the most secure nests of Hunters, and the Network came looking." He gave me a tired smile. "They wanted to help me leave the city. I told them I wanted to save you. They were reluctant until I showed them September's diary."

"And then?" I leaned into Aaron's touch as he wiped away the dirt along my nose.

"Then they took me to a safe house. I had to wait for what felt like forever before September finally came and she swore to help." Aaron finished. He tilted my head to the left then right, examining his handiwork before nodding to himself. "Well, at least you don't look like you've been living amongst wild hogs."

"I saw you in the park," I whispered. "I thought you weren't real."

Aaron bowed his head, his hands skirting to clasp my wrists. "For a moment, I thought I was in a nightmare," he whispered. "When I saw you, I thought *that can't be Burner, it has to be a mistake*, and then you started walking toward me, and I knew it was you, and the gun fired." He raised his head, his eyes searching mine. "You didn't stop. You could have been shot."

I touched his cheek, a weak smile on my lips. "Then I would have been with you one way or another." Aaron recoiled at the words. He let go of my hands and rose to his feet, avoiding my panicked gaze. "Aaron?"

"We should get going. Time's ticking." He peered at the clock partially buried underneath a pile of documents on July's desk. "Finish eating, I'll go check with Jasmin. I'll be right back." With that he left the office, closing the door behind him. The silence caused an uncomfortable prickling along my spine, so I finished eating, hoping to distract from the quiet.

I only managed to eat half of the sandwich before I finished the glass of water. I was putting it back on the tray when I heard someone yell near the stairs. The hair on the nape of my neck rose as the floorboard creaked in the hallway. I stood up, accidentally knocking my foot on the tray, a strange sort of panic curling in my gut.

The door kicked open, the glass window shattering as it bounced off the wall. Serga stormed into the room, dragging a shrieking Jasmin into the room by her hair. He threw her onto the floor and she immediately crawled into the corner, her eyes wide in panic, the room filling with her scent of fear.

I should have realized it was a distraction.

I didn't realize it until my back hit the wood-covered windows, and Serga and I were airborne. I hit the ground first, my skull throbbing from the impact, and the wind was gone from my lungs when Serga collapsed on top of me. I had a fraction of a second to prepare myself, shielding my face with my hands, before Serga raised his fist and hit my side hard enough to crack my ribs.

I gagged, clawing at his shoulders, and somehow was able to roll so I was on top. I smashed my fist against the side of his face. He snarled as his nose broke under my hand. He grabbed my hands, both of them, so I raised myself up and brought my forehead down against his.

I hope Serga saw the stars I did.

He sputtered underneath me, saliva and blood spattered my face, and somehow, he flipped us both back. I sunk my teeth into his arm when he tried to push it against my throat. Serga roared and jerked his arm back.

I used the momentum to throw myself at him and tackled him back to the ground. I grabbed his hair and slammed his head against the concrete. My ears roared as a crowd of Hunters, Deadwalkers, and wolves gathered around us. They booed, and shouted, and cheered, and—

"Burner!"

I jerked my head up, my eyes wide.

Aaron and Sam stood five feet from us. Aaron clawed at Sam's arm wrapped around his throat, Sam's other hand holding a gun pressed against Aaron's right temple. I froze, momentarily forgetting Serga below me. I didn't see the punch Serga threw, but I sure as hell felt it.

Chapter Thirty-Seven

EVERYTHING HURT.

My jaw ached, I think my ribs were broken, and I had a strange ringing tone in my right ear. I rolled onto my side, groaning at the movement, and spat out a few teeth and a lot of blood. I ran my tongue along my gums, pausing to spit out more blood and counted the ones I'd lost: left upper canine and three grinding teeth along the bottom right. They'd regrow, but it would be an incredibly painful process. I rubbed the back my head, grimacing at the stickiness I found there.

Where the hell was I? Where was Aaron?

The room was spotless, except for the pool of blood gathering around me, and brilliant with its white marble walls. Columns supported the ceiling that was painted with soft pinks, blues, yellows, and little kids with wings on their backs. I had a magazine that had pictures with them like that, but those were a, what was the word, a museum? I didn't think this was a museum.

I struggled to my feet and yelped as pain shot up through my spine before collapsing once more to the ground. Bewildered, I looked at my leg and realized the bone was sticking out.

Not good.

I rested my back against one of the columns, taking even breaths, and bent at the waist. I grabbed my ankle, and the bone just above my knee, and took a deep breath, then another one. I willed myself to calm, let myself think about

Den Mother when she did the very same thing to Fern after he'd brought back a grown boar. It'd taken all the daughters, pups, and every available hand to hold onto him when she set the bone.

At once, I snapped my ankle and leg and screamed at the top of my lungs.

I gulped down huge gasps of air until I could control the pain and I was sure I wasn't going to pass out. It was still bleeding, though, and I needed to stop it. I looked around the room again, spotting an ivory-white curtain with a long, yellow, pull cord with a tassel at the end. I crawled on my hands and good knee and ripped the cord free, the curtain fluttering to the ground. With slippery hands, I tied the cord around my leg, fighting back the awful throbbing ache. At least that would help slow the blood flow.

I gave myself a few minutes to just breathe before I tried to stand again. I bit back a groan of agony, clinging to the pillar. I hobbled over to the floor-to-ceiling window and peered out, pressing bloodied hands to the glass. It was a clear view of the field Bear and the others were being forced to plant. There was no latch, no way to open it, so I left the window and limped around the room. No food, no bed, just a gold-lined door with a solid gold door handle.

I touched it and stumbled backward as it popped open to reveal another room with similar windows, but these went from wall to wall and were darker with some sort of coating on the glass. A steel desk with a glass top was placed near the window. There was a line of liquor bottles against the wall and on the floor was a faded red and gold rug.

Another door that looked like part of the wall opened to the right and a man in a black suit with a red tie waltzed out. He was taller than me but far paler. He had a diamond ring on his right hand, and his blond hair was slicked back. He looked like he'd walked straight out of my old magazines.

The man walked right past me, his red eyes flickering to mine, before continuing to the bar. He was a Deadwalker, but his scent was covered in something musky and sweet, hiding the rot and mold from his body.

Shit. I was in no fit state to fight.

"Do you want a drink?" The Deadwalker raised a glass.

"What?" I rasped.

The Deadwalker turned to me, a perfectly brilliant smile on his face. "I said 'do you want a drink?'"

"I don't drink." I scowled, unease crawling in my gut like a sick snake.

"Ah, you're one of those club soda and lime guys, I can always tell." The Deadwalker placed two soda cans on the counter, reached under the bar, and pulled out a bucket full of ice. With a pair of gold tongs, he took three ice cubes and dropped them into a wide, fat glass. He popped open the cans and poured their fizzy contents into the ice.

When he finished, he placed the cans on the counter and took another glass. He filled it with an amber liquid from one of the bottles from the bar. Both hands full, he walked around the counter. I hobbled back, covering my nose with my hand as whatever he was wearing was threatening to make me sneeze. He placed the drink on the glass desk and sat in the leather chair. He smoothed his silk tie.

"There we go. Now, why don't you have a drink, and we'll talk business." The Deadwalker smiled again. He sipped the amber liquid.

"Why don't you tell me who the hell you are and where Aaron is before I rip your fucking heart out?" I growled.

The Deadwalker laughed. He actually laughed.

"Serga told me you were a fighter." He took a sip from his cut crystal class. "And don't worry about your boy. He's safe, for now. Please, have a drink, sit down, you look like you're about to pass out." He waved to the empty seat.

Whoever this Deadwalker was, he was like September, and nothing like the feral thing Martha had been. Uncertain, I limped to the offered chair. It took me a few tries to sit down, my leg ached at the movement, but I got there, fighting back the sigh of relief of not having to stand on it.

"For being a toothless wolf, you sure do have a certain *je ne sais quoi.*"

"Just tell me who the hell you are," I growled.

"To the point, I like that." He thumped the glass desk with his fist. "Well, my dear boy, I am King Daniel, I rule this city, and everything from Massachusetts to Washington State."

I rubbed my sore jaw. Already the roots of new teeth were starting to form. "So...you're that Deadwalker that Serga's working for?"

Daniel smiled painfully. "Yes."

I stared at him. He didn't flinch. "What do you want?" I broke the silence.

Daniel rested his elbow on the glass desk and propped his head on a closed fist. "I know it's been a while, but when you first came here, you had something that didn't belong to you. A piece of paper?" Daniel offered.

"September's map," I murmured.

Daniel nodded. "Exactly. Well, that and the wonderful fashion accessory you seem to be wearing." I narrowed my eyes, but Daniel continued, "But what I want is this. Where is September 24th Amon?"

"I'll tell you what I told Serga: September left me to die after the Hunters attacked my pack," I growled, my voice low. "I've been tracking her ever since. I found part of her book on the rooftop of a mall, but I ripped out the map parts and left the rest behind."

Daniel tilted his head, the fingers of his other hand tracing the rim of his glass. "He also said your name is Burner Lee?"

"I am." I shifted my throbbing leg; at least the wound was trying to heal shut. This Deadwalker, though, he wasn't like July. He was something else entirely. Were Kings different from the others? Like Alphas and Den Mothers in wolf packs?

"Lee is such an old, old name. From Europe, I believe. But you're not old, you're still, how do you wolves say, a puppy?"

I growled, low in my throat.

Daniel held up his hands, his blood eyes wide. "I meant no offense, Burner. I apologize. Let's talk about something else, can we? You and this...Aaron. Have you two known each other long?"

"We were bitten under the same moon," I admitted.

Daniel's eyes seem to light up at that. "Really? Now, I don't mean to be pushy, you're probably in a lot of pain with your leg there—" He gave a flourish with his hand "—but I don't think you've seen many Deadwalkers before, have you?"

I nodded, uncertain.

"Was September the first?"

I nodded, again.

"When did you see the next one?"

"On...on a farm," I admitted, "but she...she didn't act like you, or any other Deadwalker."

Daniel leaned forward, his eyes alert, focused. "How did she act?"

I ran a hand through my hair. Why was I answering his questions? He had some strange pull to him. "Feral? When I killed her, she dissolved into this goo?"

Daniel's sharp intake of breath was telling. "Goo? Are you certain? Liquefaction?"

"Goo." I frowned. "Why?"

Daniel thumbed his fingers along the desk. "Your pack, the ones you freed, where did they go?"

"Where are the Den Mothers?" I interrupted, fighting back against whatever spell he was casting.

Daniel paused, confused, possibly even startled at my question. "Excuse me?"

"Where are the Den Mothers? Everywhere I look, there are Den daughters, but they don't know their names and they aren't marked. I asked them where the Den Mothers are, and they have no idea what I'm talking about. So, you tell me, where are the Den Mothers?"

A small, quiet smile danced across Daniel's lips, and the lines around his eyes crinkled. "Instead of telling you, how about I show you?"

Chapter Thirty-Eight

THE DOOR DANIEL had entered through opened and Aaron, bruised and stunned, was shoved into the room by Sam. I jumped to my feet, fighting back a growl of pain, my leg and jaw throbbing. Aaron froze like a deer when he saw King Daniel, his blue eyes growing wide, and the room flooded with fear. King Daniel smiled, and his mouth pursed, amused almost.

"You must be Aaron," King Daniel purred. I growled low in my throat. The sound caught Aaron's ear and he glanced at me, realizing I was in the same room. His mouth opened in shock.

"B-Burner?"

I ground my teeth, the pain of my wounds a throbbing reminder I couldn't fight.

"Oh, so he *was* right. You two do know each other very well." Daniel swirled his drink in his hand before sipping from it.

"Who?" Aaron raised his brows, confused.

"Serga," I grunted.

"Oh, no, no, no, no. Not Serga." Daniel shook his head, placing the cup on the desk. "Rock, my dear boys. Rock told me all about the two of you."

If Aaron and September coming to rescue me had been a fantasy, then this was a complete and utter nightmare. I was too stunned to talk, and Aaron sputtered the word, "W-what?"

The grand doors to the room opened and Serga appeared, half his face the color of a sickly eggplant where

I'd hit him. I swallowed, jerking my head from side to side, trying to keep an eye on Daniel, Sam, and Serga, but all that crumbled when Rock entered wearing an arrogant smirk and a black, tailored suit like the King's. His smirk widened when he saw me.

"Hello, Burner."

"Dad?" Aaron's voice cracked.

The smirk wavered on Rock's lips, but he turned a steely eye to Aaron. "Hello, pup."

"What are you doing here?" Aaron's voice was a ghost, small and soft, but we all heard it.

Rock cocked his head, preparing to respond, but Daniel cleared his throat, stopping him. "Burner wants to see the Den Mothers, Rock. Will you be so kind as to show him?"

"Follow me." Rock waved toward the door.

I didn't move. Neither did Aaron.

"Move." Sam shoved Aaron and he stumbled forward, staring at Rock. A wide hand curled around the back of my neck and squeezed the muscles tight, followed by Serga's voice in my ear.

"Try anything and I'll throw him out the window." Serga's gaze was fixed on Aaron, who bowed his head, his hands shaking at his sides. I nodded, tried to, anyway. Serga clicked his tongue. "Sir, he'll pose no problem."

"Excellent. Come along, boys." Daniel finished his drink and placed it on the desk. He stood and buttoned the front of his suit jacket before stepping away from his desk and walking through the door. Rock walked two steps behind him, a pleased grin on his face.

Sam forced Aaron beside me, and side by side, we followed Daniel and Rock down a long corridor lined with massive paintings of men and women. I recognized a few of them from the two or three museum books Aaron hoarded.

I kept glancing at him, trying to catch his eyes, but he just stared at the floor. I brushed my hand against his, and he jolted, finally raising his head. I felt sick to my stomach at the absolute misery in his eyes.

"I'm sorry," I mouthed. Aaron mutely shook his head, his gaze turning venomous as he glared at Rock's back. I brushed my hand against his again, and he met my eyes. We had to get away. We needed to get out of here, escape the city. I just didn't know how.

Eventually, we reached a set of tall ebony carved doors.

"Burner, why don't you go first?" Daniel smiled. "Rock, if you would be so kind."

"Yes, sir." Rock swung them open and beckoned me in. I faltered in my steps, but Serga's grip was tight on my neck. I entered, instantly drowning in the scents of the powerful wildness of Den Mothers and...and...

My mouth parted, unable to find the proper words, the *right* words at the sight that greeted us of the room. In four corners were Den Mothers frozen in place, partially shifted into wolf form, their hands raised, their mouths opened wide ready to bite, their skin covered in thick fur. They were stuffed and on display, similar to some sick human trophy room. I glanced at the glass display in the middle of the room. A woman's skeleton was posed on her hands and feet, her spine curled forward as her skull peered up at the Den Mothers who surrounded her. The scent that clung to those bones rocked me on my heels and I almost fainted when I realized who it was:

Charlotte.

It was Charlotte's skeleton on display. There was no denying it. Even through the glass, I could smell her, her sweet perfume of clover and lavender, and if I could, then...

"Mom?" Aaron's voice broke the silence. He took two steps toward the display, his entire body shaking. "Mom?" He threw himself at the base of the display, pressing his forehead against the glass, his hands clawing at the cool surface. "No, no, no, no!" he wailed.

"She is a fine specimen. A young Den Mother," King Daniel murmured, standing just behind me, Serga letting go of my neck to step away. "I compensated Rock well, didn't I?"

"Yes, my King. Penthouse, food, drinks, women." Rock flashed us a wild grin. "Everything a wolf needs to live the civilized life."

The words seemed to draw Aaron out and he turned on Rock, his face rippling with rage and bruises. "Why did you do this? Why did you do this to Mom? She loved you!"

Rock shrugged his shoulders. "I was bored of cottage country." Rock sniffed. "It was time to rejoin humanity."

Realization hit me like a thousand-watt lightning bolt and the words tumbled out of my mouth before I could stop myself. "You did it."

Rock glanced at me, unamused. "What was that?"

"You sold out the pack. You sold them to the Hunters." My voice was flat and even. A statement of fact.

King Daniel placed his cold clammy hands on my shoulders, splaying his fingers across them. I didn't jump, didn't react to the touch.

"Damn right, I did, and I could have retired if you hadn't fucked it up. Do you have any idea how much the twins would have made in the dog pits? How much I could have made off selling Fern alone? Ruling the pack for close to twenty years made him weak. He couldn't see that times were changing," Rock spat.

My stomach lurched, bile rising in the back of my throat, but Daniel's voice was next to my ear, whispering for me to be calm and collected.

"I'll kill you," Aaron whispered.

Rock rolled his eyes and crossed his arms over his chest. "No, you won't, son. Your mother made you weak. You're a failure of a wolf."

"I said *I'll kill you*!" Aaron screamed. He scrambled to his feet and lunged for Rock who easily backhanded him. Aaron skidded several feet away, coming to rest at one of the Den Mothers' feet. My hands curled into fists as Daniel's grip tightened.

"Oh, you'll *kill* me? I'm the only reason the Hunters didn't take your sorry ass," Rock sneered, stalking toward him, curling his hands into fists. "Obviously you've forgotten your place."

Aaron raised his hands above his head, turning his face away and trying to curl himself into a small ball all at the same time.

My mind whirled in a cloud of disbelief, even as Daniel's hands started to stroke the pulse of my neck. Rock wasn't...he couldn't be *that* arrogant... Could he?

"You said she was a Den Mother, that Charlotte was a Den Mother," I murmured to Daniel.

"Yes. A small one too," Daniel said.

I craned my neck, meeting Daniel's too close face. "Charlotte was no Den Mother." Daniel's fingers suddenly tightened on my skin as my voice rose. "She would never become a Den Mother. She was a normal daughter. She had Aaron, and Den Mothers don't have sons." That last part was a complete and utter lie, but the sons of Den Mothers were nothing like Aaron or me.

Rock focused on preparing to strike Aaron until Daniel's voice carried in the small room. "Is this true?"

Rock spun on his heels, his yellow eyes momentarily startled before he sneered at me with disgust. "You can't believe a word that shit says, he'll lie, he'll—"

"Our Den Mother died the night of the attack," I continued. "She'd been shot with twenty poisoned arrows. We weren't able to remove them before she died."

"We?" Daniel's smile was tight. "Who is we?"

"Aaron and me." I didn't blink, not even when Daniel hummed, his eyes searching mine.

"And the rest of your pack?"

"The daughters killed the elders and pups. Then they turned on each other until they died, the only survivor bled to death. She told us what happened and died in Aaron's arms," I answered.

Daniel glanced at Serga. "Is this true?"

"My king, you can't believe—" Rock interrupted.

"Shut up!" Daniel snapped at Rock, focusing on Serga once more.

Serga crossed his arms. "It's what happened to my pack. The daughters don't leave anyone alive once they're certain they wouldn't be able to survive on their own. The thought of pups or elders starving to death or being hurt by others drives them crazy."

Serga had a pack? I swallowed, my Adam's apple bobbing against the collar.

"Most wolves wouldn't be so calm about the destruction of their pack," Daniel said after a few minutes.

"I'm not most wolves," I said.

Daniel's face broke into a wide grin and he laughed, tipping his head back. He clapped my shoulders and stepped back. "Oh, you are not, are you? In fact, I think I might have a business proposal for you, Mr. Burner."

Rock shifted his weight, his attention away from Aaron who lowered his arms, confusion dancing across his face. "What? No. You have to kill him. He dies tonight. That's part of our *deal*!"

Daniel waved away Rock's words. "No, I don't think so. It's hard to find good help these days, especially such young rugged ones. In fact, get out. I don't want to see you in my city. Serga?"

Serga whistled and two of his guards appeared from beyond the doors. They approached Rock who was backing away, his eyes wide in panic. "W-what? No! We had a deal!"

"I don't like to be lied to, Rock. Consider yourself banished." Daniel hummed as Rock was grabbed by his arms.

Rock struggled before he screamed, trying to kick at the guards dragging him from the room. "You can't do this to me!"

"I just did!" Daniel yelled back. He smiled sweetly at me. "Now, Mr. Burner. Where shall we begin?"

We would never be free. There was no way I could escape New York alive but maybe...maybe I could save Aaron and give him a chance at some sort of life. It might be my only chance to save at least one of us.

"Aaron is protected and given room and board. He never works in the fields," I said.

"Burner?" Aaron croaked from the floor. "What are you doing?"

"He's preparing your future in New York," Daniel mused.

"Burner, no." Aaron sat up. His hands were shaking, his eyes wide with panic.

"What do *you* want?" I focused on Charlotte's skeleton. It was easier than watching Aaron's face as he witnessed what I was doing.

"Where is September 24th Amon?" Daniel said.

I licked my lips. "I haven't seen her since the summer."

"And the pack?"

"The pack's dead," I said.

"No, no, no, my sweet wolf, where is the big pack? The one with the Den Mother as old as time and decorated with tattoos of wolves, reindeers, and wild beasts?" Daniel's smile grew to that of a shark, all pointed teeth as I sucked in a sharp breath at the realization.

Quebec. He wanted the wolf pack of Quebec. Correction, he wanted the Den Mother of Quebec. He wanted to stuff her and place her amongst his collection.

"I—" How was I supposed to answer without ending in our deaths?

"He doesn't know the roads," Aaron blurted.

Daniel looked at him curiously. "He doesn't?"

"Burner can't read, he doesn't know which sign to follow and the route changes each season," Aaron explained. His gaze locked on mine, and I *knew* that look in those gold-flecked blue eyes of his. It was the same look he'd had when I found him holding the knife at the pier. "He knows where September is, he knows where the Network is—"

"Aaron!" I shouted. Daniel's hands were claws on my arms. "Aaron, *stop!*"

"But *I* know where the wolf pack is." Aaron tipped his head up, his jaw set. "And I'll tell you, and you alone. I don't want any...interruptions, my King."

Daniel shoved me into Serga's arms and I yelped, struggling as arms as strong as iron held me tight. "Aaron, stop! You don't know what you're doing!"

"Oh, I think he knows exactly what he's doing," Daniel purred. He walked over to Aaron, extending his hand. Without hesitation, Aaron took it and let himself be pulled to his feet. "You want a taste of the good life, hmmm? Even at the expense of your...friend?"

"I'm just like my father, except I know enough to be loyal." Aaron didn't bat an eyelash, and I howled, thrashing in Serga's grip. He grunted, wrapping his arm around my throat, his other grabbing my wrists and restraining me.

"A-Aaron! You are not your father!" I sputtered.

Aaron walked to me. I calmed, my eyes searching his. He cupped my face, pressing our foreheads together.

"I am so sorry." His voice was hoarse. He pressed his lips against mine, squeezing his eyes shut while mine widened. He let go and stepped back while Serga hauled me away. King Daniel ran his hands up and down Aaron's arm, bending to whisper into his ear as I was dragged from the room.

"Aaron!"

Chapter Thirty-Nine

"LOVERS' QUARRELS ARE so heartbreaking," Serga mused.

We were back in his white room, except this time, I was hanging from my wrists by a rope attached to a hook overhead, and the tips of my feet could barely touch the ground. I'd struggled, biting and kicking and fighting the entire way there. My heart was a thrashing creature in my chest, threatening to claw its way out. I was dizzy with the reality that Aaron had betrayed me, he'd betrayed the pack. I didn't want to believe it, I couldn't, not with everything he'd done. Coming back for me, saving me, trying to save the pack. It couldn't be real.

"It's always hard when your partner betrays you," Serga continued. He cast a glance at Sam who stood in the corner, wearing a butcher's apron and a bandana over his blond hair. He was chipping at the wall with his thumbnail. "Isn't that right, Sammy?"

Sam bit his bottom lip in response.

"I said, *isn't it hard when your partner betrays you?*" Serga spat and Sam jumped. He nodded, turning to face us, his head bowed.

"Yes, Serga," Sam whispered.

"You and I are going to have a very long talk about loyalty, later." Serga eyed Sam before he unrolled the bundle of black cloth and pulled out a thin surgical knife along with several other instruments that smelled faintly of bleach.

"We're not partners," I mumbled.

Serga tilted his head, his lips pursing together. "Really?"

I barely nodded.

"Huh. I had you two figured as a bonded pair. Most wolves won't stick their necks out for another, let alone spend months trying to free them." Serga sniffed. "Well, whatever. I'm going to give you a few options, Burner."

"You are?" The words were dejected on my tongue. How could Aaron betray the pack? Me?

Serga nodded. "That, I am. You see, it's pretty damn clear that beating the shit out of you won't work. It doesn't usually work on Alphas, anyway, so we're going to have to be a bit more..." He waved the knife in the air as he searched for the word. "Extreme."

"Do what you want." The words were hoarse.

"No, no, damn it." Serga rolled his eyes. "I can't just kill you. I need answers, and you're going to tell me everything about September and the Network."

"I don't know anything."

Serga's eyes narrowed and he tapped the flat edge of the knife against my chin. "You know a lot more then you let on, Burner. Why don't we start with something simple, then, hmm? Tell me about the one who bit you, and groomed you to lead the pack, tell me about Fern."

"Rock tell you that?" I sneered.

Serga smiled, but it didn't reach his eyes. He pressed the blade against my cheek and I didn't even feel it cut, just the trickle of blood. I gasped, jerking my head away, eyes wide.

"He didn't have to. We all carry our Alpha's scent. It's a memory you can't get away from," Serga said. His eyes searched mine. "He ever tell you about where he originally came from?"

My brows furrowed. Why was Serga asking me about him?

"No? I thought not." Serga flicked his wrist again and another cut appeared just before the first one. I tried to kick him in response, but he moved out of the way. "Tell me, Burner, did he ever tell you about the family he left behind to go to Maine?" I froze, my breath caught in my throat, my eyes wide and staring into his. Serga's lips twisted into something vicious, his eyes burning bright. "He ever tell you about the son he left behind?"

"You...what?" I choked. "You're...you're his *son*?"

Serga examined me, his eyes roving over my body from filthy, blood-coated feet up to my bound wrists. "I'll take that as a no," he said coolly. He sighed, glancing at Sam who'd listened to the entire exchange but was tight-lipped. "Sammy, I want you to go get Bear and Melody, take them to the field, and shoot him. We'll use his body for compost, but we'll keep Melody. She's a decent cook."

Sam paled, his eyes as wide as saucers. "You can't be serious."

"A hundred percent, Sam." Serga's voice held no room for argument and Sam fumbled with the door handle. He opened it and was about to leave when Serga added, "Oh, and don't make one of the others do it. I'll find out." Sam nodded and shut the door behind him, leaving Serga and me alone.

"He's a good dog: obedient, always does as he's told, doesn't sleep around, but something about watching me torture people leaves him crying at night, so I don't get any sleep." Serga sighed, shaking his head. "Now, let's focus on you, hm? Are you going to tell me about September and the Network?"

I tilted my head, my eyes staring into his copper ones. He leaned close, our faces inches apart. "I'll die before I tell you anything," I whispered.

Serga grinned wickedly. "I hoped you'd say something like that."

Chapter Forty

DEN MOTHER TOLD me once that when wolves were dying, they dreamed of the ghosts of yesterday. I thought she meant literal ghosts, so I was always looking over my shoulder. When Fern asked me what I was doing, and I told him. He'd laughed it off, explaining that it was just a combination of chemicals our brains produced creating a comforting hallucination, a way to protect us and ease our way into death.

I think I was dying because I kept slipping between whatever Serga was doing to me, whatever caused the air to taste like hot copper, and the night I was bitten.

It was a blood moon. Fern said it was a good omen, that I would be strong and would lead the pack one day. I was barely eight, what did I know about running wolf packs? Den Mother had the daughters prepare a big meal to celebrate the night, and Fern said I would need my strength for the following days. Charlotte had Aaron sit beside me at the table because he was being bitten that night too.

He was shy, with curly black hair, and small. A sickly, weak runt, Rock called him. He was sick so often Charlotte kept him indoors and away from the others so he wouldn't infect them. Den Mother made sure Aaron got extra helpings of the food, trying to give him a chance to survive what came next. He coughed throughout supper, his small frame shaking each time.

After supper, we had to go upstairs and tell the Elders we were joining the pack. Aaron was struggling up the stairs, so I took his hand in mine and together we climbed to the top. He was dizzy and out of breath, but we met the Elders together and were shooed away after telling them we would be as one.

Den Mother kissed my forehead as Charlotte wept and clung to Aaron. Finally, Fern and Rock pulled us from them, all part of the ritual, Fern had whispered to me later. They led us deep into the woods and away from the pack. Fern and I built a campfire while Rock told Aaron to behave, to never ignore his advice, and to always do as he was told. Afterward, Aaron and I sat together, waiting for the moon to reach its zenith overhead.

It was a strange sort of suspense, a building of anxiety. Fern kept watch on the parameter while Rock drank from a silver hip flask he'd brought along. Then, when even the insects had silenced, and there was no sound of animals, just the crackle from the fire, Fern called me over. Aaron gave me a nervous look and I gave him a brave smile.

Fern raised my arm, his eyes practically glowing in the firelight. "Don't ever give up, you understand? Protect the pack, protect the elders, and pups, and daughters. No matter the odds."

"Yes, Fern," I said.

Fern smiled again and held my arm firm in his hands and sunk his teeth in deep, to the very bone. I screamed, thrashing in his arms until he jerked his head back and I collapsed to the ground. He smiled and showed that he was missing one of his canines. When I clutched my arm, I could feel it embedded in the bone.

Suddenly, I was sick to my stomach and the worst fever of my life coursed through me, but I faintly remembered

Fern's enraged face illuminated by the campfire light, yelling at Rock to bite Aaron and at least give him a chance at surviving. Rock relented only because Fern threatened to bite him in his place.

I spent the week buried in fever dreams of worms burrowing through my skin and spine, spreading throughout my body. The only relief was when the moon sang overhead, soothing the pain, the fever, and the ache buried deep in my guts.

When it was over, and we rejoined the pack, I felt better, a thousand times better than before. Aaron was healthy, too, and happy to be out of the house to play, wrestle, and read his books under the big trees at the ocean's edge.

"Where are you going, Burner?" Serga hissed.

I was back in the white room, and I wished I could return to the campfire with Fern.

I sucked in air, the sound oddly high-pitched like a hollow whistle. I shook my head, sobs rolling past my tongue as the agony of Serga's work hit home and I drowned in it, desperately trying to breathe, and fight against the tide pulling me under, but Serga wouldn't let me.

"Where are you going? Who did you see?" His face was covered in blood.

Behind him, the door silently opened. Bear stood there, holding a frying pan in his hands.

"The ghosts of yesterday," I mumbled, missing the way Serga jerked his head back, confused, before shock danced in his eyes as Bear slammed the frying pan against the back of his head and he collapsed to the floor.

Bear stared at me, his face paling, before Aaron, covered in rotted blood, and September, dressed in smoking clothes, crowded the entrance.

I smiled, tried to, anyway. My head fell against my chest as the group shouted my name and suddenly my hands were free and I sagged into familiar arms.

"Burner, don't leave me!" Aaron's voice was desperate and bounced off the blood-spattered walls of the small room.

The ghosts finally came for me.

Chapter Forty-One

"BURNER?"

My eyes fluttered open. Brilliant white sunlight streamed in through the cracks in the blinds. I let out a breath, my body relaxing onto the dark blue sheets, and the soft but firm mattress under my body. The bedroom was tidy, a place for everything and everything in its place. A stack of books was gradually creeping up on the other side of the bed.

I sucked in a deep breath, clearing my throat as I tried to digest the bizarre, fucked-up dream I'd awoken from. Deadwalkers and shape-shifters in post-apocalyptic America? Really?

"Burner," Aaron's voice called to me from across the room and I rolled over, stretching. My joints popped and I sighed, content. Aaron's clothed back was to me. He was digging through his dresser. "I hate to wake you, but have you seen my tie?"

"Tie?" I whispered. My voice was hoarse and raw, as if I'd been screaming for days.

"Uh-huh. The one with the little geese holding the crayons?"

I frowned and rubbed my forehead, trying to think. "You mean the one with the black-and-white ducks?"

Aaron stopped and glanced at me over his shoulder. His hair was shorter, styled into something fashionable, and he was a few years older than I remembered him. He was trying hard not to smile. "Geese, Burner. They're called geese."

I raised my hand, my fingers dancing in the air. The gold ring on my right hand glinting in the morning light. "The 'duck' tie is in the closet."

The smile dropped, and he scowled. Abandoning the dresser, he walked into the closet. "*Where* in the closet?"

"I don't know. I just saw it there." I yawned. I sat up in bed, scratching my neck. I checked the alarm clock on the bedside table and groaned at the time. Six-fifty-five. *Ugh.* I flopped back in bed, yawning again.

Aaron emerged and walked back to the dresser, working on his tie.

"Is Robby up?" I grabbed a pillow and shoved it under my head, content to watch him.

"Already eaten and getting dressed as we speak. She actually woke me up this morning." Aaron smiled.

"She did?" I frowned. "Is she okay?"

"Just nerves, I think. She's doing a presentation on bees for her science class."

"She is?" My frown deepened. Why wasn't I told?

Aaron caught my gaze in the mirror's reflection. His face softened. "You didn't notice the little black-and-yellow striped balls on the kitchen table? Or the jar of honey? Or the cards we'd written next to them?"

I sniffed and looked away, toward the bedroom's open door.

Aaron sighed and, abandoning his tie, he sat on the edge of the bed, his hand on my side. "I know you're working all hours, but..."

"I'll talk to Fern," I interrupted. "Try and get my hours shifted, so I work days at the prison."

"I don't want you to burn out."

I sighed and rolled onto my back. Aaron's eyebrows were drawn up, his eyes worried. I grabbed his hand with the matching gold ring. "I won't burn out. Not if I get to see you and Robby at the end of the day," I said.

Aaron didn't look convinced, but I grabbed the tie with my other hand and dragged him down for a kiss, smiling as he grumbled against my lips.

"Dad, we're gonna be late!" Robin shrieked at the doorway. Her blonde hair was tied back in a messy ponytail, but she was wearing one of her finest Disney dresses, and her backpack was stuffed with yellow and black *things*.

I let go of Aaron's tie and he sat up, straightening his shirt. "Oh, honey, you can't go out like that." He sighed. He pushed off the bed, shaking his head.

"I think she looks fine," I commented. Aaron shot me one of his death looks as he joined her at the door.

"Papa says I look okay." Robin crossed her arms.

"Papa would wear sweatpants, hockey jerseys, and Crocs for the rest of his life if I allowed him," Aaron growled.

"I'm not that bad!" I called back.

"Yes, you are!" Aaron called from further down the hallway.

I flopped back into bed again and glanced at the clock. Fat chance of me going back to sleep, even if it was my day off. I threw back the covers, grabbed my sweatpants from the floor, and tugged them on. I also grabbed a wrinkled T-shirt and pulled that on, as well, grimacing at the traces of stale deodorant before shrugging. It could last another day before it needed a wash. I left the bedroom, my bare feet on the carpet, and headed downstairs. I was rarely up at this hour, and I would probably crash in another hour or two.

I padded downstairs, my eyes adjusting to the light pouring in through the windows. I wandered into the kitchen and poured myself a coffee. It was fresh, dark, a bit bitter, and a thousand times better then what we had at security.

I peered through the kitchen window, noticing people getting their morning paper, and a few joggers passing by.

"Papa, you're awake!" Robin dashed into the kitchen. She dropped her backpack and wrapped her arms around my waist.

"I am, bug." I patted her hair. The messy ponytails were now smoothly brushed, and her Disney princess dress was replaced with jeans, a T-shirt with a cartoon robot holding a flower, and her favorite jacket. I knelt on the cool tiled floor and took her hands in mine. "Dad says you're doing a presentation on bees and you're a little nervous?"

Robin ducked her head, nodding.

I tipped up her chin, smiling. "You studied a lot, right?"

"Yeah. We used the internet, and we watched a lot of videos," Robin said.

"Well, if you and Dad did that, then I think you're going to be fine. Dad's a pretty smart person." I winked.

"You think it'll be okay?" Robin's voice wavered.

I pulled her into a hug. "You'll be perfect," I whispered into her ear as she hugged back.

Click.

I looked up. Aaron had his phone out, taking a photo of us, grinning from ear to ear. "That was perfect. Martha and Jessica are going to love it."

I rolled my eyes. "Not every moment of every second needs to be posted online." I stood up.

"But how else will I compete against the yummy mummies and the legions of arrogant tiger moms?" Aaron batted his eyelashes and I groaned.

"Not this again." I picked up Robin's backpack and placed it on the wooden kitchen table. I unloaded and reloaded it so it was balanced and not about to burst at the seams. "Aaron, we've talked about this."

Robin opened the fridge and pulled out her lunch container. I popped it open, making sure there was a sandwich already inside before I closed it, and placed it in her backpack.

"You never let me have any fun." Aaron pocketed his phone and grabbed a travel mug. He filled it with coffee.

"I don't know why you need strangers' approval for everything. You have my approval, what else do you need?" I gave Robin another hug before leading her, and Aaron, to the front door. I gave Robin her backpack which she slung over her shoulder.

"There are so many things wrong with what you just said." Aaron shook his head. He grabbed his book satchel, loaded heavily with his laptop, and grabbed his coat off the hook by the door. "Get some sleep, okay? You looked close to death last night."

"I will, I will. Have a good day. Try not to kill the children." I got a quick peck on the lips as a response before I opened the door and Aaron and Robin left. I waved as they got into Aaron's shitty Subaru I was constantly repairing, and they pulled out of the driveway and down the street.

I slammed the door and wandered back into the empty house. I grabbed my coffee from the counter and eased into the living room, mindful of Robin's loose Lego pieces and robot toys, and Aaron's various piles of craft projects.

I settled onto the stuffed couch, propping my feet up on the coffee table. I dug into the side of the couch until I found the remote and clicked on the TV, channel surfing past cartoons, nature documentaries, and eventually landing on the morning news.

"And that was Dunken Dan with his record-breaking giant donut. Back to you, Tim," the cheery reporter said, her smile almost as bright as the sun.

The camera switched to a man in his forties, a gleam in his brown eyes. "Thank you, Silva. Now, as I'm sure many of you have noticed, the traffic in the downtown area is miserable and congestion is at an all-time high. We sent out Deva North to investigate. Deva?"

I yawned, my jaw popping as I slid further down the couch, my eyes falling shut while the TV droned on and on. Within seconds, I was asleep. It felt like I had only closed my eyes when I heard someone pounding at the door. I wrinkled my nose as I sat up, noticing the TV was a gray, hissing screen. I turned it off and managed to find my way out of the living room as the pounding got louder.

"Just wait a minute," I yelled. I grabbed the doorknob, about to open the door.

"Little pig, little pig, open the door," a voice sang from the other side and I froze.

That voice...

"Or I'll huff, and I'll puff, and I'll kill everyone you've ever cared about," the voice continued.

It couldn't...

That was a nightmare.

That wasn't *real*.

The door was kicked open and I stumbled back.

Serga stood in the doorway wearing a bloodstained apron. He grinned, his canines longer then humanly possible and his gold eyes reflecting in the moonlight. He stepped inside, and I backed away into the kitchen, shaking my head.

"You, you're not real!" The words bubbled up from my throat. Serga, faster then I realized, grabbed me by the throat and pushed me down. He straddled my waist and raised his other hand, the bloodied surgical knife gleaming in the red light pouring through the windows.

"Now, where were we, Burner? Oh, that's right, it's time to play." He laughed, slicing into the skin of my neck. I shrieked, kicking and clawing at him. He jerked my head to the side and I saw Aaron's and Robin's lifeless bodies next to me. Aaron's hand was open, palm upward, his gold ring covered with his blood.

"Don't worry," Serga purred, "you'll be with them shortly."

Chapter Forty-Two

MY EYES FLUTTERED open and I sucked in a quick breath, holding it as my heart hammered in my chest. I looked around, confused, disoriented, and in so much pain I wanted to cry out. But I didn't. I let out a shaky breath, my chest throbbing with the movement, fighting the panic as I examined my surroundings.

I was on a bed in a small room with mismatched patched wallpaper, heavy drapes blocking windows and a fire roaring across from me. I saw a chair and, when I squinted, Robin asleep. Her head was pressed against the side of the stuffed chair, her mouth slightly parted, drawing in soft breaths. A large book with pictures of maps was about to slip off her lap and onto the old, stained, carpeted floor.

Robin was alive.

I swallowed, almost choking on the sensation, and let out another breath slowly, finally noticing the weight on my stomach. Aaron was asleep, resting his head atop his crossed arms on my waist. He was wearing brown coveralls with yellow stripes on the side, his hair longer than when I'd last seen him.

Aaron was alive.

It'd all been a dream.

I closed my eyes, Serga's face flashing in my vision instantly, and I grimaced, opening them and staring at Aaron. There were more flecks of gray in his hair, a couple of strands, different from the white from being sick as a kid.

His eyelashes flicked, his eyes moving behind his closed lids, his face tense. Lost in a bad dream.

I went to move my hand, to touch his hair, and I bit back the cry that desperately tried to crawl past my lips. Instead, I whimpered and freed my hand from the blankets. I reached out to touch him, my arm weak and heavy. I stilled when I saw the crisscross of marks on my skin and my wrists from the light of the fire.

I turned my arm, frowning as I brought it closer to my face. I looked *God, what was the monster from the book Aaron read? Frank'n'stin? No, that was the doctor's name... What was the monster's name? The one sewn together from pieces of people who eats the girl in the red cloak. No, that's not right. That's a different story...isn't it?*

"Burner?"

I peered past my arm to meet Aaron's sleep-startled gaze.

"A-are you awake? Is this a dream?" he whispered. His hands were digging into the fabric of the old quilt, his eyes taking on a haunted look. "Please, please tell me this isn't a dream."

"Mot drema," I slurred. The words weren't working right. I scowled then flinched, my jaw aching at the movement, as if I'd had a bad back tooth and it'd been removed without anything to dull the pain.

Aaron's eyes widened. "H-hold on." He reached for something behind my head, leaning closer to me. I caught his scent of old trees, and summer grass, and soot. He sat back on the chair, his hands shaking while he held a glass of water and an eyedropper filled with clear liquid.

"Dinah said four drops would ease the pain, but not make you sleep," Aaron rambled. He squeezed the eyedropper into the glass, cursing when he pressed too hard and dripped in six by mistake. "Shit! Don't worry, I'll get another glass, and we'll do this again, and I'll-I'll make it right." His voice cracked, his eyes furiously blinking.

Feeling far weaker then I'd ever thought possible, I placed my hand on hand on his, his warmth seeping into my fingertips. He stilled and bowed his head, his hair hiding his face as his shoulders started shaking.

"I'm so sorry, *I am so sorry*, Burner. I didn't think he—he would hurt you like that. I-I thought Serga would rough you up, not...not do what he did. I never in a million years—I—I didn't betray you, Burner, I never would, but it's my fault what happened, it's all my fault." He broke down, dropping the glass to the floor along with the eyedropper while tears rolled down his cheeks.

I pulled my other arm free from the blankets, sucking in deep breaths at the agony of the movement, and leaned to the side. I touched his shoulder, trying to pull him down. He resisted at first before he grabbed the blankets, burying his face in the old quilt, and cried. I sunk my fingers into his thick, black hair. My other hand rested just below his neck, and I hoped the touch alone was enough to soothe him. Eventually, he quieted, hiccupping every now and then. He turned his head, our eyes meeting. I gave him a tired smile.

"Burner?" Robin whispered.

I tilted my head, catching her wide green eyes. The book was teetering on the edge of her lap, about to drop. I raised my hand. Robin abandoned the book and rushed to my side next to Aaron. He shifted, giving her room to squeeze between us.

"R'bby," I slurred.

"You slept a really long time," Robin whispered.

"Ya?"

"September didn't think you'd wake up."

"Robby, stop." Aaron's voice was firm. Robin bit her bottom lip, nodding. "I want you to go wake up Dinah and tell her he's awake, okay?"

"Yes, Aaron." Robin pouted. She hugged me tight and I clasped a hand around her shoulders and squeezed. She let go after a few seconds and walked out of the door.

"They didn't think you'd wake up, but I told them you would, because I *know* you, and I know you wouldn't have survived this long to just to die in your bed." Aaron's voice was cracking again, so I returned my hand back to the nape of his neck, my thumb rubbing against the tense muscles.

"'Ero," I tried to grin, Aaron's lips twitched.

My eyes started to drift shut, exhaustion overriding every sense, but every time I closed my eyes, I saw Serga behind my eyelids. So, I watched Aaron, memorizing every line of his face, the curve of his eyes, his tear-stained cheeks, his mouth, and jaw, until I couldn't fight the pull of sleep anymore.

I didn't dream.

Chapter Forty-Three

"DID YOU DREAM?" Aaron's voice was soft. Robin had left the room once more to go talk to the mysterious Dinah while Aaron changed the bandages around my neck, waist, chest, thighs, legs, and biceps. Evidently, Serga had tried to carve me up like a sacrificial lamb. It'd been a few days since I'd first woken up, but at least I was staying conscious longer and able to talk. Sort of.

"Yeah," I breathed. It still hurt to talk, my jaw ached with each word, and my voice was ragged and husky.

"Were they good dreams?" Aaron carefully peeled off the bandages around my waist. I watched his hands work, boggled at the ragged scars that crisscrossed my stomach.

"Magazine."

Aaron shot me a confused look. He put the dirty bandages into a bin he'd dragged close to the bed and grabbed a brown bottle that stunk of medicinal alcohol. My nose wrinkled at the strength of it. He pressed some cotton balls to it, letting the white puffs soak up the mixture before he carefully dabbed the ragged lines on my stomach. I hissed, my muscles flexing at the cool and sharp bite that came with the contact.

"Sorry, sorry, it's rubbing alcohol. It keeps the wounds clean. You were covered in so much dirt and grime it affected your ability to heal," Aaron whispered.

I ground my jaw, resulting in a painful groan. I reached up to rub my poor jaw and felt it creak in my hand. That wasn't good.

We fell into a sort of silence interjected with me hissing while Aaron cleaned the sites still struggling to heal. When he'd finished with my stomach and cleaned the scars leading around my waist to my back, Aaron picked up a new, wider bandage and leaned close. As he wrapped it around my waist, he effectively hugged me.

I leaned close, burying my nose in his hair and breathing deep. Aaron stilled. I rested my arms on his shoulders, my scarred fingers curling through his hair as I inhaled his scent and let my eyes close. He smelled of the chemicals he painted my skin with and coal ash, but beyond that, there was the faintest scent of hot summer grass and the salt of the ocean.

"Burner?" Aaron croaked.

"I dreamed we were in a magazine," I mumbled, refusing to let go, allowing myself to drown in his scent. "We were a family. A pack. Robby and us. But as they used to live, in the magazine time. Gold on our fingers."

Slowly, Aaron eased himself away. I relinquished my hold on his hair, my hands drawing down his cheeks to hold his neck as he sat up, his eyes searching mine, his pulse fluttered like a trapped bird in a too-small cage against my thumbs. "Burner?"

I couldn't stop myself.

My fingers tightened around his throat, his eyes widening. I dragged him closer, pressing my lips against his, that warmth from the dream, of doing just the exact same curling in my stomach. Aaron came to his senses and dropped the bandage, his hands rising to curl around my hands still holding to his throat.

"Burner, stop," he whispered, his voice desperate. I tilted my head, my tongue flicking against his parted lips, deepening the kiss. A soft whine crawled up from his throat and I moaned at the sound.

This was way better than any dream, but I needed to breathe. I pulled back, breathing hard. Aaron, who'd closed his eyes, snapped them open, his pupils blown, traces of gold spiraling around the iris, his lips swollen and parted, panting.

I pressed my forehead against his, breathing in his breath.

"Burner, what have you done?" Aaron's voice was wrecked. I stroked his throat, trying to ease the way his pulse thundered under my fingertips.

"Something I should have done a long time ago," I murmured.

"Well, that explains a lot."

Our heads snapped toward the voice. September stood there, her arms crossed across her chest, a smile tugging at her lips. She was hiding in the shadows of the open doorway, maskless, her hair cut short around her neck.

I wrapped my arms around Aaron's shoulders and dragged him close, growling at her as her Deadwalker scent filled the room. Aaron squawked as he tried to pull himself free, but my grip tightened.

September rolled her eyes, her smile widening into a full-on grin. She raised her hands in mock defense. "All right, Burner, down boy. I won't take Aaron away right now. When you two are done, Aaron and I need to talk. And yes, I'll keep an eye on Robin." She gave Aaron a wink and closed the door, leaving us alone.

I eased my grip on Aaron and cupped his jaw, tilting his head up. His entire face was crimson.

"You're an idiot," he mumbled, looking away.

I dragged him back onto the bed, ignoring his protests that he needed to wrap my wounds, and buried my face in his hair, drinking in his scent. Eventually, he placed his hands on top of mine.

"I'm sorry," Aaron whispered.

"I know."

Aaron wiggled beside me until we were face to face, his eyes searching mine. "You almost *died* because of *me*."

"You didn't cut me."

"Burner, no, Goddamn it, it's because of me that Serga *hurt* you!" Aaron raised his voice. I smiled, tiredly, tried to anyway. It hurt to smile.

"You are not your father."

Aaron slowly blinked, confused. "I don't—"

"You said you were like your father, except loyal," I murmured, suddenly exhausted. "You are nothing like Rock, Aaron. You're a good person."

Aaron looked away, his lips curling in shame. "H-how can you forgive me for doing what I did?"

"I never said I forgave you," I murmured, ignoring his startled reaction. I shut my eyes, fighting the heavy weight of sleep trying to drag me down. "It just balances out all the stupid shit I've put you through over the years. We're equal now."

I was almost asleep when Aaron finally muttered a response under a hiccup of breath.

"You're *such* an idiot."

Chapter Forty-Four

AARON WAS ACROSS the room from me, fidgeting with his arms at his side as he paced back and forth in front of the fireplace. He'd been rubbing some sort of mint-scented cream along the scar that trailed the length of my spine—Serga had tried to cut it out—while I laid on my stomach, and I might have made a comment about his hands, and the cream, before he bolted off the bed.

I'd been awake for roughly a week, I think, and improving day by day. My joints were starting to heal, my muscles knitting together properly, but I was getting squirrely spending hours in the room, although Robin had taken to reading to me from whatever book she could scrounge up. So far, we'd learned about asteroids and colonies on the Moon and Mars, but teasing Aaron and watching him get flustered and turn various shades of red was by far the best way to kill time.

"Aaron, come back." I reached out, my fingers clawing at empty air.

"Not until you stop talking." Aaron shot back, his face as red as the glow from the fire.

I grinned, a broken fang peeking past my lips. "But you like it when I talk."

"Damn it, Burner. These walls are paper thin!" he hissed, waving his arms at the walls.

"So?" I raised an eyebrow.

Aaron huffed, scandalized. "Robby can hear you! Have you thought about that? Hear every *word* you say!"

I raised both eyebrows at that. "Fine, I'll stop."

Aaron's shoulders sagged in relief.

"Talking so loud. I'll just whisper." Aaron shot me an annoyed look. "Now, come back here, and make me feel better. My spine hurts," I added when Aaron didn't move. He rolled his eyes and came back to the bed. I grinned up at him as he knelt next to me.

"Not. One. Fucking. Word," Aaron warned, the blush on his cheeks disappearing down the collar of his shirt and spreading to his ears.

"Spoilsport," I sniffed, hugging the pillow close.

Aaron's hands returned to my back, the cream cool against my skin before it warmed, and he kneaded the muscles of my back, spine, and shoulders. I was melting under his hands, nuzzling into the pillow that smelled of us.

Serga haunted my dreams unless I had Aaron close. I'd awoken several times in the night confused about where I was, panicking and thinking I was still with Serga, but one sniff of Aaron's scent and I relaxed. We were safe and far from Serga's grip.

"How come..." Aaron started, his voice uncertain before he cut himself off.

"How come?" I glanced at him over my shoulder.

"You act like you've...done this before." He waved a hand between him and me.

I frowned.

"Kissing and—and cuddling," he mumbled, staring at my back.

It took me a few moments to realize what he was asking, and I gave him a small smile. "You remember Andre's daughter, Michelle? Future Den daughter of the Quebec pack?"

"Of course, why?" Aaron's brows came together in confusion.

"Well, you know that winter I ended up having to sleep in the pups' quarters for the last half of the season and wound up with all those bites and injuries from being their living chewy?"

Aaron's hands slowed. "Yes, I remember waking up and hearing you scream a few times."

"So—" I cleared my throat. "Michelle and I might have found a stash of a fermented apple cider and we might have engaged in some activities for a week or two."

"You slept with Michelle?" Aaron shouted.

If Robin was next door, she certainly heard that. "Um, yeah. Andre was really not happy, and he may have thrown me through a wall, that I ended up repairing later, but the Den Mothers managed to calm him down, got Michelle to drink some potions, and everything was good."

"Oh, my God, no wonder Mom didn't let me wander off," Aaron groaned. "I thought she was just sad about Dad not being there, I didn't realize she was afraid I'd get into trouble too." He went back to rubbing the cream on my aching back and I studied him.

"What about you?" I asked.

"What about me?" His brows came together as he worked on a knot of tight flesh, trying to smooth out the scar with his hands.

"Didn't you ever..." I offered.

Aaron's hands slowed and stopped when he realized what I was asking of him. He was silent for a long time and I was about to roll over when he finally cleared his throat.

"Rock would have killed me if he knew that...that I..." His voice wobbled.

I rolled onto my back, wincing in pain. Aaron was staring at his hands and chewing on his bottom lip. I reached up, grabbed the front of his shirt, and pulled him down with me. I put my arms around his shoulders as he stilled before he wrapped his arms around my sides and hid his face in my neck.

We laid together, Aaron holding tight while I rubbed his back, staring up at the water-stained ceiling of the room. I thought he'd gone to sleep when he spoke again.

"I can't believe he did that to Mom," he whispered. "Putting her on…on display like that." He lifted his head and I brushed away the hair from his forehead. "You dug up her grave, you must have known she was gone."

"I was afraid of what you would do if you found out she was missing," I murmured. "I wasn't sure what to do, and I panicked because Fern had guarded her grave, so nobody should have touched it." I pressed him back to my neck and he sighed, hiding his face once more. "He'll die without the King's protection," I added absently.

"Umm…" Aaron shifted on the bed and we rolled onto our sides. I bit back a groan until I shifted on the bed, stretching my legs out underneath the blankets and finding a comfortable position to lie in. Aaron plucked at the blankets.

"What is it?" I frowned.

"I, um…might have…done…something." He averted his gaze.

I slowly blinked. "Aaron?"

He let out a shaky breath, shyly meeting my eyes, that same look he did when he got into trouble and didn't want to tell me what he'd done. It was a rare look, but the way he was shifting on the bed, he'd done something major.

"Aaron," I pressed.

"You haven't asked where we are, or why September's with us, or anything since you woke up," Aaron blurted.

My frown deepened. "I assumed we're in a safe house September set up to hide from the King?"

Aaron flicked his tongue against his lips. I was momentarily distracted by the movement before he tapped my hands and I focused on him once more. "We are. Technically. Sorta."

"Technically? Sorta? What does that even mean?" I scowled.

"I might have killed the King of New York." My jaw dropped, my eyes widening. Aaron hurriedly spoke up. "I— I had to! He was going to kill you—well, Serga *was* killing you and he wouldn't stop until he found the Network. And— and September bombed Times Square, and I stabbed him in the neck with that ridiculous tie pin he had, and now, we're hiding in a mining place called Centralia in Pennsylvania while September can arrange a safe passage for all of us to Baltimore, and then to Washington, and we're sort of hiding because there's a group of Deadwalkers called Blood Hunters that want our blood." Aaron stared at the frayed edge of the blanket he'd plucked as he spoke.

"Ah."

Aaron shot me a look, panic in those blue eyes. "*Ah?* All you can say is '*ah*'?"

"Well, I mean, there's nothing to be done about it now." I shrugged, and he sputtered "Besides—" I wiggled closer to him on the bed, smiling happily. "You killed for me. Nobody's ever done that, Aaron, except for Fern. You killed to save me, to save the pack, to save us all." I nuzzled his cheek.

Aaron groaned, half-heartedly trying to push me away. "We're being tracked by monsters, and you're happy I killed someone? You're such an idiot Alpha, Burner."

"But I'm *your* idiot Alpha, Aaron." I flashed a toothy grin as Aaron huffed in response before a slow smile curled on his lips, his gaze shyly meeting mine again, warmth pouring into those blue eyes of his. He tapped my nose with his finger and I tried to nip the digits.

"Yeah... I guess you are."

"Yeah, I am," I purred and partially rolled on top of him, framing his head with my arms, bending to kiss that smile on his lips when the bedroom door was suddenly opened, and September entered, her voice panicked.

"We have a problem."

Chapter Forty-Five

IF I HAD my way, Aaron and I would have never left the bedroom. We would have stayed there, curled up in bed, wrapped around each other, just being together, and never leaving the comfort of the soft mattress to face the harsh brutality of reality.

Because reality completely and utterly fucking sucked.

The reality was Aaron helping haul me out of bed and onto jelly-like legs while I clung to him. I was weak, my muscles disused, and the world spun around me while I tried not to vomit over the motion and the pain.

My body *burned* in agony. The nerves, joints, and even my organs ached. Aaron made me drink another glass of water that he added the bitter fluid from the eye-drops. It was fast acting and made the pain shift from a raging inferno to a dull throb. I was so happy, I tried to kiss him, but he shook his head, quietly whispering we didn't have time.

He helped dress me into a pair of black coveralls, a patch on the arm showing a wolf's head and a shovel and pick, and laced my sock-covered feet into black boots. He just shook his head again when I asked him what was going on.

It was when he went to grab something from the closet that I saw a mirror and was stunned by the sight. I looked like a pup's ragdoll that had been sewn together after its limbs, its head, every inch of it had been ripped apart in complete and utter fury. My blue eye was all right, but my green eye, what had been green, was now yellow. I stared at my reflection, willing it to shift back, but it couldn't. It was stuck. Hell, I still had that damn collar around my throat.

Another wave of dizziness raced through me and I tore my gaze away, clutching the chair as Aaron turned back to me. He frowned before he closed the closet, hiding the mirror.

"It—" Aaron swallowed "—it isn't as bad as it looks. When we got you out of Serga's den, you...you were cut all apart, Burner. It was a miracle you survived."

"Did Robby see me?" My voice was low and hushed.

"Yes." Aaron gripped the zipper nestled just below my naval and drew it up until it reached the collar of the coveralls. "She cried and cried, but then September made her forget."

"How did she do that?"

Aaron shrugged, a small smile on his lips. "I don't know. She spoke Robby's language, and Robby doesn't remember anything from the time we were in July's apartment to when we arrived here."

"But you remember." I grabbed his hand.

"Knowing you were still alive... It was the only thing keeping me going."

"Aaron..."

"Come on, we have to get you moving. You need to meet October and Dinah." He flashed me a smile that didn't reach his eyes.

"Who the hell are October and Dinah?"

Aaron shook his head and carefully wrapped my arm around his shoulders. I groaned at the movement, but he ignored the sound. Together we hobbled toward the door, out of the room, and into a poorly lit maze of hallways decorated with the pictures of people; women, children, men, whole families. There were numbers with words below the pictures. I stumbled several times, distracted by the pictures, until Aaron glanced at them.

"They're missing people from during the Two Years of Darkness. October collected as many as he could, trying to build a library of sorts," Aaron explained. He frowned when I stopped moving. "Burner?"

"October... September...July... Is he a Deadwalker?" I frowned.

Aaron shifted his stance and finally, reluctantly, nodded.

"And he's part of September's Network?"

"Yes."

"We're never going home, are we?"

It wasn't a question. Aaron bit his bottom lip, worrying the flesh between his teeth. "I don't know," he said.

I didn't respond. I let Aaron lead me to a set of stairs and I struggled down them, my grip on the banister so tight my fingers turned red from the pressure. When we reached the bottom, I rubbed my nose, scowling at the mingling scent of mold and baking bread. All the windows were either boarded up or covered with thick curtains.

"This way," Aaron said, leading me down a cramped hallway covered with layers upon layers of pictures of missing persons. We went to a door, and Aaron nudged it open with his foot. Entering it gave me a sense of déjà vu because it was almost identical to July's office with the mountains of paperwork everywhere, except Aaron mumbled something underneath his breath, momentarily unsteady before he flicked a switch and suddenly the room was lit with soft, white light. I startled, eyes wide.

"It's coal operated, like in New York," Aaron explained and I glanced at him. "You...never wondered why there was electricity?"

I shrugged. I had other things to worry about.

Aaron opened his mouth to say something, probably scold me. Instead, he pressed a kiss to my cheek. "Come on, have a seat." He eased me into one of the two chairs that faced the desk.

"Goddamn," I sighed, relieved to be sitting down. Aaron squeezed my shoulders.

"Wait here, I'll get the others."

I nodded, rubbing my neck while Aaron left me alone. With the lights on, I could see the room in greater detail. There was a large map behind the crowded desk covered with colored pins and symbols that looked oddly familiar. Some areas were circled with red ink or marked with fat black Xs, and others had square lines with the symbol of a dagger through a wolf's head. I blinked slowly. It was just like September's map.

"Jesus Christ, you're alive!"

Startled, I turned in my seat, my jaw dropping open at the man standing in the doorway. He wore a similar coverall to mine, except his face was clean, the tattoo on his forehead slightly faded, and he had a wide, delighted grin. He sat in the seat next to me, grinning from ear to ear.

"Bear?" I whispered.

Bear laughed. "In the flesh."

I racked my brain for a few seconds before things clicked. "Sam was supposed to kill you. Why aren't you dead?"

The laughter died off, but Bear kept his smile. "He was. He was going to shoot me in front of my little girl—well, that's what he told me was supposed to do, but what with the bombs going off all over the city—"

"Bombs?" I raised my eyebrows.

"And fires. She might not look like it, but that September is a fierce firebug if ever I've seen one." Bear chuckled. "Anyway, the first one went off, Sam ordered the guards to go check it out and we were all alone, all three of us, and Sam raised his gun to shoot me, Melody started crying, and then..." Bear's smile turned wistful. "Sam shot at the sky and said if he ever saw me or the others in New York, we'd be killed on the spot."

"The others?" I frowned. "What others?"

"The other prisoners," Bear explained. "He threw the keys at me and said I had ten minutes to get them out. So, I did, and they scattered. I was going to leave with them, but then this guy covered in blood and yelling for you raced into the prison. Took me a few minutes before I realized he was the one you'd stared at during that day in the fields."

Bear sighed and shook his head. "When I told him you weren't there, and probably in Serga's torture room, he turned eight sheets of white and begged me to tell him where that was. I couldn't let him go alone, so with Melody's help, we got a frying pan and, well..."

"Saved my life," I finished.

"Saved mine too," Bear pointed out. "You're a lot heavier than you look, and in your shape, September and Aaron couldn't have gotten you out of the tower and into the escape car. Anyway, Melody and I got a free one-way trip to beautiful Centralia, Pennsylvania." The grin came back fully and he slapped his knees. "I never thought I'd breathe fresh air again, or that my little girl would be free."

"Well, thanks." I gave a lopsided grin and Bear winked.

"My pleasure."

I hesitated, uncertain for a second, and cleared my throat, rubbing my wrists. "So, um..."

"I don't know." Bear's voice was suddenly soft, as if was reading my mind. "I don't think *he* knows where we are, but for the moment, we're safe."

I nodded, staring at the map, my gaze tracing the string wrapped around the pins and highlighted sections. There was a soft knock at the door and we both looked toward the sound. Melody stood there. A large, pale hand patted her head and she looked up as a tall man, resembling a scarecrow and wearing a blue suit with frazzled red hair and glasses perched on a beak-like nose, entered. His red eyes made me shudder.

"You must be the infamous Burner," the man mused. He leaned down to Melody. "Sweetheart, could you go help Dinah in the kitchen?"

"Yes, Mr. October." Melody gave me a curious look before she left, and October entered. His movements were sluggish, as if it took a lot of energy for him to take each step, but as he walked around the desk, he waved at Bear who nodded curtly and stood.

"I'll go make sure the trucks are prepared," Bear said. He clapped my shoulder. I squeezed his hand before he let go and left, leaving October and me alone in the office. The only sound came from the grandfather clock ticking away in the corner.

I didn't want to admit it, but my heart was starting to pound a bit faster than normal. October was staring at me, his red eyes taking in my scars, the collar around my throat, and finally my eyes.

"He's very protective," October said.

"Who is?" I frowned.

"Your Aaron," October clarified. "He wouldn't let September or me or any of my doctors anywhere near you as soon as you arrived. It took Dinah and a few of my men dragging him away just so we could tend to your injuries. You're healing nicely."

"It still hurts."

October nodded as if he'd expected that response. "Before you leave, I'll make sure you're given a month's supply of laudanum. That should help with the pain." At my confused look, he waved a long-fingered hand. "It's that bitter stuff Aaron's been adding to your water."

"You're...part of September's Network?" I said.

"One of many." October tried to offer me a lopsided grin, but his rows of sharp teeth made me push back against my chair. He shut his mouth. "My apologies."

I shifted uncomfortably in my chair, looking toward the doorway and hoping someone would come and end the awkward silence in the room. Thankfully, September entered. She gave me a warm smile, a small pile of folded documents under her arm. Following behind her was Aaron holding Robin in his arms.

"Burner!" Robin beamed. She wiggled free of Aaron's arms and raced over to me. I couldn't help myself and hugged her, ignoring the way my muscles pulled under the skin.

"Hey, bug," I whispered, the nickname from the dream slipping out. Robin peered up at me, her eyes sparkling green before she nodded.

"Nickname accepted and tied to speaker," she chirped.

"That's good," I said, even as September shot Aaron an uncertain look. Aaron ignored September and held open the door as warm cinnamon and cedar bark filled my senses. I followed the source of the scent, startled as Melody entered holding a tray of mashed potatoes and other soft food. Behind her, a woman roughly October's age carried in a tray with glasses of water and a vial with the same eyedropper as before. She placed them on October's desk, giving me a warm smile, and I almost melted at the sight.

I *knew* what she was.

"Burner," October started, "may I introduce Dinah, the last Den Mother of Boston."

"It's good to see you awake and in one piece." Dinah stroked my hair. I let my eyes fall shut, her words not quite registering.

A sharp pinch to my arm and my eyes snapped open, meaning to glare, but Aaron sat next to me, raising an eyebrow. I focused again on Dinah who looked far too amused.

"Den Mother." I smiled.

"He'll be all warm and fuzzy while Dinah's here." Aaron shook his head.

"No, I won't." I shot Aaron an irritated look.

"Yes, you will. All Alphas get dumb around Den Mothers; it's how it works." Aaron rolled his eyes.

"No, we don't." I huffed, hugging Robin.

"Yes, you do."

"No."

"Yes."

"No."

"Are they always like this?" October asked September who only shrugged in response.

"Judging by the way they act in private, and the amount of bickering I've witnessed, I assumed they were bonded."

"We're not bonded!" Aaron shouted, his face bright pink.

"Maybe we should," I mumbled, shrinking in my chair at Aaron's death glare.

Dinah covered her mouth, stifling a laugh while September awkwardly held up her hands. "Okay, okay. Sheesh. Sorry."

"As much as I would love to sit around and discuss pack dynamics, we do need to address a serious, and dangerous, situation we find ourselves in," October interjected. I sighed. September nodded stiffly, shut the office door, and leaned against the frame.

Aaron cleared his throat, pointedly ignoring me and focusing on October. I glared at him and turned my attention to October. Dinah patted my shoulder and stood beside him, her hands on her hips. I could get a good look at her; she had white hair with a scattering of red streaks pulled back into a bun at the back of her head. She wasn't nearly as skinny as Den Mother back home was; Dinah looked like she had access to regular food. Underneath her right eye was the black tattoo of the letter "B."

October leaned forward on his desk, his elbows rested on scattered papers. "My name is October 31st Thatcher, and you have brought monsters to my town and placed the entire Network at risk."

Chapter Forty-Six

THE ROOM WAS dead silent, so I slowly nodded, trying to digest what October just said.

"Right." I dragged the word out before I cleared my throat. "So, just for those of us who've been imprisoned, tortured, and unconscious for however long, how exactly did I do this? Besides, what the hell *is* the Network?"

October glanced at Aaron, who was staring at his hands, refusing to make eye contact, and back to me. It clicked. Sort of.

"You're talking about King Daniel being dead?" I asked.

"And the fairly large explosions and fires." October glared at September who smiled sheepishly.

"Just for the record, I didn't realize that much dynamite would do that."

"Oh, and mixing it with napalm was just an afterthought?" October asked dryly.

September shrugged.

October sighed and leaned back in his chair, suddenly looking a hundred years older than his stick-thin frame betrayed. Dinah placed a hand on his shoulder and October squeezed her hand. "You can't just kill a Deadwalker King without consequences, Burner."

I frowned, opening my mouth to speak, when October raised his hand. "Within this room, we know Aaron killed him, but out there in the wider world, it's being circulated that you killed him *and* the Network was behind it."

Aaron gave me a nervous smile. Robin peered up at me. She took my hands, tracing her small fingers along the scars. I racked my brain before I came to a decision.

"I did it." My voice held no room for doubt.

October frowned. "What?"

"If it means that Aaron can have a chance at living a normal life, without being hunted or having a bullseye on him, then I accept complete and utter responsibility."

"Burner," Aaron sighed.

"I told you he'd say that," Dinah mused.

I shot her a confused look.

"Protect the pack, right?" Dinah offered. I smiled awkwardly.

"Unfortunately, that can't happen." October crossed his arms over his chest, frowning at his desk. "Aaron's name has been tied to you as a traveling companion, thankfully Robin hasn't been named, yet. As for your other question, September?"

"Right." September pushed off the frame and strolled to the map against the wall. "The Network is an underground resistance dedicated to the end of the Deadwalker Kings and Queens."

"But you're Deadwalkers," I pointed out.

"We are, yes." September nodded. "But there are a large number of us who don't agree with the Kings and Queens having total authority. Many have ruled since the Two Years of Darkness twenty years ago, and any effort to bring about change has been eradicated."

"And?"

September blinked. "Excuse me?"

"What does that have to do with us?" I gestured at Aaron, Robin, and myself. "We're going back to our pack. This isn't our war."

September's eyes narrowed, the never-ending star tattoo on her face crinkling, but Dinah shook her head. "Burner, you saw Daniel's room...the room with the Den Mothers?"

It took me a few minutes to remember. Trying to pull the memory to the front was hard because it kept blurring with the dream of gold rings and blood moons. Eventually, I could see it, the four Den Mothers and...and...

"Charlotte," I murmured.

"I have her bones," Aaron whispered. He gave me a weak smile. "I haven't buried them yet. I'm waiting for a really nice spot, somewhere she'd like."

"Burner." Dinah's voice snapped me back, and my spine stiffened. "There are only three known Den Mothers left."

I slowly blinked, my skin prickling. "*What?*"

"The Den Mothers of New Vegas, Utah, and myself," Dinah said.

"I don't, what?" I leaned forward in my chair. Robin hopped off my lap and went to Aaron who picked her up and sat her on his knee. "That's not, that isn't *possible.*"

"After Darkness fell across the world," September started, her voice soft, "the Deadwalkers emerged from the shadows and there was a war between your kind and ours."

"The paper we found in Boston from the doctor," Aaron clarified. I nodded. I remembered that.

"The Hunters started off as groups of people struggling to survive and the Deadwalkers gave them refuge and protection from others, but in return, they had to hunt wolves, specifically Den Mothers." September tilted her head, her black hair falling to partially cover a brown eye. "It was an easy trick, something about welcoming men, women, and children?"

"It's our way." Dinah's voice was tinged with sadness. "We welcome those who need our help. But they came and killed the Den Mothers and then the Alphas and cast the packs into chaos. They would place early versions of collars developed by a Deadwalker scientist to ensure our kind couldn't shift, couldn't fight back."

I sucked in a sudden breath, realization dawning on me like the sun. "That's why he never did it."

"Burner?" Dinah frowned.

"That's why Fern never brought back men with him," I said. "He only brought women and children back to the pack when he found them."

"Smart," Dinah said. "So, you understand what this means, don't you?"

I wetted my lips, staring at my hands, then up to Dinah. "Without the Den Mothers, there's no core to the packs. They'd fall apart."

"And without an Alpha, there's no one who can turn the young into real wolves," Aaron finished.

"So, you end up with mix-and-matched wolves...like Melody, and the other daughters in New York and Boston?" I frowned.

"Exactly, and the reason Serga's men were all full-blooded wolves was because they were either bitten before the Two Years, or Serga bit them while they were still young enough to survive," Dinah said.

Serga.

I shuddered at the name, and Aaron reached over to squeeze my hand. I shot him a grateful look, holding tight to his wrist. October leaned forward on his desk again, his eyes boring into mine.

"As of what is known right now, a feral Alpha associated with the Network killed the King of New York. Deadwalkers are already forming alliances across the country. There's chatter among the wolf communities about you and there are *whispers* of rebellion in the streets. For the first time in twenty years, a chance of a lifetime to change things has put the royalty on edge," October explained.

The room fell into silence, the ticking of the clock the only sound. When it chimed, I spoke, my voice low. "What do you want me to do?"

"Come to Washington with me," September said. "There, we can argue our case to the Elites for change, for them to stop the Kings and Queens and finally take things back to the way it was before the Darkness."

"Or else?" I raised my eyebrows.

"Revolution." September raised her chin, defiance flashing in her eyes.

I nodded slowly. I looked back to my hands, to Aaron's fingers that slid between mine. I peered at him from the corner of my eye. He wouldn't meet my gaze, his lips set in a thin line, his shoulders tense.

"What happens to us?" I raised my head.

"What do you mean?" October frowned.

"If we go to Washington, if we do...whatever you want us to do with the 'Elite,' what happens to Aaron, Robin and me?" There was a sinking sensation in my gut, heavy and weighted.

September and October exchanged a quick glance, something unspoken between them. Dinah looked to the map on the wall, her eyes downcast.

"Well?" I snapped.

"You'll be provided with shelter, work, a new life in the city," September said.

"We're never going home. Are we." It wasn't a question but a statement of fact, and I wanted the honest truth from *someone.*

"It's too late for that now," October admitted.

"Did you know about this?" I let go of Aaron's hand. He didn't look to me. He buried his face in Robin's hair, pulling her close. "Aaron, answer me," I growled low in my throat and he shook his head. I growled deeper and he shuddered, partially turning away on the seat.

"Burner," Dinah interrupted. I growled at her, my hands twitching. The collar buzzed faintly, a tickle against my throat, and I paused, reaching up to touch it, frowning.

"Can someone please get this damn collar off me? You'd said you knew someone who could do it." I glared at September.

September shifted, looking uncertain for the very first time in her life. "Well, ah, about that..."

"We can't get it off," October said.

I looked at them. "That isn't funny."

"It's not a joke, Burner." September dumped the files onto the desk and pressed her palms against the edge. She leaned over it, her eyebrows drawn, worried. "October had his engineers come in to examine it, try and figure out how to open it, but they couldn't. I've sent drawings and messages across the Network, even to Miami, California, Colorado and New Mexico. Nobody has any idea what it is." She bit her bottom lip, exposing a sharp fang. "The only answer is that it was specifically made for you by someone who knew you were an Alpha. Someone who understood that you would cause a whole lot of trouble, and who recognized the danger you posed if you shifted."

Before I could even form an answer, Aaron growled low and Robin looked up worried. "Rock. It had to be him. He was the only person who saw you as a threat, Burner. He would do whatever it took to get what he wanted..." His face paled.

"He'd know we would go to the mall," I finished for him. "He…must have known we'd go there, that you would stay at Charlotte's grave, and…and…" I stared at him. "Aaron, he set us all up."

Aaron slapped his hands over his eyes, groaning. "Good God, he sent him." At my confused look, Aaron waved his hand. "Rock sent Riley! He had to or else I would have been there when the Hunters attacked. Instead, Riley came to me, crying about you and holding the net. He said you'd yelled at him and wanted to go back to the pack, but he ran off into tall grasses to hide. By the time I found him, the explosion happened, and the sky lit up."

"I saw that explosion." September crossed her arms. "Natural gas, by the look of it."

"I didn't yell at him. I told him to go to you. Goddamn it," I hissed, standing up, my fingers curling into claws. I paced back and forth, my forgotten pain starting to sing as I moved. "God*damn it*! It's all Rock's fault!"

Just then the door to the room was thrown open and Bear stood there, panting, his eyes wide in panic, the room filling with the scent of terror.

October stood up. "Bear?"

"Blood Hunters!"

Chapter Forty-Seven

TIME SLOWED DOWN.

September and October raced out of the door, pushing Bear against the frame to get past him. Aaron kicked back his chair and picked up Robin, hugging her tight. Dinah grabbed the hand-sized, brown glass bottle off the desk and silently waved at us. I bit back the pain, limping after her and Aaron down the narrow hallway and into the too-hot kitchen while September left, chasing after October. I hissed, leaning against the flour-covered table.

I grabbed Aaron's arm, stopping him.

"What the hell are Blood Hunters?"

"Burner, we don't have time," Aaron started, trying to look at the other doors while Dinah hurriedly filled a satchel with bread, dried meats, and bottles of water.

"Aaron!" I snapped.

"Do you remember Martha?" Aaron blurted.

Stunned, I nodded.

"Blood Hunters are like her."

I limped to the lace curtain kitchen window and peeked out, startled by the falling white in the daylight. Was it snowing? "It's daylight. She can't be out there."

"No, Burner, you don't understand," Aaron tried again only for a black mask to suddenly appear in the window. I yelled, jumping back and landing on my sore leg. Pain shot up my spine and I cursed, the world momentarily swirling around me.

Dinah grabbed my arm, helping to steady me. Nausea rolled through my stomach, a tsunami of bile. Suddenly a bucket was in my hands and I was puking my guts out while the door opened and the Deadwalker entered.

"September! You can't scare him like that or else he'll never heal!" Aaron hissed.

"Sorry! But we have to go, now. October and about a hundred of his men are holding off the Blood Hunters by the front gates." September's voice was muffled behind her mask.

"How many?" Dinah stroked my back as another wave hit and I was throwing up something that was black and bitter tasting, and oh God *why* did it stink like rotting skunk?

"Four so far."

Dinah's hand at my neck froze and I spat the last bit of black ink into the bucket. "*Four?* Are you certain?" she whispered.

"Yes." September nodded.

"Then where's the fifth one?" Aaron's voice trembled.

"*Burrrrner Leeeee...*"

A voice, low and breathless, a whisper tumbling past a ghost's lips drifted down the hallway and curled into the kitchen, surrounding us. September twitched, her head tilted left then right, her hands curling into claws before she grabbed Aaron by the wrist and physically dragged him, and Robin, out of the room leaving Dinah and me in the kitchen.

I didn't speak, just stared into the darkened corridor as a red-cloaked figure crept from the shadows. It made no sound, even the cloak's mud-soaked edges dragging along the floor was silent.

"*Burrrrner Leeeee,*" the voice whispered again, breaking the silence of the room.

"Get back, you *monster*," Dinah snarled. She stood between the creature and me, her shoulders hunching together, her voice dragging and raw. The creature paused, its entire body shifting underneath the velvet fabric.

"*Den Moth...er...*"

"Run," Dinah hissed at me.

I couldn't move. I was fixed to the spot as a low, chuckling crackle came from the creature.

"*No...escape.*"

"I said *run!*" Dinah howled.

I shot out of the kitchen door, running blindly into falling snow that wasn't cold but tasted of ash. Dinah howled again, and I stumbled over my feet. Dinah leaped through the door and skidded in the dirt on her hands and feet, completely shifted. Her coat was brilliant red and gray, and she was *massive*. The Blood Hunter appeared in front of her, seemingly unafraid that a Den Mother was about to attack it. Dinah took a step back, her feet as wide as my arm planted in the dirt, her long limbs tensed. She threw her head back and *howled*.

It was silent for a second, and then the resounding howls made my teeth ache and my head throb. Suddenly there was a wave of wolves and men wearing soot-covered black coveralls racing toward them as Dinah howled once more, drowning out everything, and calling the pack, *her* pack, to fight for her.

The vicious heat in my belly screamed that I was a coward for turning my back on a Den Mother howling for help, and I agreed. I should have stayed, I should have fought with her, but Aaron was calling for me and his pull was far stronger than it should have been.

I jerked my head toward a row of trucks starting to move out. I raced toward his voice, fighting against the tide of people, gasping for breath as I forced my way through. The coal truck was already alive, starting to move, and Aaron was sticking out of the front passenger seat, his arm extended, reaching for me.

"Aaron!" I reached for his hand and missed by the fraction of an inch, my body drenched in sweat as I struggled to move while my muscles screamed at me to lie down and die.

"Bear, slow it down," Aaron snapped. The truck hiccupped for a second, just long enough that I could grab Aaron's wrist. He grunted, hauling me into the truck. I let out a choked yell, the stitches on my arm tearing. I collapsed onto the seat, my eyes crossed, clutching my arm as blood swept down and along my fingers.

The truck jerked underneath me and I almost slammed into the front dash, but Aaron's hands held me down as he frantically told Robin to grab the brown bottle from inside the bag and to give it to him.

With shaking hands, she did as he asked. I grabbed it from his hand and drowned a quarter of its contents in one gulp before Aaron ripped it from my fingers. I moaned at the immediate lack of pain and of worry, my eyes drifting shut even as Aaron's face rippled with fear.

"You *idiot*!"

Chapter Forty-Eight

"YOU SHOULD BE more careful with that stuff; it can lead to addiction." Bear's voice was quiet in the truck cabin. It was late, how late I couldn't tell, but the only light came from the numerous walls of trucks rumbling across the highway illuminating old stacks of cars, ancient barricades, and the glowing amber eyes of creatures slinking in the woods.

"Hmm." It wasn't really a word or a grunt. I didn't care, though, because, for the first time in a long time, I didn't hurt. My arm was freshly bandaged, and my head felt like a cotton ball floating on a summer breeze.

A quiet sigh tickled my ear and I peered down at Aaron asleep next to me, his head resting on my shoulder. Robin was curled up on his lap, holding his hands as she slept. Melody sat next to Bear, dozing. I rested my head on Aaron's, watching the road pass us with little to no interest.

"Sep'member," I mumbled. Bear spared me a glance.

"In one of the trucks bringing up the rear."

I grunted, and Aaron shifted in his sleep. I nuzzled his hair, my own eyes falling shut.

"How long?" I said after a while, fruitlessly trying to fight the cobwebs sweeping across my mind.

"Guessing by the signs, we've got about another hour of driving ahead of us before we reach Baltimore," Bear offered.

"Hunters?" I swallowed, blinking, trying to fight the wave of sleep.

"So far, nothing, but that...could...always..." Bear stared at the road ahead of him. He slammed on the brakes and I almost crashed into the dashboard again. The movement, as well as the horns of the following vehicles honking behind us, stirred Aaron. He lifted his head, whining low in his throat as he rubbed his eyes, his voice thick with sleep.

"Wha's going on?"

The high-pitched shriek of the truck's horn made us both startle in our seats, and Robin sat straight up, her eyes wide and brilliant green. Melody opened her eyes, alarmed, before she looked out of the windshield and hid her face in Bear's side. Bear fumbled with the radio, flicking a switch.

"This is King October's property and right of way! Stand aside!" Bear barked into the handset.

"Burner, look, Blood Hunters." Robin pointed beyond the windscreen.

I followed her finger to a group of ten people illuminated by the truck's lights. They all wore the same red cloaks and red-colored masks similar to September's. They were waving slowly back and forth in place. Their heads bobbed up and down like snakes, their movements hypnotic.

They were blocking the road.

"What's going on?" I braced my hand against the dashboard, blinking rapidly, trying to focus past the drugs. Aaron pressed back against the seats, his grip on Robin tight.

Bear didn't answer. He flipped a switch on the radio. "Donner, Luke. There's a fucking pack of ten of 'em in front of us, blocking the road."

The radio crackled, and September answered. "Floor it."

"Bear, what is going on?" I hissed.

One of the red cloaks stepped in front of the others. *"Burrrrner Leeee, come out, come out, so we may eat your heart!"* It was a man's voice. I shivered.

"Hold on to something. This is going to get rough," Bear said.

Aaron grabbed a handful of my coveralls, squeezing his eyes shut. His hold on Robin tightened and she turned, hiding her face in the safety of his neck. I clawed my free hand into the door handle just as the truck shot forward and barreled through several of the red cloaks. The action caused one of the red masks to be torn off and revealed a man's head with a set of a thousand teeth where his face should have been and two black holes for eyes.

A weird scream, high-pitched and desperate, and so loud my ears felt like they were bleeding. If I hadn't been in the truck, if Bear hadn't been driving, I would have been frozen to the spot. I twisted in my seat and looked through the back window as the other trucks followed us, driving over the fallen bodies. But, as I stared at their twisted and broken forms, they straightened themselves and stood once more.

"Go faster. You need to go faster," Aaron babbled.

Bear shifted gears and the truck jerked ahead. We almost lost the convoy, but as I kept watch, September, illuminated by the floodlights on top of every truck, crawled out of the last truck's window to stand on the roof. She balanced herself before she leaped onto the truck in front of her, even as one of the Blood Hunters climbed up the side of the vehicle and attacked her. She pulled a long knife from her boot and slashed viciously at the Blood Hunter, who easily ducked her attacks.

"What's happening?" Bear demanded.

"September's fighting them on the roof of one of the trucks!"

Bear grabbed the radio again. "Klaus, September's up top! Give the lady a hand," he barked.

The passenger door of the truck September was fighting on opened. A male not much older than me pulled a shotgun from the cab. He shouted, and September ducked down when he fired, and sent the Blood Hunter flying off the roof of the vehicle.

September yelled to him, the words lost on the wind. She deftly jumped onto the roof of the next truck, and the next, until she hit our roof with a heavy thump. I opened the door and squeezed against Aaron as September slid down and into the truck, next to us. She pulled off her pig mask. She was panting, her black eyes wide.

"Are they still there?" Kevin shifted gears again and the trucks behind us followed suit.

"They're chasing the convoy. I've never seen so many. I didn't know *that* many existed!" she gasped. "We need to get to Baltimore territory as soon as possible. King August won't let them in his city."

Kevin radioed the command down the line.

"Are you all right?" September turned to me, her eyebrows knitted together when she saw the fresh blood on my arm.

"I'm fine," I choked. I couldn't hear her heartbeat. She was panting, and her eyes were wide, but I couldn't hear her heart.

"What about you, Robin? Aaron? Are you okay?"

Robin nodded mutely, her face hidden in my side. Aaron gave a weak thumbs-up.

"Those things, at the house, they were them?" I said.

"Those were Blood Hunters. Vicious creatures that are really, really hard to kill." September gulped. "They're an independent group, apart from the Kings and Queens and Elites. They're the law keepers of the Deadwalkers."

"And who controls them?"

"The Ancients."

"And they're chasing us because of me?"

September smoothed her ruffled hair. "Yes."

"Because I killed the King." I dragged the word "I."

"Yes. Because *you* killed the King." September dragged the word too. She reached past me and grabbed the radio from Bear's hand. "Truck sixteen, slow down for the Blood Hunters to get close enough, and then dump your cargo and catch up to us."

The radio crackled static and moments later familiar high-pitched shrieks filled the air.

"How long until we get to Baltimore?" September glanced at Bear.

"Not long now." Bear stared at the road ahead.

"Hit top speed, and don't slow down for a second," September ordered and spoke once more into the radio. "All right, listen up, everybody, there are Blood Hunters on us and we won't be safe till we reach the gates of Baltimore. If you need to, dump your coal and floor it."

As if on cue the line of trucks behind us let out a high-pitched mechanical screech that made us all flinch at the sound. Within seconds I felt a massive pressure on my chest as the truck shot ahead and soon we were joined by others, driving side-by-side with ours. One of the drivers, who couldn't have been much older than me, gave me a thumbs-up before turning back to the road.

"Baltimore doesn't have gates," Robin whispered from Aaron's lap.

Oh, but it did.

I sat up in the seat, Aaron softly gasping as he leaned forward, his eyes staring at the massive steel gates the trucks were fast approaching.

"This is September 24th Amon, on order of King October 31st Thatcher, I demand you open the gates!" September yelled into the radio and the gates, about as tall as three dump trucks piled on top of each other, opened just as the vehicles poured through. Men and wolves armed with rifles and shotguns poured out.

We drove past them and they opened fire on the scattered few Blood Hunters that still chased us. As soon as the trucks were clear, the massive gates were slammed shut once more. Bear led the convoy to a huge set of coal-stained brick buildings that puffed up black-gray clouds into the sky, blocking out the morning sun.

September hopped out and pulled on her mask, fidgeting with the plastic straps, while Aaron, Robin and I slowly crawled out. "Aaron, remember the plan: head for the building with the half-eaten moon and wait there for me."

"Right." Aaron nodded.

I looked at him and September. "What plan? Where are you going?"

"I need to make last-minute arraignments. The Blood Hunters are here, it's only a matter of time. Just wait for me, okay?" She squeezed my arm. "Trust me."

"We'll meet you at the safe house," Aaron offered. September nodded and let go. We watched as she slipped into the darkness.

Bear climbed out the truck and jogged around to join us. Melody clung to his hand, her eyes taking in the massive chimney stacks. "Head down the main street and turn left. The building is three blocks down past the brothels. Be safe."

With Aaron's help, together, we started toward the glowing city lights of Baltimore.

Chapter Forty-Nine

IF NEW YORK City was crowded, busy, noisy, and no place for Wolves, Baltimore was worse. The stinking sweet smell of the coal and its dust was heavy in the air as it poured out from the stacks that pumped its heat into the city. The wolves, many of them wandering around as people, weren't much better.

There were drunks passed out in the crowded streets, and Den daughters wearing thick make-up giggled as they were led from building to building by packs of males. There were Deadwalkers too. They were enticing some of the older daughters with promises of drinks, and a free supper, if only for a moment alone with them. Aaron carried Robin in his arms. Her arms were wrapped around his neck and she hid her face while I limped beside him.

The scent of sex from the brothels almost drowned my other senses before we even turned down the street. A few daughters who stood near open doorways offered Aaron and me a good time, but I ignored them. With leers and wicked smiles, some men made similar offers. Those made Aaron flush red, and I glared at them until they turned their attention elsewhere.

A few individuals took a quick look at us, thinking us to be easy targets, but when they saw my scars and eyes, they stepped out of the way, parting the crowd for us to make way. I wanted to ask Aaron what plan he and September had talked about earlier, but we were in strange territory and I didn't want us to stop until we were safe, even if I was starting to sweat like crazy.

Eventually, Aaron stopped outside a building with a sign of a wolf's head and mining picks along with wording on the green door beneath it. His eyes skimmed the words before he jerked his head. "This is the place, Burner. Can you open the door?"

Without a word, I twisted the copper handle and held the door open while Robin and Aaron stepped inside. We were greeted with two doors on the left and right—the left one reeking of a bathroom and the other like rot—and a long flight of narrow stairs going up to a second floor. I groaned at the sight of it. I was *not* looking forward to that.

Aaron gave me a weary smile and opened the door to the right. He poked his head in and waved for me to follow. I shot the stairs a thankful look and followed Aaron into the room, wrinkling my nose at the all too familiar scent of Deadwalker.

Ugh. How did they stand to be around one another?

It was, once more, an office stacked to the brim with paperwork. A Deadwalker, skinny and without a right arm, was poring over documents by the flickering naked light bulbs overhead. I was going to have to ask Aaron one of these days why the hell Deadwalkers were obsessed with books and paperwork. I cleared my throat when the Deadwalker didn't speak.

"December 29th Thatcher? King October sent us," Aaron said.

The Deadwalker finally looked up.

"I am him. You must be that miserable, trouble-making, Wolf King October informed me about." I raised my eyebrows at that. Aaron blinked owlishly in surprise.

Wolf King? That's a new one.

"Although you're certainly here earlier then I thought." December pointed to the corner of the room where a ratty couch was pressed against the green-painted wall. "Sit there, don't touch anything, and Lady September will be here soon."

I nudged Aaron toward the couch and Aaron let Robin down. He gestured for her to sit, but she shook her head, fidgeting with the front of her dress. "Robby?" I frowned.

"I need to pee," Robin said.

"The bathroom is next door." December's focus was back on the paperwork in front of him.

"I'll take her. You sit down and rest." Aaron lowered a backpack onto the floor before leading Robin out of the office. I collapsed onto the couch, the metal springs squealing under my weight. I let out a soft groan, ignoring the way December's fingers twitched as he worked on the document.

I crossed my arms over my chest and leaned against the couch, tipping my head forward. My collar bone still hurt, as did my spine, but at last, my muscles were healing, and there wasn't that sharp, horrific pain that had danced along my back earlier. My legs felt better, that week of resting after I'd woken up had helped, but walking left me exhausted.

I eyed December and wondered just when I had become so accepting of Deadwalkers, and why I wasn't fighting them, and how much had changed since I first met September. The truth in my gut was I still didn't trust them, I probably would never trust them, but Aaron seemed to trust them and so long as he did, I would too.

"Burner!" Aaron yelled.

I was on my feet in seconds and racing out of the room. I almost ripped the door off its hinges in my haste to leave the office. December straightened in his chair as I opened the bathroom door. I quickly backed out, my back hitting the wall. I clamped a hand over my mouth, nearly gagging at the combined stench of harsh chemicals and burning tires. Robin was standing next to the sink while Aaron frantically scrubbed at black, oily spots along the hem of Robin's skirt with a towel. The collar of his T-shirt was yanked up, covering his nose as he worked.

"What the hell happened? Why does it smell so bad?" I choked out. The odor was making my eyes burn.

"My filter isn't working right." Robin's eyebrows were drawn up, and her bottom lip quivered. "I think it got damaged with the exposure to all the ash and coal in the air. I need to be fixed, or else I'll just get worse and worse!"

"Your *filter*?" I raised both eyebrows. What the hell was she talking about?

"Uh-huh. I need to see Doctor Lexing in Utah. She can fix me."

"Aaron?" I stumbled over to him. He shook his head, his voice muffled.

"It's the third time she's done this," Aaron explained. "The first morning, we found her, about a week when we got into New York, and now this. It'll clear up if we can get her someplace with clean air and just *stay* for a little bit."

"What is it?" I almost gagged.

"I told you." Robin crossed her arms, practically pouting. "It's debris from my filter. Robins aren't designed for—what's that sound?" She looked past me, confused.

Aaron and I both stopped. We tilted our heads toward the front door, listening as the sounds of high-pitched sirens outside filtered through the cracks in the door, and soon echoed in the bathroom. December popped his head into the room, peering at us with an unreadable expression.

"What's that sound?" I whispered. The siren gave me goosebumps.

"That would be the sound of an attack on the city," December said.

Seconds later, a thousand wolf howls filled the air and almost drowned out the sirens' shrill scream.

"And that?" Aaron dropped the towel into the sink. He picked Robin up, and set her on the ground. She smoothed out the wrinkles in her dress, scowling at the black sludge in the toilet. I had a sinking feeling we would have to figure out her problem later.

"That would be the militia calling all available wolves to arms to fight against said attack on the city," December explained dryly.

The front door opened and a pup around Robin's age raced inside. He wore yellow coveralls and a yellow hat, with two little white wings attached to the sides of the hat.

"Mister December?" The pup gasped, his gray tail partially tucked between his legs.

"What is it?"

"The King asks that you send some of your wolves for the militia and..." The pup glanced at me.

"Spit it out, puppy," December snapped.

"Lady September asks that you escort Burner and his group to the manhole on Third Street and Maine."

December rubbed his forehead. "Fine. Send a message to Ali Kincaid in the barracks that they're to fight—wait, what are they fighting?"

"Blood Hunters, Mister December, Sir," the pup chirped.

"Send the word and then go and hide in one of the brothels. Do you understand me?" December said.

"Yes, Sir. Thank you, sir!" The pup saluted. He dashed out of the door and into the noise of the streets.

"I suppose you have nothing to do with Blood Hunters attacking Baltimore, do you?" December turned to me; his red eyes glowed with anger.

Aaron and I exchanged a quick glance before I cleared my throat. "Well…"

Robin slipped past me and December, disappearing into the office before returning with the backpack. She handed it to Aaron who slipped it over his shoulder.

"Follow me." December closed his office door and pulled a key from his pocket, locking it. He shooed us out of the bathroom and outside. He had us step out first, and all I could do was stare dumbfounded as one of the massive chimneys started to collapse. Three flares were shot into the air and illuminated the night sky in eerie red.

"Unless you want to inhale some really toxic chemicals, I suggest you move," December warned.

I grabbed Robin's left hand, Aaron grabbing her right, and we held tight as December escorted us down the street and past the tide of wolves and daughters who raced toward the flares or fled into nearby buildings. I witnessed pups dressed like the one who had brought September's message race past men armed with shotguns and rifles, standing as sentinels outside the doors of the brothels.

I tried to stick as close to December as I could while he shoved wolves and Deadwalkers aside, but when I heard the monstrous screams of the Blood Hunters, all the wolves and daughters on the street came to a standstill, clapping their hands to their ears, myself included.

"Another chimney is collapsing!" Someone in the crowd yelled and coal and ash and dust filled the streets and made it impossible to see. Robin was torn from my hand and Aaron disappeared with her.

"Robby! Aaron!" I yelled, coughing as dust and ash flooded the streets like a swollen river. Even with the red light of the flares, I couldn't see an inch in front of my face. I spun around and blindly reached for him. I grabbed someone, but it was a Deadwalker in his fifties who took one look at my scars and eyes and fled in absolute terror.

"Burner Leee."

I bolted into the dust, crashing into people and wolves alike, almost tripping over paving stones and just *stuff* people had thrown to the ground in order to escape.

"Burner Leee."

I turned around, toward the voice, the hairs rising on the back of my neck. Sweat prickled my brow when I was faced with nothing but ash and dust and red light.

"Burner Leee," the voice hissed right next to my ear. I slashed wildly, spinning in a circle. Another flare shot into the sky and I realized with horror that I was completely surrounded by Blood Hunters. Their red cloaks coated with gray ash and black soot, their bodies waving in unison from side to side like snakes. But there was something different about them; the hems of their cloaks were striped with a different color, similar to tarnished gold.

Fern never prepared me for *these* things.

I swallowed, desperately wishing I could shift, but the soft buzz of the collar against my throat reminded me that if I even tried, I wouldn't be able to fight against whatever happened next. Suddenly, the Blood Hunters parted, and one wearing a filthy gold cloak stepped into the circle. It was smaller than the others, and it spoke with a breathless child's voice.

"Wolf King, Burner Lee, Wild Alpha, which of these three is thee?"

"What?" I hissed.

"Ruler, traitor, leader, which of these three is thee?" the gold-cloaked Hunter asked again.

"I don't know what you want." I ground my teeth, watching the Hunters from the corner of my eye.

"Leader, killer, wild as the sea, pick your destiny."

I growled, the sound ragged and deep, and the hood of the gold cloak twitched. "Whatever stupid game you're playing, I don't care. My name is Burner Lee and I killed the King of New York!" I snapped.

A strange wobbling giggle drifted from within the gold cloak at my words.

"We like you, so you shall be free until we meet again under the dying tree."

Small, clawed hands the color of deep purple pressed against my chest and I was falling into darkness.

Chapter Fifty

I SHOULD BE dead, but I wasn't. I was biting my hand bloody, choking back the screams that were trying their damnedest to bubble up from my throat. I'd fallen God only knows how far and landed directly on my feet. The sudden landing made everything ache and throb, even my spine was burning. Hot liquid coursed from the base of my skull down my back toward that pulsating point in my feet. Wherever I was, it was pitch black, and it stunk like a sewer.

"Burner?"

A white flare sparked to life. I rolled my head to the side, my eyes clouded with agony. September stood above me, the light of the flare mirrored in the black-tinted lens of the mask. Robin was glued tight to her side as if her life depended on it. Aaron was kneeling next to me, his hands cupping my face. I blinked rapidly, looking past him into the tunnel. Evidently, my nose was correct; we were in a sewer on a side path next to a ladder that went skyward.

"Are most Alphas usually this hard to kill?" September mumbled through her mask.

Aaron didn't answer. He silently searched my eyes, and I nodded after a few seconds. He let go of my face, grabbed my arms, and hauled me to my feet. I struggled, letting out a heavy hiss as pain crawled its way through my body. I leaned on him when I was upright and hobbled on my good leg.

September began to lead us through the sewers. We approached the end of a platform and Robin whimpered. She tugged on September's arm, shaking her head at the sludge we were about to step into. Grudgingly, September hoisted her up on a hip, holding the flare high with her other hand.

Aaron slung my arm over his shoulders. He wrapped a hand around my waist, his other holding tight to my wrist dangling over his shoulder.

"December must have shoved you into the manhole." September sounded relieved.

"It wasn't him," I grunted in response. Aaron shot me a look.

September glanced over her shoulder. "What do you mean?"

"Those *things*," I spat out the word, "surrounded me. I lost Aaron, Robby, and December in the crowd, and suddenly they were everywhere."

September turned back to me, illuminating my face with the flare's light. "But you're...still here. Why?"

"There was another one."

September's arm wavered. "What did it look like?"

I shifted on my feet. Aaron stared at me.

"Burner?" There was a nervous tinge in September's voice. "What did it look like?"

"It wore a gold cloak." The words were barely past my lips and September was suddenly wading ankle deep in the sludge toward a path. "H-hey, wait!"

"We don't have time!" September yelled. "We have to go, *now!*"

Aaron and I tried to follow her, but she was moving so fast and taking so many turns, it was only the light from the flare that was our guide.

"September, slow down!" Aaron called out.

"We have to go, we have to move. We can't stay here."

"Damn it, September, what the hell is going on!" I yelled. My voice echoed amongst a hundred paths.

Suddenly, September was in front of us, and through her scent of rot, past the overwhelming stench of sewer, I could smell her, and she was *afraid*. Robin had covered her eyes with her hands, trembling in September's grasp.

"*They're* coming," September whispered.

"Who are *They*?" I sputtered.

September shook her head. "It won't matter if we don't get out of here. We're not far from an exit pipe. I've got a vehicle waiting for us, then we drive straight for Washington, D.C."

"And the Blood Hunters? Won't they just follow us to Washington?" Aaron asked.

September hesitated, and glanced at me. "The Counsel is stationed in Washington. They have a treaty with the Ancients; I'm just hoping it still stands, but if one met you then..."

"Burner met an Ancient?" Aaron breathed.

"As soon as we're out, I'll explain everything, but we have to go *now*," September hissed.

Aaron and I shot each other another look, and, as quickly as we could, we followed her deeper through the sewers. Eventually, we came to a cross point and we climbed onto another platform. I was barely on it before she was moving again. She led us through a massive drainage tunnel, but we had to duck down, and hell if that didn't make my spine ache.

We fell into a tense silence until Robin softly spoke.

"Ms. September?"

"Yes?"

"Why do all of the Deadwalkers have names based off of a calendar year?"

September stopped. Aaron and I almost crashed into her, but I squeezed Aaron tight, grateful for a breather.

"How did you—?" She stared at Robin, dumbfounded.

Robin tilted her head. Her eyes glowed green, like she was examining September.

"She's a strange thing," Aaron murmured. He nudged September forward with an elbow.

"Do you know about the Two Years of Darkness?" September asked Robin.

"Is that when the connection was lost with the Cloud and network?" Robin chirped.

"Yes," September said, "that was when the Deadwalkers rose and the world was never the same. There were just so many that there needed to be a way to keep track of all of us. So, it was decided by the Council at the time that we would be named after the month we were turned, the day, and the name of the Deadwalker who turned us. So, for me, my full name is September 24th Amon."

"But what was your birth name?" Robin frowned.

September hesitated. She cleared her throat as she stopped at another junction, holding the flare aloft. Silently, she waited until the light of the flare flickered, and she went in the opposite direction. I understood then why she'd done that; I saw light coming from the end of the tunnel.

Finally.

After what felt like an eternity, we were out of the sewer. My arms and legs were shaking, and I was drenched with sweat. Aaron wasn't in any better shape; he was panting hard. September was shaking too as she followed up behind me. Once she was out of the sewer, she looked around at our surroundings and dropped the flare to the ground.

We were surrounded by the burned ruins of old houses, but in the distance, I saw Baltimore with its tall walls and smoke plumes as the fire devoured the city. More flares lit the sky, and sirens and wolf howls could be heard, even as far away as we were.

"Come on, we have to move before the Blood Hunters figure out we aren't in the city," September said. Quietly, we made our way through the ruins until we came across a patch of bare road without debris on it and a—

"What the hell is that?"

"It's a motorcycle with a sidecar." September dragged us toward the black motorcycle with the peeling white star on the gas tank. "I got it in Las Vegas a little under eight years ago as a reward for a favor I did for the Den Mother there. Robin, Aaron, you two climb into the sidecar and Burner... What?"

"No."

"What?"

"Not until you tell me about the damn Ancient."

September climbed onto the seat of the motorcycle and fidgeted with the handles. "Did...did it ask you anything?"

"Yes." I frowned and repeated what it had asked me. September stilled.

"It...said it'd meet you again under the dying tree? You're sure?" she whispered.

"Yes."

"What's the dying tree?" Robin peered up at Aaron.

"It's not real, it's just a rumor from the Old World." September shook her head. "Some of the Ancients, they lose sense of reality. First off, they're Blood Hunters, and those are Deadwalkers made wrong, so Ancients are just insane, but if one spoke to Burner, and let him *live*, then something big is happening, something beyond the Network's knowledge. I won't know more until we get to Washington, so, Burner, could you *please* get on the bike?"

Reluctantly, I slid into the bike's seat behind her. I grabbed her waist by reflex as she flipped the bike stand up and kick-started it. The motorcycle came to life, the high beam lit up, illuminating the street ahead, and my grip on her tightened considerably. She twisted the handles, the engine roaring underneath us, and we were driving down the road at breakneck speed.

In the distance, the siren abruptly stopped and I could only hold tighter to September as the last chimney fell in the city. It was horrific and terrifying, and I hoped that the pups and daughters were safe. Judging by Aaron's worried look, he shared the same thought.

"How long to Washington?" I yelled above the roaring motorcycle.

"Sooner than I hope," she called back, turning hard on a street corner.

Familiar prickles on the back of my neck again, my name whispered in the wind, and I glanced back over my shoulder. Chasing after us was a Blood Hunter, covered in black soot, scrabbling on all fours like some twisted crab, his wide mouth with its many white teeth snapping at us.

"Blood Hunter!" I yelled. It had to have been one of the ones that followed us in the trucks.

September wavered, cursing as the motorcycle fishtailed and she almost lost control. I caught her gaze in her side-mirror. Soon it was joined by another, and another, until there were five in all. Aaron was cursing in the sidecar, gripping the edge, and trying to keep Robin hidden.

There was absolutely nothing we could do except attempt to outrace them.

September revved the engine and we were going faster than I thought possible. The motorcycle growled underneath us as we gained distance from the Blood Hunters. I caught Aaron's eyes, holding his gaze until September yelled, "Don't let go!"

I swiveled my gaze toward the front and saw a roadblock of old cars ahead of us. September wasn't slowing down. She angled the motorcycle toward them, and I squeezed my eyes shut. I didn't need to see our deaths as they happened. Aaron's hand grasped my ankle, and I ground my jaw.

Instead of crashing into the roadblock, we were airborne, and I opened my eyes just in time to see September had used one of the vehicles as a ramp. We hit the ground with a heavy *whump*, the motorcycle groaning under our weight, my spine burning in agony at the landing, the sidecar squealing unhappily at the impact, but we were a lot further ahead of the Blood Hunters who shrieked behind us.

"Take this and squeeze it." September pushed something into my hand. It was small and round, about the size of an apple with a red button on top.

I squeezed the button and almost jumped from the loud explosion of the cars behind us that the Blood Hunters had started to crawl over and around. Their gnarled bodies were sent skyward, their limbs shattered when they crashed into the pavement, and I hugged September's waist as we were pelted with their rotted, sick blood.

"Fireworks!" Robin squealed. Aaron clamped his hand over her eyes.

Chapter Fifty-One

AFTER THE EXPLOSION, the Blood Hunters abandoned us. Whether they were injured or dead, I don't know. What I do know is that we arrived in Washington, D.C. just before dawn. September's head was drooping as the sun began to rise, and the motorcycle slowed. Her breathing was starting to turn ragged as if she was struggling against an invisible weight trying to press her down.

The only people on the streets in the early light were wolves and daughters in human form. Unlike in New York, and Baltimore, these wolves and daughters all wore tailored suits and dresses similar to my old magazines. Many of them also wore badges with symbols on their sleeves, or as pins on their chest. Symbols of birds, dogs, books, and guns; all were separate and equal.

September pulled up to a house with huge white columns and a sign of a black-painted fox chasing its own tail. She kicked out the kickstand and I eased my grip on her.

"Are you okay?" My leg had stopped its persistent throb and now the bones inside sewed themselves against the muscles and marrow. I could walk, even if just for a few feet, without the pain from before. My spine, however, was still burning with that liquid heat.

"Sun...up soon," September mumbled in her mask. "We need to...to...get to the station."

"Where is it?"

She gestured somewhere ahead of her. I turned to Robin, who'd fallen asleep in Aaron's arms. His eyes were still wide, mixed with panic.

"Aaron?" I whispered.

Aaron blinked, finally noticing where we were. He sat up, waking Robin with the movement. He looked at the house, then at all the other buildings with the tall column and one building surrounded by a tall metal fence, a large domed ceiling, and boarded windows.

"We're in Washington, D.C.?" He cleared his throat.

September slumped back against me. Her head rolled to my shoulder as the sun's rays peeked above the clouds and across the city.

"Hello there."

Startled, I turned to the soft voice and saw a daughter several years older than me with a tattooed "T" under her right eye. She held open the door to the house with the black fox sign. Her eyes were a soft copper and she had russet-brown skin and styled hair. She wore a pin of a funny-shaped gold T on the front of her tailored blue and purple shirt.

"You should bring Lady September and yourselves inside before you attract any more attention." The daughter stepped aside.

"Who are you?"

"I'm Tallah, and I tend to King October's house here in the city. Now, come in before she bursts into flames. The clothing will only help so much," Tallah urged.

"Give us a hand?" I pleaded and Tallah stepped out of the house. Between us, we dragged September into the house. Tallah closed the door behind us and led us into another room with blue-painted walls, a white couch, inlaid designed tables, and fresh flowers in ceramic vases. I felt as if I was in a living version of one of the magazines I'd loved so much.

"On the couch." Tallah pulled the heavy embroidered curtains across the windows and blocked out the sunlight. She lit two oil lamps and placed one on a little coffee table next to the couch. She reached up and pulled off September's mask and set it on the table.

"Lady September? Can you hear me?" Tallah peered down at her.

"Blood... Hunters..." September mumbled softly, her eyes shut.

Tallah sighed and picked up September's arms. She crossed them across September's chest then covered her with a blanket from her feet to her head.

"She won't be able to help you in her current state," Tallah explained.

"What's wrong with her?" Aaron's voice was rattled, and I gripped his arm tight.

Tallah lit the other coal oil lamp. "She's sleeping. She'll stay that way until dusk. But in the meantime, follow me."

"Where are we going?" I swallowed.

"Well, I'm going to get you into a hot bath, feed you, and give you some clean clothes. All three of you stink of coal and shit," Tallah said bluntly. She turned and walked out of the room.

I didn't move. Neither did Aaron. Robin peered up at us, blinking her wide eyes.

"I am never riding in a sidecar again," Aaron whispered, breaking the silence. He took Robin's hand and followed Tallah out of the room. I followed him, limping with each step.

Chapter Fifty-Two

THE WATER WAS so hot, I was sure I looked part lobster.

It felt like ages since I last had a hot bath. Not since the summer with the pack, at the very least. Hot water did something to wolves. I'm not sure what it was, but it was this huge sense of *warmth* that spread throughout my body, causing my injuries to heal faster than normal, or at least as fast as if I could have shifted.

Tallah had divided the three of us among the bathrooms in the house and swept Robin away to bath her, much to Aaron's objection. Tallah had glared at Aaron and he'd given up, shuffling into a bathroom just down the hall from the one I was shoved toward. As soon as I was standing on white tiles, I'd shed my clothes in a pile and dropped them into the basket Tallah gave me, before popping it outside the door. There was a similar basket outside Aaron's bathroom.

I took a washcloth and scrubbed myself down, ridding myself of as much of the soot, ash, and shit as I could, before I crawled into the too-hot water the clawed foot bathtub offered. I picked up a different washcloth from its place on the side of the tub and wrung it, soaked it in the hot water, and rested it across my eyes and forehead. I sunk deeper into the water even as my knees popped up just above the water's edge.

Silence.

I tapped my fingers on the edge of the bathtub.

It was too quiet.

I cleared my throat, looking around the pristine room at the white floor tiles, the white toilet, the white towels, and wallpaper. It was so *white* it made my eyes ache. My gaze fell on my arm and hands, and I examined the lines of scars crisscrossed across my body. I wasn't sure if they would ever heal; some scars just didn't, especially the ones inside, festering like diseased wounds that drove people crazy on sultry nights with the memories of yesterday.

I slowly blinked and before I knew it, I was out of the bathtub, sloshing water all over the floor. I grabbed a fluffy white towel off the counter and wrapped it around my waist. I left the room, steam spilling into the hallway as I marched down the hall. I was about to knock on the door when I heard crying from inside.

I grabbed the door's glass handle, twisted it, and pushed it open. Aaron was sitting in a bathtub, his knees drawn to his chest, his face buried in his arms. He jerked when the door opened.

"Burner? What the hell? I'm taking a bath," he croaked.

I stepped inside, shut the door behind me, and twisted the little knob underneath the handle, locking it.

"Burner?" That same uncertain tone again and I ignored it. I stepped toward the bath and pushed on his shoulder.

"Move."

"What? No, this is my bath, you have your own," Aaron snapped.

I rolled my eyes. "Move *forward,* you dummy, so I can get in there too."

Aaron froze. "What?"

I fought back the grin at the way his voice cracked. I waved my hands again, and, finally, he slid forward. I tossed away my towel. I crawled into the bathtub behind him, momentarily annoyed that he got the much bigger tub. I wrapped my arms around his shoulders and pulled him flush against my chest. I stretched out my legs, sighing happily.

Aaron didn't move, didn't relax for the longest time until he finally did. He grasped my wrists, tilting his head to the side to catch my eyes. "Why are you in here?"

"You have a bigger bathtub." I shrugged.

Aaron blinked before he scowled. "That's not what I meant."

"You're in here?" I offered, flashing him a smile.

Aaron sniffed, looking away toward the end of the bathtub where our feet were pressed before he glanced at me again, his face somber, his eyes soft.

"It was the silence, wasn't it?"

This time, I looked away. I pulled one of my arms free from around him and rested it on the edge of the tub and propped my head on a fist. "Do you remember when we were kids and one of the pack hunters came back with Albe and Danbe and their mom?"

Aaron relaxed his head against my shoulder, humming to himself. "Yeah, we'd been chasing chickens most of the morning."

"Do you remember when the Den Mother came out?"

"I do. I translated for you because she didn't speak English," Aaron said.

"We'll never see her again."

Silence.

I cleared my throat, staring at the tap at the end of the bathtub. "We'll never see Albe or Danbe again, we'll never see Eric, or Riley, or any of the other pups. We'll never see Jessica, or Yun, or any of the daughters. We'll never see Den Mother or...or..."

"Fern," Aaron whispered.

"We'll never see home again, Aaron. And even if we were to try, we'd lead Blood Hunters, Hunters, and Deadwalkers right back to them." My voice was cracking. Aaron shifted in the tub. I let go of him, breathing in deep as he turned around and straddled my lap. I swallowed, distracted by the way the water ran over his lithe frame. Only focusing once he cupped my jaw and I stared into his blue and yellow eyes.

"Burner..."

"What exactly did we accomplish? Now, we're in a completely fucked up *world* that doesn't make any sense. Hell, Aaron, we're trusting *Deadwalkers*! We have Robby! Cities have fallen because of us! We're being chased by monsters! What the hell have we done?" I rambled.

Aaron leaned in and pressed his lips to mine, his eyes watching me. I stared back, his forehead pressed against mine.

"*We* didn't burn down the cities, they did. And back home, we were being hunted by predators, Burner. Just instead of wild boars or cougars, it's just another creature but with a scary name." Aaron nuzzled my cheek against his, his voice dangerously soft. "You set out to save the pack, and that's what you did." I pressed a kiss to the corner of his mouth, smiling as he licked his lips. "You saved a group of humans when they should have died." He kissed my jaw and I bit my bottom lip. "You saved Robin, Bear, and Melody..."

I ran my hand up Aaron's back, drinking in the shudder he gave at the touch.

"*We* saved them, Aaron. Together, *we* did it. I would have died without you," I whispered against his lips, my eyes searching his.

Aaron made a humming sound, his pupils blown, his arms around my neck. "In the grand scheme of things," he murmured, "we did what we set out to do. Our pack might be smaller now, but we're still one, right?" There was a note of uncertainty at the end, and I kissed him, hard.

Aaron deepened the kiss, his lids falling shut. I poured everything I had into the kiss, leaving us both breathless. Soon the room filled with panting moans and soft groans.

Chapter Fifty-Three

THE WATER WAS cold, and Aaron wouldn't meet my eyes. I grinned and leaned over the edge of the tub to pinch his ass as he roughly dried his hair with a towel. He yelped, jumping away from my fingers, and spun away, throwing the towel at my face. I snatched it, grinning wider as he hurriedly wrapped another one around his waist, the blush on his cheeks spreading down from his neck and across his shoulders.

"I can't believe we... we..." He stumbled, grabbing a different towel to finish drying his hair *and* keep as far from my hands as possible. "In a bathroom, with a Deadwalker downstairs!"

"You're actually a lot louder than I would have thought," I said thoughtfully, fighting back the laughter at Aaron's scandalized look.

"*What?*"

"I'll have to keep that in mind for next time," I mused, catching the second towel he threw at me.

"I swear to God, Burner," Aaron hissed.

There was a hesitant knock on the door. Aaron glared at me before he unlocked it. "Robby?"

"Is she okay?" I frowned.

"What's wrong?" Aaron asked.

"Um, there's a-a Deadwalker downstairs. He wants to talk to Burner," Robin mumbled.

Aaron glanced back at me and I looked at the little window. The sun was streaming into the bathroom.

"Why isn't he asleep?" I frowned.

"He says he's very old. He wants to talk to you," Robin said. "Oh, and Tallah said to have this."

"Where's September?" Aaron asked.

"Tallah had to wake her up. She was summoned," Robin explained.

Aaron shot me a worried look and I shook my head.

"I'll be there in a moment," I called out.

"Thank you, Robby." Aaron closed the door, his face troubled but his arms loaded with clothing. I stood up and eased myself out of the bathtub. I dried off with a towel and examined the clothing Aaron was laying out on the counter. Two green sweaters with a T-shirt underneath and blue jeans with a clean pair of socks, and boots about my size. I dressed in what he'd picked out for me, some of the muscles and tendons in my arms and legs pulling at the movement, but I was startled when I caught sight of our clothed reflection in the mirror of the bathroom.

We looked like one of Sam's men from the prison.

I shivered, the hairs rising on the back of my neck, while Aaron averted his gaze. We left the bathroom and found Robin sitting at the top of the stairs wearing jeans and a sweater, her blonde hair tied back into a short ponytail.

Without a word, I offered my hand to her and she took it, blinking up at Aaron and me. Together, we walked down the stairs and met Tallah who sat on a chair outside another room. I wanted to ask her what was going on, but she raised her hand for me to be silent and led us into a private library that reeked of Deadwalker.

A Deadwalker in his late thirties, early forties, leaned against a dark mahogany desk, a book in his hand. He wore a tailored suit with a gold eagle pin on his chest. He had a streak of white in his black hair and was taller than me by a good foot.

Tallah cleared her throat.

"Senator Rue, this is Burner Lee." Tallah gestured to me.

Senator Rue paused before he closed the book and placed it gingerly on the table. He turned to us. He ran his blue gaze across my body as though I was a rare insect he'd never seen before. He turned a similar eye to Aaron and I wanted to growl.

"You may leave us, Tallah." Senator Rue's voice was husky and smooth.

"Yes, Senator," Tallah said.

I tried to grab her wrist, but she shook her head. She took Robin's hand and led her out of the room. Aaron shot her a confused look, but Tallah mouthed "it'll be okay," before she closed the door and left us alone with Rue. I focused my attention on him, even as he crossed his arms and watched us curiously.

"You two are quite the troublesome wolves," Senator Rue mused.

I clenched my fist, growling low in my throat. Aaron's shoulders tensed, his eyes narrowing, his hands curling at his sides. I prepared to be attacked, but when Senator Rue didn't speak, just watched us, Aaron shot me an uncertain look.

"What do you want?" I asked quietly.

"What makes you think I want anything? Maybe I just want to gaze upon the wolf who killed the King of New York, survived Serga's torture, caused the city of Baltimore to fall from a crazed horde of Blood Hunters, and has the protection of September 24th Amon, one of the very few

Deadwalkers who has the favor of the Counsel's President." Senator Rue shrugged. "For someone who was born feral, word does travel fast. Especially about a wolf who believe in the old ways, who seeks the Den Mothers, and who poses a challenge to everything that my fellow Deadwalkers and I have struggled to rebuild since the world devoured itself, and yet still wears the traitor's name of Lee."

"What. Do. You. Want?" I gritted my teeth.

Senator Rue hesitated. Then he chuckled. He pushed off the desk and sauntered toward me. I took a step backward, Aaron sucking in a deep breath as he too stepped backward. My back hit the wall of the room as Rue closed the distance between us and before I realized it, he was in front of me.

Rue cupped my jaw and brought his face close to mine. My hands clawed, and I grabbed his wrist, snarling as the collar buzzed unhappily. Aaron growled low in his throat. Senator Rue winked at him before he pulled from his pocket a small pair of scissors. I hesitated, confused as he smiled.

"May I take a lock of your hair?"

I blinked, taken aback by his questions.

"What?" Aaron gave voice to my question. Senator Rue just chuckled again.

"Don't worry, I'm not here for *that*." He curled a short piece of my hair behind my ear around one finger and deftly, with the same hand, snipped the hair. He let go of my jaw and examined the small lock. He pulled a handkerchief from his pocket and carefully wrapped the hair before he placed it in the protection of his inner coat pocket. He flashed me another smile and withdrew a pocket-sized red book with a black edge and a gold eagle on the front.

"Give this to Lady September when she comes back and tell her to head to the CDC in Atlanta. Tell her I want my usual order, and that as long as she does it, her little

Network is safe and sound, and her pets will be protected. Do you understand?" He pressed the red book against my chest and I grabbed it.

I nodded, silent.

"Good boy." Senator Rue stepped back, looking me over from top to bottom before he gave Aaron a wink and left.

Before I could even figure out what had happened, Aaron was ripping the red book from my hands and rapidly flipping through the pages. Tallah and Robin returned, a frown creasing Tallah's features.

"What did he want?"

"I'm not sure?" I said even as Aaron gasped. "What is it?"

"He's given us a passport to travel on the Midnight Train." Aaron held it up.

"What the hell is the Midnight Train?" I frowned.

Chapter Fifty-Four

WHEN DUSK FINALLY started to settle, the front door opened and slammed shut. September walked into the kitchen, pulling off her mask and tossing it onto the counter and came to join Robin, Tallah, Aaron and me. I was eating mashed potatoes and roast beef when September sat next to me at the table.

"God, I hate politics, did I miss anything?" she groaned and rubbed the bridge of her star-tattooed nose.

Aaron pulled the red book from his pocket and placed it on the table next to her.

"Senator Rue came while you were gone. He wanted me to give this to you and tell you to go to the CDC in Atlanta, and that he wanted his usual order," he said.

September froze and her eyes widened. She grabbed the book from the table and flipped through the pages. "What? He was here?"

"Yes."

"Did he take anything?"

I didn't have to be a wolf to hear the worry in her voice.

"Just a lock of my hair," I said.

"Did he want anything else?" Her voice was soft, much softer.

My fork hovered inches from the potatoes before I scooped up another pile of buttery mash. "No."

September narrowed her gaze, and I ignored her and Aaron's thin lips.

"How come he was able to walk around in the daylight when you were so tired?" Robin interjected.

"Senator Rue is much older than me, and the older ones can walk in the sunlight, but only for a short amount of time." September shifted in her seat and opened the booklet once more.

"What is it anyway?" I chewed on a mouthful of mash.

"It's a passport to use the Midnight Trains. I lost mine a while back. October's man, December, was supposed to give me another one, but in all the chaos, that didn't happen," she explained. "It allows me to travel the rail network."

I put my fork down, glancing at Aaron who pushed his own plate forward. When we didn't say anything else, September shifted in her seat again, looking up and noticing our stares.

"What?"

"What about us?" Aaron asked, his voice firm. "What do *we* do now?"

September cleared her throat, looking down at her passport. "Do you...know where I went this afternoon?"

"No," I said.

September sighed. "I spoke with my contacts about the Ancients taking an interest, the Kings and Queens, the Hunters and Blood Hunters. It's impossible to move either of you out of the city. At the moment," she clarified.

"How long is 'a moment'?" Aaron's voice was strangely cool.

September flinched. "It...might take a year for things to calm down. As it is, there's just too much focus on you two, so your best bet would be to just...just..."

"Just...?" I stared at her.

"Disappear."

"What?" Aaron and I shouted in unison.

"No, no, not like that. Okay, listen, the Network has done this before, but with a wolf looking for his mother in California. You two were born feral, right?"

Aaron nodded while I scowled. "What does that have to do with anything?"

"Nobody, not a Blood Hunter, not a Hunter, not even the Deadwalkers will expect you two to live in a city like this place. The Network will provide new identities, jobs, and I will ensure you have houses if you want to live separately—"

"Packs live under a single roof." I scowled.

"Okay." September raised her hands once more. "And, once the heat has died down, if you choose, I'll take you two to California, or if you want to stay here and build a life together, I will help in any way I can."

"What about giving testimony about the Kings and Queens? What about revolution?" I raised an eyebrow.

September fidgeted. "I've been informed by my contacts that if you even set foot within the White House, you'll be executed on the spot. Apparently—and I swear neither I nor the Network was aware of this—Daniel had some very powerful old friends on the Council, and to make matters worse, the Ancients are apparently descending into chaos over the destruction of Baltimore because Deadwalkers were harmed during the collapse. Like I said, it's too dangerous to move either of you right now."

Aaron squared his jaw and I reached over to grab his wrist. He stared at me. I rubbed my thumb against the back of his hand.

"Your choice," I said. "What do we do?"

Aaron looked at our hands, then to Robin who was shoving her mouth full of vegetables and completely ignoring our conversation. He let out a nervous breath.

"We stay, for now, and let things calm down."

September clapped her hands, relief on her face. "Excellent! Aaron, I have the perfect job idea for you, and Burner, I'll make sure you spend the majority of your time somewhere where you won't be found out."

"Sounds like a plan."

Epilogue

SIX MONTHS LATER

The Washington Harbour maintained a constant buzz of activity. Much like a beehive that never slept. Boats loaded with goods, stipends, and gifts to the Grand Council unloaded in a near constant stream of clothing, food, items of trade that would then be distributed along the railway system to Deadwalker kingdoms across the US.

It was confusing at first, trying to figure out which crate went where, which crates stayed in D.C., and which ones went West or South. Thankfully, every twenty-four hours, Donald, the harbormaster and wolf, put up a large sign marked with symbols and locations, similar to the pins that the wolves running around the capital wore on their clothing, to help us.

The first few days of working at the Harbour had thrown me for a loop. I couldn't read the signs or symbols, and the short talk the others used to pass messages was downright confusing, but Donald had taken me under his wing. After a week of crashing into people, dropping a few cargo boxes, and getting lost twice, I'd settled into a daily routine.

Rise in the morning with dawn's light and pick up the newspaper some pup delivered every morning to our door. I could read a small amount, just a few words, thanks to Aaron. While I skimmed the paper, my fingers tinging black with the fresh ink, Aaron would come downstairs, usually still sleepy, and start breakfast. I'd go and wake Robin, and by the time she was awake, we'd eat and get ready for the day.

I'd walk Aaron and Robin to the Library where he worked poring over the text and translating some of the more archaic books from French to English. I would head to the docks and work there until late, come home, eat an amazing supper Aaron would have made, have a bath, and fall face first into bed with Aaron softly snoring next to me.

It was exhausting work, but coming *home* each night and seeing Aaron and Robin's grinning faces made it all worthwhile. It meant the world to us, that unlike the other wolves who lived in the cramped apartments, we had a house. September's gift to Aaron and me.

Today was different, though. Today, they'd shut down the Harbour over some sort of containment issue and Donald had given everyone the rest of the day off while the Deadwalker council guards flooded the area. I wasn't about to complain. I walked home, watching the purple sunset over the Obelisk and White House as I headed for the library.

Deadwalkers and wolves in their human forms and wolf forms filtered in and out of the building, passing the white columns. I wandered inside, heading for the archives department. I found Aaron standing in front of a chalkboard, speaking French and scrawling words onto the blackboard with white chalk. He glanced over his shoulder and caught my gaze. I waved at him. He smiled before clearing his throat and turning to face the crowd around him.

"That's it for today. We'll pick this up tomorrow," Aaron said. There was a murmur among the crowd before they parted and left the room, casting me disapproving and curious looks. I didn't care about them. I cared about Aaron who closed his book and tidied up his desk before he joined me at the door. When he clapped his hands together, dust covered the front of his pale blue shirt. "You're off early."

"Harbour problems." I shrugged. "Thought we could hit the market together."

Aaron's eyes lit up. "Yeah, let me grab Robby."

I followed him out of the room and we walked a few doors down to a room crammed with old electronics and technology. Robin was sitting in the middle, twisting cables with her fingers. A blank black computer screen was positioned in front of her, reflecting her small form.

"Come on, Robby." Aaron carefully stepped over the tech scattered across the floor. "We're going to the market."

Robin's eyes flicked pale blue to iridescent green and she nodded, dropping the wires to the floor. "Can I play again tomorrow?"

"Sure can," I said. She jerked her head toward me and she squealed, taking Aaron's hand, and climbing from her small clear island. I picked her up, holding her in my arms while Aaron led us out of the library.

"I think I found it," Robin whispered to me, her voice low.

I raised an eyebrow. "Found what?"

Robin glanced at us before she spoke, her eyes deadly serious. "The Cloud. I found the Cloud."

"Really?" I mused. "And where is it?"

"New Mexico."

I raised both of my eyebrows. "New Mexico? And how do you know that?"

"The coffeemaker told me." Robin stuck her chin out.

"The coffeemaker?" Aaron fell into step beside me.

"Yeah," Robin pouted. "It lasted longer than all the other tech, and that's where its last transmission came from."

"Huh." I glanced at Aaron and he shook his head. "Well, let's get something for supper, and then you can tell me all about the talking coffeemaker."

Robin's pout deepened, and she wrapped her arms around my neck, grumbling. I bit back a laugh as we turned down the street toward the market and the tantalizing aroma of freshly cooking food filled my nose, leaving my stomach to growl. Aaron's hand brushed mine and I grabbed it, curling my fingers with his. He cast me a side glance, a soft smile on his lips.

Aaron tugged on our hands, leading us toward a human woman selling a dozen varieties of beans and different types of herbal plants. After he bought what he wanted, he led us toward a wolf selling carrots and garden turnips. Robin tugged on my arms and I let her down but held onto her hand so she wouldn't get lost among the growing dinner crowd starting to flood into the market.

When I straightened my back, I bumped into someone and apologized, my gaze drifting across the crowd until I froze.

Gold eyes stared back at me, pinning me to my spot. A wicked smile framed by a neatly trimmed goatee on an all too familiar face. I swallowed, suddenly nauseous.

Serga.

I squeezed my eyes shut, then opened them again, taking in a ragged breath and looking toward the spot where I'd seen him, but he was gone, the crowd moving in a wave as if he'd never been there, like he was a fragment of my imagination. I rubbed my forehead, looking back to Robin who was watching me curiously.

"I got us a new type of carrot, it's purple, but Teddy says they don't taste any different," Aaron said, digging into the bag to produce the carrot in question. When I didn't respond, he waved it in front of my face. "Burner?"

"Yeah?" I stuttered. My eyes skimmed the crowd again. "Can we go home now? Like, now?"

Aaron slowly blinked before he nodded. He grabbed my hand again and pulled me toward one of the nearby exits. Once outside, I could breathe. He didn't say anything, not on the long walk home, but he didn't let go of my hand either, not even when I craned my neck back, looking toward the market.

When we got home, I locked the front door, grabbed one of the dining room chairs, and shoved it under the handle. Not that it would work, it would take one boot against the door, but at least it was something. Aaron took Robin into the kitchen with him and worked there while I checked the house, locking each window, pulling the curtains shut and casting the rooms into darkness, except for the kitchen, because Aaron stopped me, his hands on my wrists.

"Robby, go change out of your day clothes and put on your home clothes," he told her. Robin nodded, leaving Aaron and me alone in the kitchen. Silently, we stared at each other, his eyes flicking between mine. "Who did you see?"

I swallowed. "I didn't—"

"Who?"

I looked away and focused on his hands around my scarred wrists. "Serga."

Aaron pulled me into a hug and I clung to him, wrapping an arm around his waist, and burying the other in his hair. I ducked my head into his neck, inhaling his scent. He nuzzled his face against mine.

"Sometimes," he started, "sometimes I see Rock at the archives."

My fingers tightened.

"I just glance up, and he's there, but then I blink or rub my eyes, and he's not there." Aaron lifted his head. I pressed our foreheads together. "I know you miss home—"

"It's not that," I whispered, my eyes searching his. Aaron frowned. I sighed. "I do… Sometimes I think about the pack. Where they are now, what they're doing." My lips twisted. "Sometimes, I wish we could just go back to where we were, to our old lives, to the summer before the Hunters attacked, and September entered our lives and all of that, but—" I wetted my lips "—but then I wouldn't be with you, like this." I thunked our foreheads together and Aaron bit his bottom lip. "And we wouldn't have Robin and…" I took in a shaky breath. "If that means going through what Serga did to me again and again for us to be together, to be with Robin, for the pack to be safe, for September and the Network to be trying to help the wolves I saw in cages in Boston, then seeing ghosts is a small price to pay."

"Burner," Aaron murmured. His eyes fell half shut and he pressed his lips to mine.

I hummed into the kiss, deepening it, even as he sunk his fingers in my hair and somehow Aaron ended up backed against the kitchen counter. Our lives weren't perfect, the world wasn't perfect, everything that happened wasn't perfect, but as long as Aaron was with me, and Robin was safe, then nothing else mattered.

It's our happy ending.

Acknowledgements

Thank you to:

All of the wonderful hard-working people at NineStar Press, and Elizabeth for editing this novel.

My parents, Roxanne and Michael, for always encouraging me.

The wonderful people at The Writer's Studio Online with SFU and my fantastic writing group who helped me revise this and provide feedback, and a special thank you to Eileen, my mentor and friend. This has taken a long time to write with many versions. Thank you, everyone!

About the Author

J.M. Goguen is a pen name for a Canadian author. A graduate of Simon Fraser University, The Writer's Studio, and a current MFA creative writing student at UBC, she is known to spend more time world-building than writing. Growing up with a love of paranormal, horror, romance, and speculative fiction, she will happily chat about topics ranging from interstellar ark ships, werewolves, and the zombie apocalypse, to the dangers of lightsabers and space lasers.

Her previous work has appeared in *Micro Madness* and *Emerge 16*, and she does manuscript consultations. She lives on the Sunshine Coast of British Columbia, Canada. In her free time, she plays video games, takes too many photos of her cats, and watches the local wildlife.

Email: jgregoryauthor@gmail.com

Twitter: @Jocelyne001

Website: www.jgregoryauthor.wordpress.com

Also Available from NineStar Press

Connect with NineStar Press

Website: NineStarPress.com

Facebook: NineStarPress

Facebook Reader Group: NineStarNiche

Twitter: @ninestarpress

Tumblr: NineStarPress